'May I present my friend, Richard, Viscount Braybrooke?'

The man behind Mr Gosport stepped forward and the whole roomful of people gave a combined sigh, including Sophie, who had told herself she was immune to masculine vanity. If vanity it was. He seemed unaware of the impression he had created, and yet, as she looked more closely she realised he did know, for there was a twinkle of amusement in his brown eyes and a slight twitch to the corners of his mouth.

Here was a tulip of the first order, and tulips were very definitely not what she was looking for, but beneath all that finery she sensed a man of great strength and power. She had a sudden vision of him unclothed, all rippling muscle, and a flood of colour suffused her cheeks.

Born in Singapore, **Mary Nichols** came to England when she was three, and has spent most of her life in different parts of East Anglia. She has been a radiographer, school secretary, information officer and industrial editor, as well as a writer. She has three grown-up children, and four grandchildren.

Recent titles by the same author:

DEAR DECEIVER

MISTRESS OF MADDERLEA

Mary Nichols

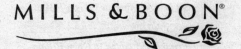
MILLS & BOON®

All the characters in this book have no existence outside the imagination of the author, and have no relation whatsoever to anyone bearing the same name or names. They are not even distantly inspired by any individual known or unknown to the author, and all the incidents are pure invention.

First published in Great Britain 1999
Harlequin Mills & Boon Limited,
Eton House, 18-24 Paradise Road, Richmond, Surrey TW9 1SR

© Mary Nichols 1999

ISBN 0 263 81657 5

Set in Times Roman 10½ on 12¼ pt.
04-9905-72132 C1

Printed and bound in Great Britain
by Caledonian International Book Manufacturing Ltd, Glasgow

Chapter One

1817

'This is no good, no good at all,' William Hundon muttered, reading a letter which had just been brought to the breakfast table. 'Something must be done.'

'My dear, do not frown so,' his wife said, glancing up from the piece of toast she was buttering to look at him. 'You will give yourself wrinkles.'

'Wrinkles!' he exclaimed. 'If that were all I had to concern me, I should count myself fortunate…'

'That is a letter from Mr Sparrow, is it not?' she went on. 'Only Mr Sparrow could put you in such an ill humour.' Although an invalid and a martyr to rheumatics, his wife insisted on coming downstairs in a dressing gown to have breakfast *en famille,* which included their daughter, Charlotte, and her niece, Sophie, who had lived with them for the last two years.

Sophie, alerted by the mention of Mr Sparrow's name, looked up at her uncle. 'Is there something untoward at Madderlea, Uncle William?'

'There is always something untoward at Madderlea.' He stopped speaking to tap at the letter with the
back of his hand. 'This time he wants money for repairs to the stable block, last week it was the roof of
the west wing that was leaking. I do not know
whether he is incompetent or criminal...'

'Surely not criminal?' his wife asked, taken aback
by his vehemence.

'Could you not employ another agent to manage
Madderlea?' Sophie asked.

'And how could I be sure another would be any
better? It is a highly unsatisfactory arrangement. We
live too far from Madderlea for me to be constantly
going to and fro to see that the man is doing his job.
Besides, he does not own the place and one cannot
expect him to have the same care as the family.'

'But, Papa, there is no family, except Sophie,'
Charlotte put in, then stopped in confusion when her
mother gave her a look of disapproval. The loss of
her family was hardly ever mentioned in Sophie's
hearing to save her pain.

'Precisely,' he said.

Madderlea Hall was the home of generations of the
Roswell family. Her father had always referred to it
as home, even when they lived in Brussels, and it was
to Madderlea he had taken her when Napoleon's con-
quests and tyrannical rule had made living on the continent too dangerous for an Englishman. It had been
a terrifying journey for a fifteen-year-old.

Because of the blockade of European ports, they
had been obliged to travel eastwards to Gdansk where
British ships were bringing guns and ammunition to

the Russians who were retreating before Napoleon's march on Moscow, and she had seen sights which were indelibly printed on her memory. Troops were left to forage for food from a countryside laid waste by its people in order not to feed the invaders. The fields remained untilled or scorched by fire, the livestock slaughtered. Men and horses starved, even during the advance.

It had taken all her father's savings and her late mother's jewellery, everything they possessed, except the clothes they wore, to buy food and a passage home in a cargo ship which pitched and tossed on the rough sea until she was sick as a dog. From London, where they landed, Papa had taken her to her uncle, the Earl of Peterborough, and then gone off and got himself killed fighting in Spain.

The experience had made her seem older and wiser than her years, able to take the ordinary ups and downs of life in her stride, resourceful and unafraid. Nor was she often sad; life was too short for that and the serious side of her nature was balanced by a sense of fun.

Uncle Henry had treated her like the daughter he never had and she had loved him and his wife as a second set of parents. It did not diminish the fond memories she had of her mother, who had died years before, nor of her brave and loving father, but Madderlea had become her home too, a safe haven, a beautiful and happy place, the villagers content because the people at the big house cared about them. Until…

She didn't want to think of that day, but it would

always be there in the back of her mind, a day in her life she would never forget, a day which had transformed her from a bright happy young lady looking forward to her first Season, into a quiet, withdrawn woman, who was never free of pain, both physical and mental. Almost two years on, her body had miraculously healed, but the mental images were still with her and would be to the day she died. Even now, sitting at the breakfast table in her Uncle William's comfortable but unpretentious house, they returned to haunt her.

They had been on their way to London for the Season and she was to have a come-out. She had been full of happy anticipation, making plans, talking about the gowns and fripperies she was going to buy, confident of finding a husband among the many *beaux* who would attend all the social occasions. Aunt Margaret had assured her she would be the catch of the Season and she had no reason to doubt her.

She did not consider herself beautiful, being rather too tall and slim for the current fashion, and her hair was red-gold at a time when dark locks were favoured, but she carried herself well and her complexion was good. Her greeny-grey eyes were her best feature, or so her aunt had told her. She had been promised a considerable dowry too, provided her choice met the approval of her aunt and uncle, but that was only fair and she had no qualms about it.

The weather had been fine when they set out in the family coach from Madderlea in Norfolk, but by the time they reached Newmarket Heath, black clouds had gathered and it became almost as dark as night.

Long before it began to rain, lightning flashed across the heath and thunder rumbled ominously. There was nowhere to stop and take shelter. Her aunt had wanted to turn back but, as Uncle Henry pointed out, the clouds were moving northwards and turning back would mean travelling with them instead of against them; if they kept going they would soon be under clear skies again.

It was the most terrible storm Sophie had ever witnessed and the terrified horses, intent on turning away from the flashes that continually rent the air in front of them, galloped off the road across the rough heathland, bumping the carriage up and down so that the occupants were hard put to hold onto their seats. They had heard a scream as the coachman was thrown off and though the groom who sat beside him on the box tried to retrieve the reins, he could not. Helplessly, they hung on until a wheel hit a rock and the whole vehicle turned over to the sound of rending wood, screaming horses and cries of terror, hers as well as her aunt's. And then there was black silence.

How long Sophie had been unconscious she did not know. She had come to her senses when she heard rough voices. 'They're dead, every last one of them.'

'Well, we can't leave them here. Best find out who they are, send for help.'

It was then she had cried out, unsure whether she had made enough sound to alert them, but then a man's head peered at her over the edge of the mangled vehicle, where she had been trapped with the dead weight of her aunt on top of her.

'There's one alive in here. Help me get her out. There, there, miss, you're safe now.'

Safe yes, but badly injured. The rest of that day and the weeks that had followed were a blur of pain and misery, but there had come a day when she had woken to find herself in a pretty bed chamber and the sun shining in through the window. Aunt Madeleine, her mother's sister, had been smiling down at her, her pale face full of gentle concern.

'How did I come to be here?'

'We fetched you, just as soon as we heard the dreadful news that you were lying at death's door in the infirmary at Newmarket.' Her aunt had lived in England since her marriage and her English was perfect but there still remained a trace of a French accent which reminded Sophie of her mother.

She had a hazy memory of being carried, of being put in a vehicle of some kind, of groaning at the pain and of wishing only to be left alone to die in peace. But then there had been soft sheets and someone stroking her brow and muted voices, of returning consciousness which was too painful to bear and of drifting back into sleep. 'When?'

'Two months ago.'

Two months! 'Uncle Henry? Aunt Margaret?'

'I'm sorry, Sophie, you were the only one found alive and we thought we might lose you too. Now you are going to get well again. Charlotte will come and sit with you.'

Only later, when they thought she was strong enough, did they tell her that she had inherited Madderlea Hall. 'It is not entailed,' Uncle William had told her. 'Your grandfather had a daughter and when it looked as though he would have no more children, he took steps to break the entail. The irony of it was that his daughter died and then, late in life, he had two sons, your Uncle Henry and your father. Now both are dead and you are a considerable heiress.'

She was mistress of Madderlea! But under the law, being unmarried and female, she could not have control of her inheritance, even if she had been well and strong. Until she married, it had to be administered by a trustee. In his will, her Uncle Henry had appointed William Hundon who, besides being her Aunt Madeleine's husband, was also a lawyer. Uncle William had employed an agent-cum-steward to live at Madderlea Hall and look after its affairs while she remained with her uncle and aunt and her cousin Charlotte at Upper Corbury, growing stronger day by day.

It was an unsatisfactory position. Madderlea needed more than an agent; it needed someone who cared about it. She ought to live there herself, but when she suggested it, her uncle and aunt threw up their hands in horror. 'You know that's not possible, Sophie,' her uncle said. 'Even if the law were to allow it, I, as a trustee, certainly should not. You would be the target of every rake and fortune hunter in the country.'

'But it is such a worry to you, Uncle and I would not, for the world, burden you with it if I could help it. You have done so much for me already.'

'There is only one sure remedy,' her aunt put in. 'You must find a husband.'

A husband. A husband, to have and to hold, for better or worse, to obey, to share her burdens, someone to take over the running of her affairs and manage Madderlea, to produce heirs. But where was she going to find a husband prepared to take on Madderlea, who was not a rake and a fortune hunter in a quiet backwater like Upper Corbury? She could count the eligible bachelors in the county on the fingers of one hand. There were widowers of course... She shuddered.

'You will have to marry sooner or later, Sophie dear,' her aunt went on. 'Now you are fully recovered, I think you should have a Season and William agrees with me.'

'A Season? In London?'

Her aunt smiled. 'Yes, London, where else?'

Charlotte, eyes shining, echoed, 'A Season! Oh, Sophie, how wonderful. I wish...' She stopped. There was no question that she could be brought out in that way; her parents did not move in those exalted circles and it was unkind of her to express the wish.

'But, Aunt, surely that will be too much for you?' Sophie said, knowing her aunt could only walk a few steps and that very slowly with the aid of sticks. 'I am persuaded it can be very exhausting.'

'Your aunt will not be going,' her uncle said. 'And neither will I. I would not dream of leaving her. Besides, I have an important case on at the County Court and it is set to last all summer.'

'How, then?' asked Sophie, mystified.

'We shall find a lady to take you under her wing and bring you out with her own daughter. It is sometimes done, I believe, in return for a contribution to the expenses.'

'In other words, I am to pay for my hostess's daughter as well as myself?'

'Yes, but you see—'

'And suppose I do not care for the lady or her daughter?'

'Sophie, please do not be difficult,' begged her aunt. 'It is the only way.'

'I would much rather pay for Charlotte to accompany me. In truth, I would like that very much. It is not fair leaving her behind and showering money on a stranger.'

'Oh, Sophie,' Charlotte breathed. 'I should like that above everything.'

Sophie gave her an affectionate smile. She loved her cousin dearly. At nineteen, she was almost the same age as Sophie, but shorter and rounder. Her hair was very fair and her eyes blue as the summer sky, giving her an innocent, almost childlike look which was deceptive. Sophie turned back to her uncle. 'Could you not find a lady without daughters, a widow, perhaps, who would sponsor both of us?'

Her uncle looked doubtful and she added, 'Please, Uncle William. I am quite determined on it. If you wish to see me married and have the burden of Madderlea lifted from your shoulders, then Charlotte must come too. I do not care how much it costs.'

Charlotte was aghast at the way Sophie had spoken, but her father seemed not to be offended. 'That sounds very like blackmail, Sophie, or bribery…' The twinkle in his eye belied his words.

'Oh, Uncle, I did not mean that. Please forgive me.'

'Very well. I will try to find a mature lady to take you both under her wing. And the sooner the better. Charlotte, you must look after your mother, while I am away. I shall not be gone above two days, I hope.' With that he left the table and called his manservant to help him to pack.

Charlotte could not contain her excitement, though Sophie was more subdued. In the previous two years she had become so used to taking life very quietly and avoiding agitation in order to aid her recovery that it had become a habit. No one would have believed she was once animated and brimming over with energy. The family physician had said she would recover her spirits in time, they must all be patient. Now, it seemed he had been right for a little of Charlotte's enthusiasm was beginning to affect her and she began to be impatient for her uncle's return.

'Do let us go out for a walk,' Sophie suggested when her aunt had been helped back to her room, where she would dress with the help of her maid and sit reading or sewing until the pain in her hands forced her to stop. 'I shall die of boredom if I'm confined to the house a day longer.'

For the first time that year the air was balmy, the rain which had kept the young ladies indoors all the previous week had lifted and everywhere was fresh and green. Daffodils and gilly flowers were blooming in the garden and Sophie had noticed violets out along the edge of the drive. It was a day for walking and breathing deeply and thanking God you were alive to enjoy it.

'We'll walk through the woods,' Sophie said, as they donned cloaks to cover their light wool morning gowns and buttoned their feet into sturdy boots. 'Round over Corbury Hill, down through Little Paxton and back through the village. We can call on old Mrs Brown on the way and see how she is. What do you say?'

'But, Sophie, it's all of five miles. Are you sure you're up to it? '

'Of course. I'm perfectly well now, or Uncle William would not have suggested going to London. I am persuaded one needs a great deal of energy for all the balls and *soirées* and visits to the theatre, not to mention picnics and riding in the park.'

Charlotte laughed as they left the house behind and made for the footpath to the woods which ran alongside the garden. 'You have left out the most arduous exercise of all, Cousin.'

'Oh, what is that?'

'Finding a husband, of course.'

Picking her way carefully over the damp grass, Sophie contemplated the prospect. The only men she had really been close to were her father and her two uncles and the thought of being touched or kissed by anyone else sent a frisson of fear, mixed with a strange surge of excitement, through her whole body. And then she thought of Madderlea and her fortune and knew that those two facts alone would ensure a flock of suitors. But how to choose? How to be sure that whoever offered for her was looking at her for herself and not her inheritance?

'It will not be easy.' She sighed. 'There are times

when I almost wish I had no fortune, no Madderlea. It is a weighty responsibility, you know.'

'How so?'

'It is not only Madderlea Hall which is old and always in need of repair—there are servants, indoors and out, and the tenants, who look to the Hall to repair their cottages and keep the land in good heart, and the villagers, whose welfare must be considered, and the parson, whose living is in the gift of the Lord of the Manor. I must choose a husband who will be as careful of all those responsibilities as Uncle Henry was, who will love Madderlea as much as I do.'

'You have not said one word about him loving you. Do you not believe in marrying for love?'

'Of course I do, but how can I be sure of any man? Madderlea will be a great enticement to deceive, don't you think?'

'Oh, Sophie, you must look for love as well. You will be so unhappy if you do not.'

They had entered the woods, taking a well-defined track between the trees. Sophie lifted an overhanging branch, its new leaves glistening with raindrops, and stooped to pass beneath it, holding it for Charlotte to follow.

'Oh, Charlie, I should not care if he were as poor as a church mouse, if he loved me. In fact, I think I should be averse to a man with a fortune. Men with deep pockets are almost always arrogant and unfeeling and think that money will buy anything, even a wife. I am thankful that money is not one of the attributes I shall be seeking.'

'Oh, and what qualities would you be looking for in a husband?'

'He must be handsome and well turned out, but not vain of his appearance as some dandies are. I think it is far more important that he should have an interesting face and be able to converse sensibly without being condescending. He must allow me to be myself and not try to mould me to his idea of womanhood. He must, of course, be honourable in everything he does. He must be good with children, for I should like children, and be kind to his servants.'

Charlotte raised an enquiring eyebrow. 'Oh, is that all?'

'No, he must be considerate and tenderhearted and not haughty or domineering. But not soft. Oh, no, definitely not soft.'

'Goodness, Sophie, where are you going to find such a paragon? You ask too much.'

Sophie sighed. 'I know, but I can dream, can I not? Don't you ever dream?'

'Yes, but only of Freddie.'

'Mr Harfield, ah, yes, I had almost forgot him. You will be able to enjoy your Season, safe in the knowledge that you have him to come back to.'

'I am not so sure, Sophie. Freddie told me that his father wants him to marry someone with a substantial dowry; you know I don't have that.'

Sophie laughed. 'I have not heard that Mr Harfield is making any push to obey his papa. He has never so much as looked at anyone else.'

'No, but Sir Mortimer is the squire of Upper Corbury, which I own is nothing compared to Madderlea, but in our little pool, he is a big fish, and no doubt Freddie will have to give in in the end.'

'Then he is not the man I took him for,' Sophie said.

They had come out of the woods on to a lane which wound up and over Corbury Hill. The dark fields, here and there showing the tips of winter wheat, stretched on either side of them. On the skyline, they could see the hunt, galloping behind the yelping hounds.

'Do you think they've found the scent?' Charlotte asked, as the sound of the hunting horn drifted across to them.

'I hope not. I feel for the poor fox.'

'Oh, Sophie, and you a country girl!' She stopped. 'There's Freddie. Don't you think he is handsome, the way he sits his horse?'

Sophie smiled. 'I am persuaded that you do.'

The young man had spotted them and turned his horse to meet them, pulling it up in a shower of damp earth, almost at their feet.

'Freddie!' Charlotte said, brushing down her cape. 'You have made us all muddy.'

He grinned, doffing his hat to reveal blond curls. Two years older than they were, he still had the slim figure and round face of a youth, but had been rapidly maturing over the previous two years and would soon have all the mamas for miles around looking at him with an acquisitive eye.

'I beg your pardon, Miss Hundon.' Then, to Sophie, 'Miss Roswell.'

Sophie smiled. 'Mr Harfield.'

'It is so pleasant to be out after all the rain,' Charlotte said, teasing him. 'And we might not be able to do so much longer.'

'What do you mean?'

'We are both going to London for a Season. What do you think of that?'

'Season?' he echoed in dismay. 'You mean you are to have a come-out and mix with all the eligibles?'

'I mean exactly that,' she said, laughing.

He dismounted and walked over to grab both her hands, a gesture which Sophie knew she ought to discourage as being highly improper, but she had no heart to do it.

'Charlie,' he said, using the familiar name of childhood. 'You wouldn't… Would you?'

'Now, who's to say? I might…'

'Oh, no, please say you are only teasing…'

'I am only teasing.' She looked at him with her head on one side, while Sophie pretended to examine something in the hedgerow. 'But you know, Freddie, if your papa has his way, I should be holding myself back in vain.'

'I will bring him round. Promise me you will be patient.' He could hear the hunt fading in the distance. 'I must go.' He put her hands to his lips and reluctantly released them. The next minute he was astride his horse and galloping away.

'You know, that was highly indecorous conduct,' Sophie said, as they resumed their walk. 'If anyone had seen you…'

'But they didn't, did they?' Charlotte was smiling at the memory of her swain.

'No, but it will be very different in London, you know. What might be acceptable behaviour in Upper Corbury would be enough to ruin your reputation in the capital. Do remember that, Charlie.'

'There is no need to ring a peal over me, Sophie, I know I must be prim and proper when we go to London. Besides, Freddie will not be there and I shall not be tempted to stray.'

Sophie was not so sure. Temptations there would be, she was certain, not only for Charlotte but for her too—she must not allow herself to forget Madderlea and why she was there.

Three weeks later, they set off for London in the family coach, accompanied by Anne, who had been promoted from parlour maid to ladies' maid, and escorted by Joseph, Mr Hundon's groom, riding Sophie's grey stallion. Joseph's nineteen-year-old son, Luke, was riding Charlotte's smaller horse. Joseph and the coachman were to return with the carriage immediately because William needed it, but Luke was to stay in London to look after their mounts. They would be relying on their hostess's equipage to convey them around town.

'Her name is Lady Fitzpatrick,' William had told them on his return. 'She is a distant cousin on my mother's side. You have not met her because she moved to Ireland on her marriage and we did not correspond. She was widowed some years ago and returned to live in London. I went to ask her advice and she offered to sponsor you herself, which is very agreeable of her and saved me a great deal of time and trouble. She has a town house in Holles Street, not a top-of-the-trees area, but respectable enough.'

'Some years ago,' Charlotte echoed. 'Does that mean she is old, Papa?'

'No, I would not say old,' he told them. 'Mature and well able to deal with high-spirited girls.'

'A dragon.'

'Certainly not. In fact, she is a sympathetic sort and will stand well *in loco parentis*. I believe she might be a little short-sighted, for she uses a quizzing glass all the time, but that is of no account. I am sure you will like her; she impressed me very much with her sensibility and knowledge of what is right and proper.'

This description hardly filled the girls with rapture, but it could not have been easy for him, a country gentleman not used to the *haute monde*. They were going to London for the Season and that was all that mattered.

'Now, Sophie, you will have a care, will you not?' he had said the day before, when they were in the throes of last-minute packing. 'There will be unscrupulous men about and I do not want you to be gulled. Be guided by Lady Fitzpatrick and, whatever you do, do not commit yourself to anyone until I have seen and approved him. You do understand?'

'Of course, Uncle.'

'And the same goes for you, my love,' he told his daughter. 'And though you will not be the object of fortune hunters, you are a lovely girl and perhaps susceptible to flattery...'

'Oh, Papa, I am not such a ninny. Besides, I am

going to enjoy myself, not look for a husband. The man I want is in Upper Corbury.'

He had laughed at that and said no more, though Aunt Madeleine, tearfully coming out to the carriage to wave goodbye to them, had reinforced everything he had said and more, extracting a promise from them that they would write every other day.

'Oh, this is so exciting,' Charlotte said, when they stopped for their first change of horses. Anne, who was a bad traveller, had curled herself up in the corner and gone to sleep. The girls allowed her to slumber on; it was easier to exchange confidences without eavesdroppers, however unintentional. 'What time will we arrive, do you think?'

'With luck, before it becomes dark,' Sophie said.

'I do hope Lady Fitzpatrick is not a dragon. I mean to enjoy myself, meeting all the eligibles. It will not hurt Freddie to think he has some competition.'

Sophie envied her cousin her untroubled mind. 'You may look forward to it, Charlie, but I am not so sanguine.'

'Why not? You are rich as Croesus. Think of all the splendid gowns you will be able to buy, the pelisses, riding habits, bonnets and silk shawls. A new dress and a new bonnet for every occasion. And you will have all the young men dangling after you. In your shoes, I would be in ecstasies.'

'I wish you could be in my shoes, Cousin, dear, for I would willingly trade places.'

'You surely do not mean that.'

'I do. Then I could choose a husband without him knowing who I am.'

'And afterwards? He would have to know in the end.'

'Yes, but by then we should have discovered we suited and he would not mind.'

'No, I do not suppose he would, considering he had landed an heiress and not the simple country girl he thought he had won. Oh, Sophie, if you go about with that Friday face, you will surely put them all off.'

Sophie laughed, her greeny-grey eyes danced with light and her face lit up with mischief. 'I must not do that, must I?'

'Certainly you must not, if you wish to catch that paragon you told me of.'

They talked on as the coach rattled through the countryside, which gradually became more and more inhabited as one village followed another in quick succession. Then they were travelling on cobbles and there were buildings each side of the street, houses and inns and shops, and the streets were crowded with vehicles and people, in spite of the lateness of the hour. They leaned forward eagerly to look about them when they realised they had arrived in the metropolis. Sophie had seen some of it briefly on her way from Europe to Madderlea, but to Charlotte it was new and wonderful.

Fifteen minutes later they turned into Holles Street and the carriage drew to a stop. The girls, peering out, saw a tall narrow house with evenly spaced windows and steps up to the front door, which was thrown open when Joseph lifted the knocker and let it fall with a resounding clang. A footman and a

young lad ran down the steps to the carriage and began unloading their luggage, while the girls extricated
themselves and made their way, in some trepidation,
up the steps and into the front hall, followed by Anne,
still half asleep.

'Ladies, ladies, welcome. Come in. Come in. Is that
your maid? Tell her to follow the footman, he will
show her your rooms. She can unpack while you take
some refreshment. I do hope the journey has not tired
you excessively.'

The rush of words ended as suddenly as they had
begun and the girls found themselves staring at a
dumpy little woman in a mauve satin gown and a
black lace cap, who was peering at them through a
quizzing glass. Her eyes, small and dark, were almost
lost in a face that was as round and rosy as an apple.

'Good evening, Lady Fitzpatrick.' Sophie was the
first to speak. 'We—'

'No, don't tell me, let me guess,' their hostess said,
lifting her glass closer to her eyes and subjecting them
to individual scrutiny. They were dressed similarly in
plain travelling dresses and short capes, though Sophie's was a dark russet, which heightened the red-
gold of her hair, and Charlotte's was rose-pink. Sophie's bonnet was dark green straw, trimmed with
matching velvet ribbon, and Charlotte's was a chip
bonnet, ruched in pale blue silk.

Her close inspection completed, her ladyship
pointed her lorgnette at Charlotte, who was standing
silently trying not to laugh. 'You are Miss Roswell. I
can tell breeding a mile off.' She turned to Sophie.
'And you are the country cousin.'

Charlotte was too busy trying to smother her giggles to contradict her. Sophie dug her sharply in the ribs with her elbow and smiled at their hostess. 'Why, how clever of you, my lady. I did not think it so obvious.'

'Sophie!' breathed Charlotte in alarm, but Sophie ignored her and smiled at Lady Fitzpatrick.

'I can see that no one could gull you, my lady. Not that we should try, of course. I am, indeed, Miss Hundon.'

Her ladyship leaned towards her, cupping a hand round her ear. 'You must learn to speak clearly, child, it is no good mumbling. I am sure Miss Roswell does not mumble.'

Sophie realised that, besides having poor eyesight, Lady Fitzpatrick was also hard of hearing. Had Uncle William known that?

'Charlotte, for goodness' sake, don't stand there giggling,' she murmured. 'Say something.'

'What can I say? Oh dear, Sophie, what have you done? You have landed us in a bumblebath and no mistake.'

'Bath,' said Lady Fitzpatrick. 'Of course, you may have a bath. I will order the water to be taken up to your rooms. But first, some refreshment.' She led the way into the drawing room, where a parlour maid had just arrived with a tea tray which she put on a low table beside a sofa. 'Now, Sophie, you sit here beside me and Charlotte can sit in the armchair opposite.'

Charlotte obeyed and then gasped when her ladyship looked askance at her. 'I meant you to sit beside me, my dear, but it is of no real consequence.'

Sophie relinquished her seat and motioned Charlotte to take it. 'My lady, you have misunderstood,' she said, speaking very precisely. 'I am Sophie. This is Charlotte.'

'Oh, I see. You know, Mr Hundon spoke very quickly and I did not always catch exactly what he said. So Miss Roswell is Charlotte and Miss Hundon is Sophie, not the other way about. No wonder you were amused.'

'But...' Charlotte spluttered and then dissolved into the giggles she had been trying so hard to suppress and Sophie found herself laughing. It was the first time for two years that she had really done more than smile a little, and it felt wonderful.

Lady Fitzpatrick, mistaking the cause of their laughter, allowed herself a rueful smile. 'I have it right now, do I not?'

'Yes, indeed,' Sophie said, accepting a cup of tea and sipping it. She knew Charlotte was staring askance at her, but refused to look her in the eye.

'Sophie, whatever are we going to do?' Charlotte, unable to sleep, had padded along to Sophie's room in her nightdress. 'We cannot possibly keep up the pretence.'

'Why not? Lady Fitzpatrick's mistake is fortuitous and it would be a shame to disillusion her. You said you would like to be in my shoes, so now you may.'

'But, Sophie, Anne and Luke know which of us is which...'

'Oh, I told Anne when she queried why you had

been given the best room. I promised her five guineas and assured her she would not be in trouble over it.

'Five guineas! Why, that is a small fortune to her!'

'It would not serve to be miserly. As for Luke, he thought it was a great lark, when I offered him the same inducement.'

'Sophie, I cannot do it, really I can't. I shall die of mortification when we have to go out and about and meet people.'

Sophie thrust her conscience firmly into the background. Fate had taken a hand in the matter and made Lady Fitzpatrick make that mistake. It could not and should not be ignored. 'No one knows us in town and you will manage wonderfully. Wouldn't you like to play the heiress for a few weeks? It will flush out the fortune hunters and we can have a little fun at their expense. And, who knows, I might even meet that paragon.'

'And when you do?'

'Why, we will confess the truth and the toadeaters will come home by weeping cross and serve them right.' She paused. 'Charlotte, say you will do it. At the first sign our ruse is not working, I shall make a clean breast of it, I promise, and I shall say it was all my doing.' She could see the idea growing on her cousin and pressed home her advantage. 'Go on, tell me you are not tempted by the thought of playing the lady and having all the eligibles at your feet. You will, you know, because you are very fetching. You will return to Freddie with such a tale to tell, he will be filled with admiration and no harm done.'

Charlotte laughed and gave in.

* * *

Lady Fitzpatrick's carriage was old, creaky and scuffed and the unmatched horses leaner than they should have been. It took them safely about town to do their shopping but the image it created was certainly not the one Sophie had in mind. Even though she intended to stay in the background, she wanted Charlotte to shine, for how else were they to flush out the fortune hunters as she had so succinctly put it to Charlotte the night before?

Mentally she put a new equipage on their shopping list, though that would have to wait for another day; buying gowns for morning, afternoon, carriage rides and balls, not to mention riding habits, bonnets, pelisses, footwear, fans and underwear took the whole of their first day.

Sophie's choice of garments, while not exactly dowdy, was certainly not in the first stare of fashion. She chose plain styles and muted colours and let Charlotte be the peacock, encouraged by Lady Fitzpatrick.

'Charlotte, my dear,' her ladyship said, as the young lady eagerly pounced on a pale-green crepe open gown over a satin slip, while Sophie chose brown sarcenet, 'I do not wish to scold…do you not think you could be a little more generous towards your cousin? She is to be brought out, too, you know.'

'But Sophie is…' Charlotte, who had been going to say Sophie held the purse strings and could buy whatever she wanted, stopped in confusion.

'I am quite content, ma'am,' Sophie said, all innocence. 'Any man who offered for me must take me as I am. It would be wrong of me to pretend I am of greater consequence than I am.'

'Sophie, Lady Fitzpatrick is right,' Charlotte said. 'It will look mean of me, if you do not choose at least one or two fashionable gowns for special occasions.' Blue eyes twinkling, she added, 'Please do not consider the cost, you know I can easily afford it.'

Sophie choked on a laugh; Charlotte was doing better than she had hoped. 'Very well, but I shall not be extravagant.'

They returned home with the carriage piled high with their purchases and more to be delivered the following day, all to be paid for on Miss Roswell's account, which would, of course, go to her uncle. The only thing they lacked was that first important invitation.

It arrived the following day. It was for a *soirée* being given by Lady Gosport, an old friend of Lady Fitzpatrick's.

'It will only be a small gathering, but it will set the ball rolling,' her ladyship said.

The girls looked at each other. The time had come to test their masquerade and they were half-eager, half-fearful.

Chapter Two

The two men had enjoyed a morning gallop across the heath. The horses had gone well and now they were walking them back towards town. Both were tall and sat their mounts with the ease of cavalry officers used to long hours in the saddle; both wore impeccably tailored riding coats of Bath cloth, light brown buckskins and highly polished riding boots. Richard, Viscount Braybrooke, the older at twenty-nine, and slightly the bigger of the two, had been silent ever since they had turned to go back.

'What ails you, Dick?' Martin asked. 'You've been in the dismals ever since you went home. You found no trouble there, I hope?'

'Trouble?' Richard roused himself from his contemplation of his horse's ears to answer his friend. 'No, not trouble exactly.'

'Then what is wrong? Grandfather not in plump currant?'

'He says he isn't, but that's only to make me toe the line.'

'What line is that?'

'Marriage.'

Martin shrugged. 'Well, it comes to us all in the end.'

'It's all very well for you, you haven't got a dukedom hanging on your choice. It would not be so bad if I had been born to inherit, but Emily was the only child my uncle had and the estate is entailed. My own father, who was the second son, died when I was still in leading strings and my uncle died of a fever while we were in Spain, so I came back to find myself the heir.'

'You knew it might happen one day.'

'Of course I did, but I thought I would have plenty of time to look about for a wife. The old man is holding my cousin Emily over my head like the sword of Damocles.'

Martin grinned. 'Quite a feat for an elderly gentleman. I believe she is quite a large girl.'

Richard smiled in spite of himself. 'You know what I mean.'

'She is not to your taste?'

'She was a child when I went away to war and it is as a child that I think of her, my little cousin to be petted and indulged, not as a wife.'

'She is of marriageable age now, though.'

'Seventeen, but her mother has spoiled her abominably and she is still immature, without a sensible thought in her head. I should be miserable legshackled to her and so would she.'

'Has His Grace given you no choice?'

'Oh, I have a choice. Find a wife of whom he will

approve before the end of the Season, or it will have to be Emily.'

'Why the haste? You have only just returned to civilian life, a year or so enjoying the fruits of peace would not come amiss.'

'So I told him. I also pointed out that Emily should be allowed more time to grow up and make her own choice, but he says he has no time to waste, even if I think I have. He is an old man and likely to wind up his accounts at any time. He wants to see the next heir before he goes.'

They had arrived at the mews where the horses were stabled and, leaving them in the charge of grooms, set out to walk to Bedford Row where the Duke of Rathbone had a town house.

'Do you know, I begin to feel sorry for Emily.'

'So do I. Choosing a wife is not something to do in five minutes at a Society ball. It needs careful consideration. After all, you have to live with your choice for the rest of your life.'

'Some don't,' Martin said, as a footman opened the door of the mansion and they passed into a marble-tiled vestibule. A magnificent oak staircase rose from the middle of it and branched out at a half-landing to go right and left and up to a gallery which overlooked the hall. 'They marry someone suitable to continue the line and then discreetly take a mistress. Look at the Prince Regent…'

'I would rather not look at him, if you don't mind,' Richard said, before turning to the servant who had admitted them and ordering breakfast for them both before leading the way to the library, a large room lined with bookshelves and containing a reading table and a couple of deep leather armchairs either side of the fireplace. 'I may be old-fashioned, but I would rather find a wife I could care for and who cared for me. Emily has no feeling for me at all but, with my uncle's death, my aunt was deprived of her chance to be a duchess and so she is determined on her daughter fulfilling the role. She will hound me to death as soon as she hears of my grandfather's edict.'

Richard sprawled morosely in one of the chairs and Martin, always at ease in his friend's company, sat opposite him. 'Then there is no alternative, my friend—you must mix with Society as one of the eligibles and hope for the best.'

'The best,' Richard echoed. 'Oh, that I could find such a one.'

'A great deal depends on your expectations, Dick. Tell me, what attributes will you be looking for in a wife?'

Richard gave a short bark of a laugh, as if considering such a thing had never crossed his mind, though he had been thinking of little else since the interview with his grandfather. 'Let me see. It goes without saying she must come from a good family, or Grandfather will never sanction her. Beautiful? Not necessarily, but she must have a pleasing face, a certain style and presence, so that I can be proud to have her on my arm in public. She must be able to converse intelligently; I should hate anyone vacuous or missish.'

'An educated wife…that might be asking for trouble.'

'A little education does no harm, but I wouldn't

want a blue stocking; they are always trying to score points. She must want and like children because the whole object of the exercise is to beget an heir and I do not hold with women who have babies and then hand them over to nurses and governesses to rear.'

'That's quite a list.'

'I haven't done yet. I would expect her to be considerate towards those beneath her and tenderhearted when they are in trouble, but not soft, not easily gulled. She must enjoy country pursuits because I shall wish to spend much of my time in Hertfordshire on the estate. Not a hoyden, though. Don't like hoydens above half.'

Martin was smiling at this catalogue of virtues. 'What about a dowry?'

'Most important of all she must not be a fortune or a title hunter. In fact, it would be a decided advantage if she had her own fortune.'

'Why? You are a pretty plump in the pocket already.'

'I know, but if she has her own fortune, she will not be marrying me for mine, will she? I want someone accustomed to wealth so that she will fall easily into my way of living and not be overawed by it. Besides, I will not be truly wealthy until I inherit and, for all his protestations to the contrary, my grandfather is fit as a flea.

'It would be better if my wife could afford all the extravagant fripperies she needs without my having to go to him for an increase in my allowance. If she is already independent, she would not fetter me with extravagant demands. She would be prepared to let me go my own way in return for being able to lead her own life, within certain decorous limits, of course.'

'Do you know, I am sure I heard you say you were not interested in taking a mistress.'

'I should like to keep the option open.' He spoke so pompously that Martin burst into laughter. 'You may laugh,' Richard told him. 'You aren't constrained by other people's expectations.'

'It is your own expectations which are the more demanding, old fellow. Such a paragon of virtue does not exist.'

'More's the pity.'

A footman came to tell them that breakfast was ready and they got up to go to the small dining room, where a repast of ham, eggs, pickled herrings, boiled tongue and fresh bread was laid out for them.

'Then you do agree that you must be seen in Society?' Martin queried, watching Richard fill his plate. His problem seemed to have had no effect on his appetite.

'I have no choice.'

'Well, do not sound so reluctant, you will never attract your paragon like that. You must be agreeable and well turned out and…'

'I know, my friend, I do not need a lecture on how to conduct myself.'

'Then we'll start this evening. Mama has arranged a little gathering at home and I promised to attend. It is very early in the Season, but she assures me there are to be several young ladies up for their first Season and a one or two of the competition too, I'll be bound.'

'Then I had better do something about my wardrobe. Everything I had before I went into the army is far too tight.'

'That's hardly surprising,' Martin said laconically. 'You were little more than a boy when you left and a man when you returned.' He looked critically at his friend's large frame. 'Not a small one, either. Do you wish me to accompany you?'

'No, of course not, I am perfectly able to choose clothes. I'll meet you at Jackson's at four. There will just be time for a short bout before dinner at five.'

Martin laughed. 'Do you expect to have to fight for your lady's hand?'

Richard smiled. 'No, but it is always a good thing to maintain one's ability to defend oneself.'

'Oh, come, Dick, you have no enemies, a more affable man I have yet to meet.'

'It would be a fortunate man who managed to go through life without acquiring a few enemies,' Richard said.

'Name me one.'

Richard needed time to consider. He was indeed fortunate that he was popular and well-liked by his peers and the men he had commanded, except for those who had flouted the tight discipline he maintained as an officer. 'There was Sergeant Dawkins,' he said, remembering the man he had had courtmartialled for looting, something Wellington had expressly forbidden.

The offence had been exacerbated by the fact that

the goods the man had stolen had come from a Portuguese family who were allies. His defence, which had not been upheld, was that the family had been consorting with the enemy. The sergeant had been flogged and dishonourably discharged. Left to find his own way home from Lisbon, he had threatened Richard with revenge.

'That threat was made two years ago and in the heat of the moment,' Martin said. 'You surely do not think he meant it?'

'No, of course not, the poor fellow likely never made it back to England. He probably settled down in the Peninsula with a Spanish señorita. You asked for an example and I gave you one.'

'Point taken. But I hope you will rid yourself of your aggression and ill humour against Gentleman Jackson in the boxing ring this afternoon and present yourself in my mother's drawing room at seven this evening, in a sweet temper, ready to act the agreeable.'

'Have no fear, my friend,' Richard said, as both men left the table. 'I shall be a model of the man about town.'

Sophie and Charlotte had arrived at Lady Gosport's in Denmark Place a few minutes after seven to find her drawing room already buzzing with conversation. Most of the company seemed to be of Lady Fitzpatrick's generation and Sophie's spirits sank. This was not her idea of London Society at all. She looked across at Charlotte and exchanged a rueful grimace, before their hostess caught sight of them and hurried over to greet them.

'Harriet, my dear, so glad you could come.' She kissed Lady Fitzpatrick on both cheeks and then looked at the girls, taking careful note of Charlotte's white crepe open gown trimmed with silk forget-me-nots over a pale blue slip, and moving on to examine Sophie's cambric high gown with its overskirt of pale green jaconet, which her ladyship considered more suitable for day than evening wear. 'So, these are your charges.'

'Good evening, Beth.' She took Charlotte's arm and drew her forward. 'May I present Miss Charlotte Roswell. The Earl of Peterborough's niece. God rest his soul.'

'Indeed, yes. My commiserations, Miss Roswell.'

Reminded of her superior station by a dig in the ribs from Sophie, Charlotte executed a small polite bob, not the deep curtsy she had intended. 'Thank you, my lady.'

'You are fully recovered from your ordeal?'

'Yes, thank you.' It was obvious that the girl was painfully shy and would have to be brought out of her shell if she were to take well. Her ladyship turned to Sophie. 'Then you must be Miss Hundon. Miss Roswell's companion, I collect.'

'Oh, no,' Charlotte put in. 'Sophie is my cousin and friend, not a paid companion. We share everything.'

'That is to your credit, my dear,' Lady Gosport said. 'But you will find that the possession of an estate and great wealth, as I believe you have, will make your advance in Society very unequal.' Then to Sophie, 'I do hope, dear Miss Hundon, you have not been led to expect the same attention as your more illustrious cousin?'

'No, indeed,' Sophie said, though she longed to bring the lady down to size with some cutting remark. Only the thought of their masquerade being exposed stilled her tongue.

'Come, let me introduce you to the company.'

There were a few young ladies present, they realised, as they were conducted round the room, and one or two young men, who stood about posing in tight coats and impossibly high pointed cravats, twirling their quizzing glasses in their hands and speaking in affected voices which made the girls want to laugh aloud. Instead, they bowed politely and exchanged greetings and longed to escape.

'This is quite dreadful,' Sophie murmured to her cousin when they had done the rounds. 'If the whole Season is to be like this, I shudder to think how we shall go on.'

'It is early in the year,' Charlotte whispered. 'The Season is not yet under way.'

'I hope you are right.'

Just then a commotion by the door heralded the arrival of latecomers. 'Why, it is Martin,' Lady Gosport cried, hurrying over to drag her son into the room. 'You are very late. I had quite given you up.'

He gently removed her hand from the sleeve of his green superfine coat and smiled at her. 'I am sorry, Mama. Pressing business delayed me. May I present my friend, Richard, Viscount Braybrooke?'

The man behind Mr Gosport stepped forward and
the whole roomful of people gave a combined sigh,
including Sophie, who had told herself she was immune to masculine vanity. If vanity it was. He seemed
unaware of the impression he had created, and yet, as
she looked more closely she realised he did know, for
there was a twinkle of amusement in his brown eyes
and a slight twitch to the corners of his mouth.

He was clad in a blue satin coat which fitted him
so closely the muscles of his broad shoulders could
be detected as he bowed over her ladyship's hand.
His waistcoat was of cream figured brocade and his
blue kerseymere trousers, in the latest fashion,
reached his shoes and were held down by straps under
the instep, making his legs seem impossibly long. His
cravat, though nothing like as high and pointed as
those she had noticed on the other young men, was
so skilfully tied, it drew exclamations of admiration
from them.

His dark hair, cut short so that it curled about his
ears, was the only slightly dishevelled part of him,
but Sophie knew it was a style much favoured among
the gentleman of the *ton*, called Windswept. Here was
a tulip of the first order, and tulips were very definitely not what she was looking for, but beneath all
that finery she sensed a man of great strength and
power. She had a sudden vision of him unclothed, all
rippling muscle, and a flood of colour suffused her
cheeks.

She turned away to scrabble in her reticule for a
handkerchief in order to compose herself. Whatever
was the matter with her? She had never ever thought

about a man's nakedness before. Had he deliberately set out to have that effect? It was disgraceful in him if he had and even more disgraceful in her to succumb.

Charlotte, beside her, was openly staring. 'My, would you look at that peacock,' she murmured. 'Oh, goodness, Lady Fitzpatrick is bringing them both over.'

Sophie, struggling to regain her usual serenity, was aware of Lady Fitzpatrick presenting the two men to her cousin. 'Miss Roswell is the niece and ward of the late Earl of Peterborough,' she was saying. 'Being abroad, you will not have heard of the tragedy two years ago which left poor Miss Roswell all alone in the world.'

'Not quite alone,' Charlotte said, determined to include Sophie, not only because she felt overwhelmed, but because it wasn't fair on her cousin to shut her out, as Lady Gosport seemed determined to do. 'My lord, may I present my cousin, Miss Sophie Hundon?'

Sophie found herself subjected to a brown-eyed scrutiny which made her squirm inside and when he took her small hand in his very large one, she felt trapped like a wild bird in a cage which longed to be free but which hadn't the sense to fly when the cage door was opened. Here, she knew, was a very dangerous man. Dangerous because he could make her forget the masquerade she and Charlotte had embarked upon, could make her disregard that list of virtues she had extolled as being necessary for the man she chose as her husband, dangerous for her peace of mind. And all in less than a minute!

She hated him for his extravagant clothes, for looking at her in that half-mocking way, for his self-assurance, for making her feel so weak. But no one would have guessed her thoughts as she dropped him a deep curtsy and then raised her eyes to his. 'My lord.'

'The cousins are to be brought out together,' Lady Fitzpatrick told him. 'Which I hold very generous of Miss Roswell.'

'Indeed,' he said, though she could not be sure if he was expressing surprise or agreement.

'Not at all,' Charlotte put in, making him turn from Sophie towards her. 'We have always been very close, ever since…' She stopped in confusion. She had been going to say ever since Sophie's accident brought her to Upper Corbury, but checked herself. 'Since the tragedy.'

'Your soft heart does you credit, Miss Roswell,' he said. 'May I wish you a successful Season?'

'Thank you, my lord.' She curtsied to him and he moved off. Sophie breathed again and managed a smile for Mr Gosport as he followed in his friend's wake.

'What do you make of that?' Sophie whispered, watching the backs of the two men as they were introduced to the other young ladies.

Sophie made sure their sponsor had moved out of earshot, which, for her, was not very far. 'I think Lady Fitz fancies herself as a matchmaker.'

'Who?'

'Why, you and Lord Braybrooke, of course.'

'But she thinks I am you. Oh, Sophie, we are truly in a coil now.'

'No, we are not. You do not fancy him for a husband, do you?'

'No, I do not. He is too high in the instep for my taste. Besides, he might already be married—he is surely nearer thirty than twenty.'

'Yes, but you heard Lady Fitz mention he had been away in the war. And she would not have dragged him over to us if he were not eligible.'

'What are we going to do?'

'Nothing. Enjoy ourselves. If he offers for you, you can always reject him. I'll wager that will bring him down a peg or two.'

'You do not like him?'

'No, I do not think I do.'

'Why not?'

Sophie was hard put to answer truthfully. Across the room the two men were enjoying a joke with a young lady and her mother to whom they had just been introduced and Sophie felt her heart contract into a tight knot, which she would not recognise as anything but distaste.

'He doesn't fit my criteria in any respect.'

'How can you possibly know that?'

'I just do.'

The two men were taking their leave. Lady Fitzpatrick returned to the girls after talking to Lady Gosport. 'What a turn up,' she said, smiling broadly, making her round face seem even rounder. 'We could not have hoped for a better start. Lord Braybrooke will

undoubtedly be the catch of the Season. He was particularly interested in you, my dear Charlotte.'

'Oh, no, I think not,' Charlotte said. 'He did not
say above a dozen words to me and those most condescending…'

'There you are, then! We must make what plans
we can to engage his attention, and soon too, before
he is snapped up.' Sophie burst into laughter and received a look of disapproval. 'Sophie, finding a husband for such as Miss Roswell is a very serious business and not a subject for mirth.'

Sophie straightened her face and remembered to
speak very clearly, close to her ladyship's ear. 'You
are quite right, my lady, marriage is a solemn under-
taking. I beg your pardon.'

'If you are lucky, you may engage the attention of
Mr Gosport, though from what I have seen, he does
seem to be tied to his mother's apron strings and dis-
inclined to wed. I should not say it, of course, for
Beth Gosport is my friend.'

Sophie wondered why she had said it, unless it was
to emphasise what a difficult task lay ahead in being
able to suit the less important of her two charges.

'I think we can safely take our leave now,' Lady
Fitzpatrick went on. 'It is polite to arrive a little late
and leave early if one means to stamp one's superi-
ority on to these little gatherings.'

'As his lordship has done,' Sophie said, winking at
Charlotte, a gesture which was lost on the short-
sighted Lady Fitzpatrick or she would have earned
another reproof.

* * *

'God, Martin, is that what I have to do to find a wife? I'd as lief forget the whole thing. I would, too, if it didn't mean falling into a worse case and having to marry Emily.'

The two men were walking towards St James's Street, where they intended to spend the remainder of the evening at White's.

'Oh, it was not as bad as all that,' his friend said, cheerfully, 'There was that little filly, Miss Roswell. Pretty little thing, blue eyes, blonde curls and curves in all the right places. And a considerable heiress, to boot. My mother told me the story.'

'I collect Lady Fitzpatrick saying something about a tragedy.'

'Yes. Her father, the second son of the second earl, married a Belgian lady and Miss Roswell was born and raised in Belgium...'

'Really? She does not give the impression of a well-travelled young lady. I would have taken a wager that she has not stirred beyond the shores of England. More, I should have been inclined to say she had never come up to Town before.'

'How can you possibly tell?'

'The polish is lacking. She has a simple charm that is more in tune with country life.'

'That is good, surely? It fits in well with your criteria.'

'Does it?' Richard turned to grin at him. 'And are you going to remind me of that whenever we meet and discuss one of the hopefuls?'

'Probably.'

'Then carry on. I might as well know the rest.'

'I believe her mother died some years ago. Her father brought her to England to stay with her uncle and his wife and then bought himself a commission and died in the Battle of Salamanca, a hero of that engagement, I am told. Her uncle, the Earl of Peterborough, adopted her.'

'What do we know of him?'

'Nothing out of the ordinary. He was a quiet gentlemen who stayed on his estate most of the time. I have heard nothing against him. On the contrary, he was well respected, even loved, on his home ground.'

'Go on.'

'Two years ago they were all travelling to London for Miss Roswell's come-out when they were caught in a terrible storm; the horses took fright and the carriage turned over. Miss Roswell was the only survivor. Unmarried and seventeen years old, she inherited Madderlea. Quite a catch, my friend.'

'Then why is she being sponsored by that antidote, Lady Fitzpatrick? Are they related?'

'I do not think so.'

'Related to the country cousin, maybe?'

'I don't know that either. I suppose it is possible. Since the accident, Miss Roswell has lived with her cousin.'

'Miss Hundon,' Richard murmured, finding himself remembering the feel of her small hand in his, the colour in her cheeks and the flash of fire in greeny-grey eyes which had looked straight into his, as if challenging him. She made him feel uncomfortable and he didn't know why.

'Yes, but she is of no consequence, not out of the

top drawer at all and must be discounted. Your grandfather would not entertain such a one.'

'No. So, I am to make a play for Miss Roswell, am I?'

'You could do a great deal worse. It was fortuitous that we went to my mother's *soirée*. Unless you make a push she will be snapped up.'

'I do not intend to make a push. I cannot be so cold-blooded.' They had arrived at the door of the club and turned to enter. 'But if, on further acquaintance, I find myself growing fond of her...'

'Oh, I forgot that love was an item on the list.'

Richard laughed and punched him playfully on the arm.

'Very well, I shall call on Lady Fitzpatrick tomorrow and suggest a carriage ride in the Park. And now, do you think we can forget the chits and concentrate on a few hands of cards?'

Lady Fitzpatrick and the two young ladies were sitting in the parlour the following morning, discussing the previous evening's events, when the footman scratched at the door and, flinging it wide, announced in a voice which would have done justice to a drill sergeant, 'My lady, Lord Braybrooke wishes to know if you are at home.'

'Braybrooke?' her ladyship queried, making Sophie wonder if she was losing her memory as well as her other faculties.

'He was at the gathering last evening, Lady Fitzpatrick,' Charlotte said. 'Surely you remember?'

'Oh, Braybrooke! To be sure. Rathbone's grandson. Show him in, Lester. At once.'

He disappeared and she turned to Charlotte. 'Who would have thought he would call so soon? He must have been singularly taken by you. Now, do not be too eager, nor too top-lofty either, my dear. Conduct yourself decorously and coolly.' Fussily she patted her white curls and adjusted her cap, took several deep breaths and fixed a smile of welcome on her face, just as the footman returned.

'Viscount Braybrooke, my lady.'

Richard, dressed in buff coat, nankeen breeches and polished hessians, strode into the room and bowed over her hand. 'My lady.'

'Good morning, Lord Braybrooke. This is a singular pleasure.' She waved a plump hand in the general direction of the girls. 'You remember Miss Roswell and Miss Hundon?'

'How could I forget such a trio of beauties, my lady? Quite the most brilliant stars in the firmament last evening.' He turned and caught Sophie's look of disdainful astonishment before she could manage to wipe it from her face and his own features broke into a grin. He was bamming them in such an obvious way, it made her furious, all the more so because Lady Fitzpatrick was simpering in pleasure and Charlotte's cheeks were on fire with embarrassment. He plucked Charlotte's hand from the folds of her muslin gown and raised it to his lips. 'Miss Roswell, your servant. I hope I see you well.'

'Quite well, thank you, my lord.'

'And, Miss Hundon,' he said, turning to Sophie almost reluctantly, 'you are well?'

'Indeed, yes.' He was having the same effect on her as he had had the previous evening. A night's sleep and time to consider her reaction had made not a jot of difference. He exuded masculine strength and confidence, so why act the dandy? Why pretend to be other than he was? This thought brought her to her senses with a jolt. She was acting too, wasn't she?

Lady Fitzpatrick indicated a chair. 'Please sit down, my lord.'

'Thank you.' He flung up the tails of his frockcoat and folded his long length neatly into the chair.

Sophie watched in fascination as he engaged Lady Fitzpatrick in small talk. To begin with he was frequently obliged to repeat himself, but as soon as he realised her ladyship was hard of hearing—a fact she would never admit—he spoke more clearly, enunciating each word carefully, winning her over completely.

Sometimes he addressed his remarks to Charlotte, smiling at her and flattering her, but rarely turned to Sophie. She was glad of that. He was far too conceited for her taste and she sincerely hoped Charlotte would not be such a ninny as to fall for a bag of false charm.

It was several minutes before he could bring himself to speak of the true reason for his visit. It had been a mistake to come, but Martin had nagged at him unmercifully, reminding him of his grandfather's ultimatum and in the end he had concluded it could do no harm. Little Miss Roswell was pretty; she had a rosy glow about her and an air of insouciance he found at odds with her position as heiress to a great estate.

But the other, the country cousin, disturbed him. Her eyes, intelligent, far-seeing, humorous, seemed to follow his every move, to understand that he was playing a part dictated by Society. He was not behaving like his normal self and he was afraid she would call his bluff and expose him for the clunch he felt himself to be, a feeling with which he was not at all familiar. How could she do this to him?

He had come to ask Miss Roswell to take a carriage ride with him, but she would have to be chaperoned and it was evident that was the role Miss Hundon was to play. Her watchful eyes would be on him every second, protecting her cousin, reducing him to an incompetent swain.

'My lady,' he said, addressing Lady Fitzpatrick. 'I came to ask if you and the young ladies would care to join me in a carriage ride in the park tomorrow afternoon.'

'Why, how kind of you,' she said, while both girls remained mute. 'I should very much like to accept, but… Oh, dear, I am afraid I have undertaken to visit Lady Holland.' She paused. 'But I do not see why you should not take the young ladies. Miss Hundon will chaperone Miss Roswell and their groom can ride alongside. If you are agreeable, of course.'

'I shall look forward to it.' He rose and bowed his way out, leaving two thunderstruck young ladies and a very self-satisfied matron behind him.

'Well…' Lady Fitzpatrick let out her breath in a

long sigh. 'I never thought you would engage the attention of someone so high in Society so soon.'

'No doubt he has heard of my...' Sophie paused and hastened to correct herself '...my cousin's fortune. Madderlea is a prize worth a little attention, do you not think?'

Charlotte's face was bright pink. 'That is unkind in you, Sophie,' she said. 'Do you not think he likes me for myself?'

Sophie was immediately contrite. 'Of course, he does, my dear, who could not? But you must remember that you, too, are superior and have something to offer.'

'Quite right,' her ladyship said, after asking Sophie to repeat herself. 'Now, we must discuss clothes and what you will say to him, for though it is one thing to attract his attention, it is quite another to keep it.'

'What do you know of the gentleman, my lady?' Sophie enquired, for Charlotte seemed to be in a daydream, and someone had to ask. 'Apart from the fact that he is grandson to the Duke of Rathbone. Is he the heir?'

'Indeed, he is. His father was a second son and did not expect to inherit, particularly as the heir was married and in good health, but the old Duke outlived both his sons. There is a cousin, I believe, but she is female.'

'Can she not inherit?' Charlotte asked.

'Unlike Madderlea, the estate is entailed. Richard Braybrooke came back from service in the Peninsula to find himself Viscount Braybrooke and his grandfather's heir.'

'A position, I am persuaded, he finds singularly uncongenial,' Sophie put in.

'Yes, he is a most congenial gentleman,' Lady Fitzpatrick said, mishearing her. 'Such superior address and conduct can only be the result of good breeding.'

Sophie choked on a laugh, making Charlotte look at her in alarm. 'If good breeding means one is insufferably arrogant, then he is, indeed, well-bred,' she murmured, while wiping tears of mirth from her face with a wisp of a handkerchief.

'I do not know what ails you, Sophie,' her ladyship said. 'Your cousin is also well-bred and she is most certainly not arrogant. Indeed, it were better if she could adopt a more haughty attitude, for she is far too shy.'

'I cannot change the way I am,' Charlotte said.

'Nor should you,' Sophie said. 'If the gentleman cannot see that you are sweet and kind and would not hurt the feelings of a fly, then he is blind and does not deserve you.'

The gentleman could see it. He was well aware of Miss Roswell's virtues and it only made him feel unworthy. She deserved to be wooed for herself, by some young blood who appreciated the very qualities he found so cloying. He wanted and needed someone with more spirit, someone to challenge him as Miss Hundon had done. When he had said as much to Martin, his friend had laughed and reminded him of his list of requirements. Challenge had not been mentioned at all. 'You have hardly had time to make a reasoned judgement, Dick,' he had said. But then reasoned judgement and instinct did not go hand in hand.

He called for the young ladies the following afternoon, not at all sure he was going to enjoy the outing. It might be the way Society dictated a man should court a lady, but it was not his way. It was too artificial. He felt a sham, dressed to make a killing in double-breasted frockcoat of dark green superfine, soft buckskin breeches and curly-brimmed top hat. He was not averse to dressing well, but to do so to catch a young lady smacked of hypocrisy.

Sophie and Charlotte were waiting in the drawing room for him. There was still a keen edge to the wind and so Charlotte had chosen to wear a blue carriage dress in fine merino wool which almost exactly matched the colour of her eyes. It was topped by a blue cape and a fetching bonnet trimmed with pink ruched silk in a shade that echoed the rose in her cheeks. She looked delightfully fresh and innocent.

Sophie, on the other hand, determined not to shine, was dressed in grey from head to foot and would not be persuaded to change her mind, when Charlotte said she had made herself look like a poor relation.

'But that is exactly what I am, Charlotte dear,' she had said. 'I am your chaperon, after all.'

There was no time to go back to her room and change, even if she had wanted to, for his lordship was announced at that moment and, after the usual courtesies, they made their way out to his lordship's barouche. And what a carriage; it made Lady Fitzpatrick's town coach, which stood beside it ready to convey her ladyship to her appointment, look even shabbier.

It was a shining black affair with the Rathbone coat of arms emblazoned on both doors and seats comfortably upholstered in red velvet. The driver, in impeccable uniform of tailcoat, striped waistcoat and knee breeches, was sitting on the box, whip in hand. His lordship put a hand under Charlotte's elbow and helped her into her seat, then turned to do the same for Sophie, but she was already climbing in, disdaining his assistance. He smiled at this show of independence and took his own seat and, giving the driver an almost imperceptible nod, they set off, with Luke riding demurely half a head behind on Charlotte's little mare.

Chapter Three

It was a perfect late spring day and the carriageway in the park was crowded with vehicles of all shapes and sizes, and as they were all going at little more than walking pace it was almost like a parade. Richard seemed to know or be known by almost everyone and they frequently drew to a halt for the girls to be presented to the occupants of other carriages. They were also hailed frequently by riders from the nearby gallop, who reined in to speak to Richard, while casting admiring glances at Charlotte, who sat smiling beside him, enjoying every minute.

Sophie hardly rated a second look, but that had its advantages in that she could take time to gaze about her, to make her own assessment of the wide range of characters who took part in the traditional afternoon procession. They ranged from dowagers to schoolgirls, not yet out, Lady This and the Countess of That, as well as some whom Sophie was sure came from the *demi-monde* and rode by with all the aplomb and self-confidence in the world, twirling their parasols.

There were dandies and rakes, army officers resplendent in uniform, a few naval officers and more than a sprinkling of hopefuls who did not fit into any category but wished they did. Not one took her eye…except the man sitting in the seat opposite her and conversing so easily with her cousin at his side.

He was handsome in a rugged kind of way, his features lined by exposure to sun and wind. He exuded masculinity; it came over so strongly it took her breath away. If only… She sighed and suddenly found his attention focused on her. 'You do not agree, Miss Hundon?'

She had not been attending to the conversation and found herself at a loss. 'I beg your pardon, my lord, I was daydreaming.'

He smiled. Her eyes had held a faraway look, as if she were thinking of some absent admirer. In Upper Corbury in the county of Leicestershire, perhaps. He had just learned from Miss Roswell that that was where the Hundons had their home. 'Miss Roswell was commenting on the number of officers still in uniform and expressing the hope that the peace may last and they will no longer be needed to fight.'

'Oh, to that I most heartily agree, but my sympathies are with the common soldiers, who know no other means of earning a living. I think it is shameful just to turn them loose, after they have fought so well for their country. We worry about Spain and Portugal, France and Austria, send delegates to the Congress of Vienna to ensure justice on the continent and we ignore the problems nearer home. It is no wonder there are riots. And ranging militia against unarmed men and women who are only trying to have their voices heard is not the way to go on.'

He was inclined to agree with her, but the challenge was there, in her voice and in her greeny-grey eyes, and he could not resist the temptation to rise to it. 'Law and order must be kept or we will descend into anarchy.'

'Oh, that is the answer we are given for every act of repression. Shoot them, cut them down. Throw them in prison and hope everyone will forget them. Suspending the Habeas Corpus Act was a monstrous denial of justice.'

He smiled. 'I collect your father is a lawyer. Have you learned such sentiments from him?'

In her fervour, she had forgotten her uncle's profession and she had not heard him express any views on the subject. He was not a man to discuss either his clients or the state of the economy with his daughter and niece. Young ladies, in his opinion, did not need to know of such things. She glanced at Charlotte from beneath the brim of her bonnet, but her cousin was staring straight ahead, a bright pink spot on each cheek.

'No, my lord, but I read a great deal and have always been encouraged to think for myself.' She knew she was on dangerous ground and hurriedly reverted to the original subject under discussion. 'If work could be found for the discharged soldiers, they would not be discontent.' And then, because she could not resist having a dig at him. 'It is all very

well for the officers, for they have families and estates
and education to help them…'

He laughed. '*Touché*, my dear Miss Hundon. But,
you know, families and estates bring their own responsibilities.'

She smiled at that, thinking of her own situation,
but he saw only sparkling greeny-grey eyes and a
mouth that was made for smiling. And kissing. God
in heaven, what had made him think that? She was
nothing more than a country mouse, a little grey one.
No, he amended, that description was inaccurate, for
she was tall and her movements were not the quick
scurrying of a tiny rodent, but the measured move-
ment of a stalking cat.

'Yes, my lord, the responsibility to marry well, to
produce heirs. It is, I am persuaded, a form of vanity.'

'Sophie!' Charlotte cried. 'How can you say that
when you—'

'Miss Hundon is entitled to her opinion, Miss Roswell. Do not scold her.' He was looking at Sophie as
he spoke and she felt herself shrink under his gaze,
though she would not let him see it. 'You are surely
not implying your cousin is vain?'

'Nothing was further from my thoughts, my lord,'
she said truthfully. 'No one could be less vain or more
sweet-natured than my cousin. But her case is excep-
tional. She is a young lady who has inherited a large
estate, but cannot have the governing of it. Society
has decreed that that can only be done by a man. She
must have a husband or give up her home entirely.'

'Sophie, please…' Charlotte begged. 'You are being excessively impertinent, when Lord Braybrooke

has been so kind as to invite us to share his carriage. He does not wish to hear…' She stopped in confusion.

'Oh, my dearest, I did not mean to put you to the blush,' Sophie said, contrite. 'I don't know what came over me.'

What had come over her was a strong desire to pierce Lord Braybrooke's self-assurance, to stop him looking at her in that half-mocking way and take her seriously. But why? Why did it matter so much?

They had come to the end of the carriageway and the driver turned the barouche skilfully and set out on the return journey, while the two girls chatted, their disagreement forgotten.

Richard was intrigued, not only by Miss Hundon, but by the relationship which existed between the two girls. That they were close he did not doubt, but they were so different. Miss Hundon was outspoken and opinionated, almost the blue stocking he had decried, and her dress sense left a great deal to be desired but as he was not considering her for a wife, he told himself it was of no consequence.

On the other hand, Miss Roswell, who did have many of the attributes he had so carefully listed to Martin, including her own fortune, did not stir him to any kind of passion, either of desire or anger. Her skirts, brushing against his leg in the carriage, did not make him want to increase the pressure, to touch her, to kiss her, pretty though she was. Perhaps that would come, when he came to know her better, when she relaxed a little in his company and opened out to him.

At the moment she was stiff and tense, almost as if she were afraid of him. Miss Hundon was not afraid.

He pushed thoughts of Miss Sophie Hundon from him and turned to converse with Miss Roswell, trying to bring her out, to show her there was nothing to fear, but she had suddenly gone mute. He could get nothing out of her but 'Yes, my lord' or 'No, my lord' or 'Indeed?'

Sophie, now that his attention was engaged elsewhere, was able to relax a little. The carriage bowled smoothly along and she found herself thinking that they must be seen in the park more often, but it would not do to be too frequently in the company of Lord Braybrooke. He was not the only eligible in Town and he needn't think he was! They certainly could not drive out in Lady Fitz's town coach; they would be a laughing stock.

She would buy an equipage of her own, one with the Roswell crest emblazoned on the door, and drawn by matched cattle which would be the envy of the *ton*. The thought brought a smile to her lips, a smile not lost on Richard Braybrooke, who was taken aback by the way it lit her whole countenance and made what he had hitherto considered a somewhat unexceptional face into a beautiful one. He was lost in wonder and a sudden arousal of desire which made him squirm uncomfortably in his seat. It was the second time she had done this to him, and he resented it.

He was supposed to be searching for a wife, a wife with very particular virtues, not lusting after a poor country cousin. Did she know the effect she was having on him? Was it deliberate? If so, she might be agreeable to a little dalliance if he made it worth her while. It might serve to bring him back to his usual salubrious self and he could then concentrate on the task in hand, wooing the heiress.

He allowed himself to savour the prospect for a few delightful seconds before banishing it. He was not in the army now, he could no longer take whichever wench fluttered her eyelids at him in invitation. He had never had to pay for his pleasures, but neither had he bedded an unmarried gentlewoman. The idea was unthinkable. And yet he had thought it. He shook himself and made more strenuous efforts to engage the attention of Miss Charlotte Roswell.

'Tell me about Madderlea,' he said, deciding that was surely a subject on which she would find it easy to converse, but apart from telling him that it was near the north Norfolk coast and very extensive, she volunteered no information. In fact she seemed very agitated. Did she think he was more interested in her inheritance than in her? He smiled and dropped the subject.

When they drew up outside Lady Fitzpatrick's front door, he jumped out to hand Charlotte down while the coachman knocked at the door, then turned to help Sophie.

About to step down behind her cousin, she held out her hand for him to grasp, but instead she found his lordship's hands spanning her waist. Startled, she said nothing as he lifted her down and deposited her on the pavement. He did not immediately release her, but stood smiling down at her, his brown eyes looking into hers, almost as if he were trying to read her thoughts. She moved her gaze to his mouth and wished she had not. It was a strong mouth, so close to hers, she could feel the warmth of his breath. Even as she looked, it seemed to move closer. Surely he was not going to kiss her, not here, in the street? Why couldn't she move away? Why couldn't she speak?

'Miss Hundon,' he said, and managed to convey a deal of meaning in it. 'I enjoyed our little sparring match. I hope you will afford me the opportunity of a return bout before too long.'

She had no idea what he meant and her legs were so shaky she thought she would fall if he released her, but she did not intend to be intimidated. She stepped back and found the ground stayed beneath her feet, the sky was in its correct position above her head and, though her breathing was erratic, she was in no danger of swooning. She forced a smile. 'My lord, such a manly pursuit as fisticuffs is hardly in my repertoire.'

He grinned and turned to escort her to the door, where Charlotte stood looking back at them. 'You and Miss Roswell do ride, though?'

'Yes, indeed.'

He looked up at Charlotte as they approached her. 'Miss Hundon tells me you both ride,' he said. 'Would you care to join Mr Gosport and me for a gentle canter tomorrow morning? If you have no mounts, I can easily find some for you.'

Charlotte hesitated, looking to Sophie to indicate whether or not she wanted her to accept. 'I am not sure what engagements we have,' she said.

'Why, Charlotte, we said we were going to bespeak a carriage tomorrow and Lady Fitzpatrick recommended Robinson and Cook, don't you remember?'

Charlotte remembered no such thing, but she smiled and said, 'Oh, yes, I had quite forgot. I am sorry, my lord.'

'Another time, then,' he said, smiling affably. 'But, forgive me, who will advise you on your purchase? Lady Fitzpatrick…' He left the sentence hovering in the air.

'We shall take Luke, our groom, with us and he will consult the proprietor,' Sophie said.

'I doubt that will ensure a satisfactory deal,' he said. 'Allow me to offer my services.'

Charlotte appealed to Sophie and, receiving a slight nod, turned back to him. 'That is excessively kind of you, my lord, we should be most happy to accept.'

What else could she have done? Sophie asked herself, after he had arranged to call for them the following morning at ten and taken his leave. It would have been ungracious to have spurned his help, especially when she acknowledged they probably needed it.

'He has fastened himself to us like a leech,' Charlotte said as they went up to their rooms to divest themselves of their outdoor clothes. 'It is Madderlea and your fortune he has in his sights and I wish it were not so. We shall both be ruined when the truth comes out that I am not mistress of Madderlea and have no fortune.'

'Why?' Sophie threw her bonnet on the bed and followed it with her cloak, glad to be rid of the outmodish garments. 'Young gentlemen of the *ton* are forever playing tricks on people. They bam their way into select gatherings, pretend to be coachmen or highwaymen and no one thinks anything of it. Why shouldn't we?'

'We are not young gentlemen.'

'No, but we have gone too far to turn back now. We will tell everyone when we return to Leicestershire at the end of the Season. No harm will be done because you are going back to Freddie and as for me…'

'Yes? What about you?'

'Unless I can find a man who comes up to my expectations and has humour enough to laugh at our masquerade, I shall go back single.'

'What about Lord Braybrooke? Are you not a little taken with him?'

'No, I am not,' Sophie retorted, far too quickly to be convincing. 'He is too arrogant and you heard all those questions about Madderlea. He is undoubtedly counting his chickens.'

'He does not need Madderlea, he is heir to a dukedom.'

'Then he is also greedy.'

It was all very well to find fault with the man, to try to convince herself that he had not come within a mile of her expectations; the truth was that, in the space of two days, he had touched a chord in her, made her aware of feelings and desires she never knew she had. The pressure of his hand, the light in his eye, the soft cadences of his voice when he was not sparring with her, even his disapproval, excited her and lulled her at the same time. He was a threat to her peace of mind. She must remember Madderlea and her responsibilities and perhaps the danger would go away.

'He is not the only fish in the sea,' she said. 'We must make a push to meet more people and buying a carriage is the beginning of our crusade.'

'Chickens! Fish!' Charlotte laughed. 'Are we to make a tasty dinner of him?'

They both fell on to the bed in paroxysms of mirth at the idea. 'Served with potatoes and cabbage and a sharp sauce.' Sophie giggled. 'Followed by humble pie.'

There was nothing humble about Viscount Braybrooke and Sophie was obliged to acknowledge that when he called to accompany them to buy the carriage. He was dressed in frockcoat and pantaloons with a neatly tied cravat peeping over a yellow and white striped waistcoat. His dark curls were topped by a high-crowned hat with a curled brim which made him seem taller and more magnificent than ever. She was determined not to let him undermine her confidence and treated him with cool disdain, an attitude he seemed hardly to notice, being equally determined to pay particular attention to Charlotte.

But when it came to discussing the different carriages on offer at Robinson and Cook's premises in Mount Street, Charlotte, aware that it was Sophie who would be paying for it, once again fell silent. It was Sophie who found questions to ask about the advantages and disadvantages of curricles, phaetons, high-perch and low-slung barouches, landaus and tilburys, and their comparative prices, and it was Sophie who asked about horses once they had chosen a barouche because it could seat four easily and Lady Fitzpatrick would inevitably be accompanying them on most of their jaunts.

Once the arrangements had been made for it to be finished in dark green and the Roswell coat of arms to be painted on the doors, they left and were driven by Richard to Tattersall's where he purchased a pair of matched greys on their behalf and arranged for them to be delivered to the mews which served the houses in Holles Street. Luke would be in seventh heaven looking after them, Sophie knew, and prompted Charlotte politely to decline his lordship's offer of interviewing coachmen.

They arrived home in good time for nuncheon and he stopped to pay his respects to Lady Fitzgerald, treating her with great courtesy and earning her enthusiastic approbation.

'We are beholden to you, my lord,' she said on being told of the successful outcome of their visit to the coachbuilder. 'I am sure Miss Roswell could not have made such a bargain without you.'

'Indeed, no,' Charlotte said. 'We are in your debt.' He smiled and bowed towards her. 'Then, if you wish, you may discharge it by coming riding with me tomorrow morning. Mr Gosport has said he will be delighted to escort Miss Hundon.'

Surprisingly she did not consult Sophie before accepting. 'Thank you, we shall be delighted.'

Sophie's feelings about that were so ambivalent she spent the remainder of the day going from depression to elation and back again in the blinking of an eye. Richard Braybrooke had, all unknowingly, wormed his way into her heart while so patently wooing the Roswell fortune embodied in her cousin. Mentally she went over the list of attributes she had decided were required for the master of Madderlea and incidentally, the husband of its mistress, and realised she knew very little about Richard, Viscount Braybrooke.

True, he was handsome and well turned out, but he was also conceited and arrogant. Was he kind to his servants, good with children, an honourable man? She did not know and only further acquaintance would tell her, a prospect that filled her with joyful anticipation, until she remembered that his attention had been almost entirely focused on Charlotte, the supposed heiress, which made her wonder if his grandfather, the Duke, was not as plump in the pocket as everyone had supposed and her fortune was the main attraction. Or was she maligning him—was his heart really set on Charlotte?

Jealousy and her love for her cousin raged within her so that she could not sit still, could not sew or read, was snappy with everyone and then immediately sorry. Charlotte could not bring her out of it, because Charlotte herself was worried about the deception they were practising and what she was going to say to his lordship should he offer for her.

'I like him well enough,' she told Sophie in the privacy of her room. 'But I would never consider him as a husband. I am determined on marrying Freddie and nothing and no one will change that. Besides, as soon as he discovers that you are the heiress and he has been deceived…'

'He will want neither of us,' Sophie snapped. 'So there is no need to put ourselves into a quake over it.'

It was a relief to find a pile of invitations on the breakfast table the following morning. Lady Fitzpatrick, in a housegown and with her hair pushed under a mob cap, was delighted. 'I knew it would happen, as soon as you were seen out with Lord Braybrooke,' she said. 'None of the mamas of unmarried daughters are going to let you have a clear field where he is concerned. And the ladies with sons will not allow him to take all the limelight when you have so much to offer, dear Charlotte.'

She chuckled. 'Oh, this is going to be a very interesting Season. Now, girls, go and dress for your ride. I have already sent for your mounts to be brought to the door.' She waved the bundle of invitations at them. 'When you return we will decide on which of these to accept and make plans for your own come-out ball.'

'A ball?' queried Charlotte as they mounted the stairs together. 'How can we possibly have a ball here? There is no ballroom and the drawing room is too small, even if we moved all the furniture out.'

Sophie was too tense to worry about the answer to that question. 'No doubt her ladyship will find a way. Let us take one day at a time. Today is the day for riding.'

In spite of her mental anguish, Sophie longed for

the exhilaration of a good ride and made up her mind that she would enjoy it and not spend precious time worrying about what could not be helped. She had not bought a new riding habit because the one she already had was perfectly serviceable. Frogged in military style with silver braid, it was of deep blue velvet and fitted closely to a neat waist, becoming fuller over the hips. Her beaver hat, trimmed with a long iridescent peacock feather which curled around the brim and swept across one cheek, was a creation to turn heads.

Without revealing her true identity, she would set aside the undistinguished country cousin and be more like herself, just for a day. It was vanity, she acknowledged, but necessary if she were not to sink into self-induced oblivion. She went downstairs when she heard his lordship arrive, determined to be cool, but her resolve was almost overturned when she saw Lord Braybrooke looking up at her from the marble-tiled hall.

He was neatly but not extravagantly dressed for riding, in a double-breasted coat with black buttons, supple leather breeches and boots with enough polish to mirror whatever was immediately above them, in this case, his outstretched arm as he came towards her hand to take it in greeting.

'Miss Hundon.'

'Lord Braybrooke.'

Why was it that even the small touch of his fingers could bring a hot flush of colour to her cheeks and turn her legs to jelly? She was vastly relieved when Charlotte, becomingly attired in leaf green, followed her downstairs and distracted the viscount, giving her time to give herself a severe scolding and collect her scattered wits. She picked up her crop from the hall table and led the way outside, where Martin and Luke stood with the horses.

Luke, who naturally knew that the stallion was her mount, threw her up, leaving Richard, taken by surprise, to see Charlotte into her saddle, then the three men mounted and the little cavalcade set off at walking pace, carefully weaving its way in and out of the traffic until they reached the gates of Green Park.

Sophie on horseback was a very different person from Sophie playing the country cousin in a Society drawing room, or being a nondescript companion riding in a carriage. Sophie on a horse was strong and fearless and competent. Before long she became impatient with their steady plod and, as soon as she saw a wide expanse of green in front of her, set off at a canter, which the others were obliged to follow. Laughing, she increased the pace to a gallop.

Richard was torn between going after her and staying with Charlotte, who showed none of the recklessness of her cousin.

Reckless perhaps, but magnificent. When he had first seen the stallion he had thought it too strong for either of the girls and assumed the young groom would ride it. His initial astonishment at Miss Hundon's changed appearance was increased when he realised the big stallion was hers. She sat it easily at a walk, as if moulded into the saddle, but now she was flying away from them, a born rider.

Martin, at his side, chuckled. 'Go on after her, you

know you want to,' he said in an undertone. 'I'll stay with Miss Roswell.'

Richard spurred his mount and was gone, leaving Martin to turn ruefully towards Charlotte. 'He will see she comes to no harm.'

'Oh, I doubt Sophie will fall, she is too good a rider. At home she always outruns me.'

'I suppose it is not to be wondered at. Leicestershire is good hunting country and if you have been all your life among hunting folk, you have a feel for it.'

'Oh, but Sophie has not…' She stopped in confusion and began again. 'She does not care for hunting.'

'And you?'

'I follow it sometimes, but in truth, I fell off when I was little and broke my arm. I was lucky it was no worse, but it has made me a nervous rider. Sophie is very good, she encourages me and does not usually gallop off like that, but I expect she could not resist the opportunity to stretch Pewter's legs.' She looked up to where the two riders could be seen approaching a small copse of trees. 'See, she is pulling up and his lordship has caught up with her.'

'Are you run mad?' Richard demanded, pulling his own horse to a quivering stop beside the big grey at the very edge of the trees. 'You could have been thrown.'

She smiled mischievously and slid easily to the ground. 'Did I look in danger of falling off, my lord?'

He had to admit she had not and that his annoyance was not so much directed at her as at his own strange emotions. He wanted to shout at her, to tell her she had frightened him to death, to shake her until her teeth rattled, but that was tempered by another desire, one so strong it was almost overwhelming him. He dismounted and stood beside her, looking down into her face which showed more animation than he had seen in her before.

Her greeny-grey eyes sparkled, her cheeks glowed and her mouth, slightly open, tantalised him with a glimpse of white teeth and the tip of a pink tongue. Did she know how provocative she was being? Was it a well-rehearsed ploy? God in heaven, he was not made of stone! Throwing off his hat, he reached out and pulled her into the cover of the nearest tree where he took that smiling mouth in a kiss which was almost brutal in its intensity.

She was taken completely by surprise and did not move, could not move. His mouth on hers was hard and unyielding, borne of anger, but as the kiss went on, the tension drained from him and the pressure of his lips softened. When she could have pulled herself away, she did not. She found herself responding, allowing him to explore her mouth with a feather-light tongue which swept her into heedless rapture. Her surroundings disappeared and only their two bodies, so close she could feel his heartbeat against the material of her habit, held any meaning for her.

Somewhere, deep inside her, she felt herself turn to liquid. It was as if the very essence of her was dissolving, merging, becoming one with him. The hands she had raised to push him away crept up and round his neck. Her fingers tangled themselves in his hair and pulled him even closer. Her skirt became entangled round his legs as if they were one being. Time and place were irrelevant; who he was, who she was, were irrelevant. She could smell the maleness of him, taste his saliva and it was like a drug. She was lost.

The sound of horses alerted him and he thrust her from him, breathing heavily. She stood staring at him, unable to speak.

What she ought to have been was furious with him, but that would have been hypocritical, when she had wanted the experience as much as he did. It would be more to the point to be furious with herself, for betraying her feelings, for succumbing, for forgetting she was mistress of Madderlea.

He was the first to regain his composure, but not for a moment would he admit, even to himself, that she had bewitched him, that forces stronger than reason had impelled him to act as he had. But an apology was called for. 'I beg your pardon,' he said softly. 'I did not mean to hurt you in any way.'

'What did you mean, then?' she demanded, brushing her hand against her swollen lips and trying very hard not to cry.

'Nothing, Miss Hundon.' He was almost back in command of himself. 'Temptation in the guise of a beautiful and enticing young lady is always hard to resist and I am weak when it comes to resisting temptation.'

Before she could think of a suitable reply, Charlotte's voice came to them from the other side of the

bushes. 'Sophie! Where are you? Have you hurt yourself? I saw you disappear…'

Sophie sank to the ground—her legs were weak in
any case—and smiled up at Charlotte as she ducked
under the overhanging branches of the tree to join
them. 'I twisted my ankle on a hidden root when dis-
mounting,' she said. 'It is nothing.'

'Oh, dear, do you think you can ride?'

'Of course, it was only a little twinge. And it is not
my stirrup foot.' She made to rise unaided, but Richard was at her side in a moment, picking her up ef-
fortlessly and setting up such a jangling of her nerves
that she was hard put to appear calm. He carried her
to her mount and set her in the saddle. Neither of
them spoke.

Luke and Martin were waiting by the horses and
they set off for home, silent now because every single
one of them had thoughts they could not utter. Richard and Sophie were deep in contemplation of what
had happened and what it might mean; Martin, guessing the truth, wondered whether his intrepid friend
had at last found his match; Charlotte, surmising that
something important had passed between the viscount
and her cousin, worried about the deception they had
perpetrated; and Luke was fearfully hoping that he
would not be blamed if Miss Sophie had really hurt
herself.

When they arrived at Holles Street, Richard declined Charlotte's invitation to come in and have
some refreshment and the two men saw the young
ladies safely indoors and turned to leave.

'Well?' Martin demanded, as they walked their horses back to Bedford Row.

'Well, what?'

'Miss Hundon did not stumble, did she? Except into your arms. I wonder you were so cork-brained, considering Miss Roswell was only a few yards behind. It was all I could do to hold her back when you both disappeared from view.'

'I do not need a scold from you, my friend, and if that is all you have to talk about, I would as lief you remained silent.'

'Then silent I shall be. But I won't stop thinking.'

They rode on without speaking for about fifty yards, then Richard laughed. 'I am sorry, Martin, you are too much of a friend to be treated in that rag-mannered way. And over a little bit of muslin.'

'Only she is not just a little bit of muslin, she is a gentle young lady, an innocent.' He turned to Richard with a gleam of humour in his eye, though he did not yet feel comfortable enough with him to laugh outright. 'And she does not meet your criteria.'

'She is lovely when she chooses to leave off those dowdy country-cousin clothes and she is fond of outdoor pursuits. She sits a horse better than some troopers I have met.'

'That could be construed as being hoydenish and I distinctly recall you saying you do not like hoydens. Besides, her family, though undoubtedly respectable, are not out of the top drawer and she has no dowry to speak of. Insuperable obstacles, my friend. And what about Miss Roswell, who has hitherto been the object of your attentions?'

'I said I was sorry, I did not ask you to renew your attack. If you must challenge me, let's go and have a few rounds at Jackson's.'

They left the horses to be rubbed down, watered and fed by grooms at his lordship's stables and walked to Bond Street where they stripped off and spent an hour in the ring, then they dressed and wandered to St James's to have coffee in Hubbold's and read the newspapers. It was late in the afternoon when they finally left and parted. Martin had undertaken to dine with his mother and Richard decided to go for a walk. He wanted to be alone to come to terms with that revealing kiss and what it meant.

Sophie, sitting in Lady Fitzgerald's drawing room, was tired of discussing balls and routs, musical evenings, visits to the opera and theatre, not to mention the gowns they would wear and the people they might meet. Her mind was too full of Richard Braybrooke to think of anything else. Indeed, she had developed a dreadful headache which was exacerbated by having to speak loudly and clearly to Lady Fitzgerald while avoiding meeting Charlotte's eyes. She knew her cousin was longing to ask her about the incident in the park and she knew she could never bring herself to speak of it.

The last straw was when Lady Fitzgerald began talking about their own ball, telling them that her old friend, Lady Gosport, had offered the use of her ballroom. 'It is excessively kind of her,' she was saying. 'And will suit our purpose well, for young Martin is a close friend of Lord Braybrooke's and the tabbies can make what they will of that. For my part, I do not subscribe to the common opinion that his lordship is a rake and is only looking for a wife to please his grandfather. The right gel will soon make him change his ways and if you should be so fortunate, my dear Charlotte, as to take his fancy, I shall consider my efforts well rewarded.'

Charlotte began a half-hearted protest, but Sophie could not stay and listen; she rose and excused herself. 'I have a dreadful headache, my lady, I need some fresh air.'

'Would it not be more efficacious to lie down and take a tisane, my dear?'

'No, my lady, I have sometimes had these headaches before and the best remedy is a walk.'

'Very well, but if you leave the garden, make sure Anne or Luke accompanies you. Charlotte and I have much to discuss and will remain here.' Her main responsibility was towards Miss Roswell, Mr Hundon had made that clear, and if the cousin chose to go out, then her duty was to see she had an escort, no more.

Sophie had been counting on that. Throwing a burnouse over her afternoon gown of striped jaconet and donning a small brimmed chip bonnet tied beneath her chin, she let herself out of the house, conveniently forgetting to alert either Anne or Luke. She wanted to be alone to think.

Where her footsteps took her she could not afterwards have said, but half an hour later she found herself in Covent Garden. The stalls and barrows had long since gone and it was not yet time for the theatregoers to begin arriving. The huge open space was comparatively free of crowds. The only people about were one or two walkers, like herself, a crowd of barefoot children playing tag and two or three beggars. It was only when one of them accosted her, dirty palm uppermost, that she realised that they were wearing the tattered remnants of uniforms.

She smiled and dug into her reticule for a few coins. 'You are soldiers?' she queried.

'Were soldiers, miss,' one of them answered her. 'Soldiers no longer, there being no call for military men now there's peace.'

'Where do you come from? You do not sound like a Londoner.'

'Norfolk, miss, but tain't no good going back there, is it? They've troubles enough of their own.'

'You have no work?'

'No, miss.'

She handed over all the money she had with her, which was only a couple of sovereigns and some smaller coins. 'I'm so sorry. I wish I could do more.'

'Oh, no, you don't.' The coins were snatched from the man's hand. 'Be off with you or I shall feel obliged to call a constable.'

She turned towards the speaker, eyes flashing angrily. 'Lord Braybrooke, how *dare* you interfere? I gave the men that money of my own free will and I wish I had more to give them. Please return it to them.'

'They did not threaten you?'

'No, of course not. Why should they?'

He handed over the money with a wry grin. The man tugged at his forelock and gave Richard a wink of understanding, which only a few short months before he would never have dared to do. 'Thank you, lady. God bless you.' And with that he turned on his heel and joined the others who had been watching the exchange with interest.

Sophie turned to Richard, still angry enough to ignore the swift beating of her heart at his unexpected appearance. 'Did you follow me?'

'No, why should I do that? I merely saw what I perceived to be a lady in trouble and came to the rescue. I apologise if I mistook the situation, but you should not be out alone. Where is your escort?'

'I do not need an escort, my lord. I have nothing worth stealing.'

'Except your good name.' It was out before he could stop it and he knew he had laid himself open to a sharp retort and he was not disappointed.

'That, my lord, was stolen earlier in the day and by someone I should have been able to trust.'

'It was not stolen, it was freely given,' he said, equal to the challenge.

'Lady Fitz said you were a rake and how right she was,' she said, ignoring the truth of his remark.

'And you are a tease.' He was angry now. He had thought she was in danger from ruffians, had expected gratitude, not this bitter exchange of accusations. Rake, indeed! 'If you behave like a demi-rep, then you must expect to be treated like one.'

It was as well Sophie did not understand the epithet or she would undoubtedly have stung his face with the flat of her hand. As it was, she was hard put to desist. He was the outside of enough. Not a gentleman. Not kind and considerate, not even honourable. Dastardly. She turned on her heel and walked away, tears stinging her eyes.

She had gone only half a dozen paces when she realised he was still beside her. 'Why are you following me? Are you hoping I will be so weak as to succumb a second time?'

'I wish I could be so fortunate,' he said, with a melodramatic sigh. 'Your generosity does you credit as I have just witnessed, but twice in one day is more than I can expect or deserve.'

'And there you are right, sir, so why dog my footsteps?'

'I may well have dug my own pit as far as you are concerned, Miss Hundon, but I am not so lacking in sense as to allow you to continue alone. You have given away all your money—what will the ruffians demand next, I wonder?'

She shuddered at the prospect. 'I am going home.'

'Then allow me to escort you.'

She nodded, unable to bring herself to admit she would be glad of his company. In spite of their harsh words, she felt safe with him, safe and protected.

At her door, he bowed with a flourish and strode away. She watched him go with a terrible ache in her heart. He failed her expectations in so many ways, but she loved him and everything else paled into insignificance beside that bittersweet knowledge.

Chapter Four

The Season began in earnest and the girls found themselves caught up in a flurry of social engagements. Accompanied by Lady Fitzpatrick, they drove out in the new carriage on most afternoons when the weather was fine, either in the park or to make calls. They left cards all over the place, went out to tea, visited the theatre with supper afterwards, attended musical gatherings and simple country dances but, until they had officially come out, they could not attend the big balls, which was where the higher echelons of the eligibles gathered. Lady Fitzpatrick, anxious to remedy that, was deep in negotiations with Lady Gosport to hold their come-out ball early in the Season.

It was thus that Martin was privy to all the arrangements and gossip that went on between his mother and the girls' sponsor, which he passed on to Richard. 'It is going to be a fearful crush,' he told him one day when the two men were relaxing at their club. 'Lady Fitzpatrick is determined that Miss Roswell will be launched in style.'

Richard laughed. 'What does she know of style, unless it be thirty years out of date. She will have us in knee breeches like they do at Almack's.'

'It is to be a costume ball. And she is being guided by Mama, so you need not fear being made to look foolish.'

'I am not concerned for myself, but the young ladies. Do they really suppose Lady Fitzpatrick is all the crack?'

'No, they are not blind. And both have a sense of refinement, particularly Miss Hundon. There is a quiet dignity about her which would be more appropriate in the heiress than the country cousin. Miss Roswell, on the other hand, delightful though she is, does not have that presence, that spirit of independence, which is so evident in her cousin.'

'Fustian! Miss Hundon is a hoyden, you said so yourself.'

'I was simply reminding you of the requirements you listed, I did not say I agreed with you.'

'I wish I had never spoken to you about them, if you are to be continually flinging them in my face. They are not writ in stone, you know. I may be flexible.'

'I am glad to hear it.'

'Why are you extolling the virtues of Miss Hundon? You know my grandfather would not countenance the daughter of a lawyer.'

'Have you asked him?'

'Certainly not. There is no need, I have no plans to offer for Miss Sophie Hundon.'

'Miss Roswell, then? She is excessively wealthy,

but you would not know it to speak to her, for she is modesty itself. And Madderlea is a great house, I am told, though, according to Mama, it needs repairs and renovation. She really must marry soon or it will go to rack and ruin for want of someone to care for it. Once the Season gets underway, the competition will be fierce.'

'I thought it already had.'

'No, what we have had are only preliminary skirmishes, the real battles are to come. I am looking forward to it.'

'So you may be. You are not constrained by duty as I am.' Richard chuckled suddenly. 'But I intend to mix duty with pleasure. I shall flirt lightly with every unmarried miss between the ages of seventeen and thirty and keep them all guessing. I shall sometimes be disdainful and superior and sometimes flattering and eager and see what transpires. It will serve the dowagers right for putting wealth and title before character. Time enough to be serious when I have made up my mind.'

'By then you will have earned the reputation of being a rakeshame and none will have you. Certainly Miss Roswell will not.'

'I am persuaded that is already my reputation,' he said, reminded of Sophie's accusation. 'I may as well live up to it.'

'Why?'

'Why?' he echoed. He did not know. He was not a conceited man, nor was he vindictive, but he hated this notion that a single man in want of a wife must parade himself before hopeful mamas, his address and

conduct scrutinised, his prospects and fortunes ana-
lysed, until it was impossible to sneeze without it being the subject of gossip. If he were not the Duke of
Rathbone's heir, if he were still a simple soldier, no
one would be the least interested in him.

'I suppose it is because I dislike the idea that my
faults should be weighed against my title and fortune
and not against my virtues,' he said slowly. 'I am
curious to know how far the scales will tip before one
outweighs the other.'

'That is a dangerous game to play, my friend. You
may put off the avaricious, though give me leave to
doubt it, but you will also give the lady of your choice
a hearty aversion to you.'

He had already done so, he realised with a jolt that
shook him to the core. Miss Hundon, the country
cousin, an entirely unsuitable young lady in the eyes
of his grandfather, had never been far from his
thoughts ever since he had met her. She had more
than most to gain by becoming the Duchess of Rathbone. Had she deliberately set out to trap him into
that kiss, hoping for a declaration? Had she galloped
away, knowing he would follow and that if she fluttered her eyelashes at him, he, being a man, would
be bound to do what he had? It was easier to convince
himself of that than to admit he had fallen in love.

His conviction was sorely shaken when he next
came across Miss Roswell and Miss Hundon after a
visit to the opera one evening when he discovered
they were included in the supper party Lord and Lady
Howard had arranged afterwards. Paying attention to

the Howard daughter while uncomfortably aware that Sophie stood only a few yards away and could hear every word was unnerving. He felt an almost uncontrollable urge to turn towards her and tell her he was only acting the part, to grab hold of her and hurry her away some private place where he could taste her lips again, feel her body pressed up against his, to know her passion matched his.

Instead he completed his conversation with Miss Howard and, turning as casually as he could towards the object of his discomfort, swept her a leg of such exaggerated proportions that he made her smile. 'Why, Miss Hundon, I did not know you were to be here. How do you do?'

'Well, my lord, thank you.' Having had a few moments to compose herself while he talked to Miss Howard, her voice was cool and distant. He must not know how his very presence in the same room set her heart fluttering uncomfortably in her throat. Lady Fitzpatrick's informant had been correct: his behaviour, now the Season's events were following each other thick and fast, was definitely rakish. His eye roved over the company at every gathering, stayed on her for a second that seemed like a month, and moved on. He danced with every debutante, talked a great deal of nonsense, leaving the mamas twittering and the young ladies sighing.

How had she come to be so deceived in him? Why, even now, did she tremble whenever he was near? Why could she not be like Charlotte, relieved that his attention had moved on, able to laugh at his antics and thank goodness for her escape?

'Has this been your first visit to the opera?' he queried, almost at a loss for a safe subject for conversation.

'No, my lord, my father took me to…' Goodness, she had almost said Vienna '…the local operatic society amateur performances but, naturally, they were nothing like this. I enjoyed tonight's singing very much, but I did think the soprano had a tendency to shriek on the high notes.'

'So she did.' He smiled, thankful not to have to flirt with her. He could talk to her in a sensible fashion about all manner of subjects and he allowed himself to enjoy the experience. She was not in the running for Duchess of Rathbone and he did not have to pretend she was. 'Her talent is fading now, but she had a fine voice when she was younger. I heard her sing in Milan years ago, just before the war, when I went on the Grand Tour. But when hostilities began, her planned visit to London had to be cancelled.'

'The war spoiled so many pleasures, took so many good men's lives,' she said softly, thinking of her father. 'And many of those that survive are in dire straits.'

'You are thinking of those soldiers you spoke to?'

'Yes, and others. I cannot get them out of my mind. Surely something could be done to help them?'

He decided to humour her, simply to prolong the discussion. 'What do you suggest?'

'Work could be created. Repairing the roads, for they are in a parlous state, building houses. Give them plots of land so they may be self-sufficient…'

'My goodness, a Radical!'

'I did not expect you to agree with me,' she said, stiffly. 'Brought up as you have been in comfort. You cannot know what it is like to be poor.'

'Not poor, perhaps,' he said. 'But my father was a second son and had to make his own way and I have been a soldier myself. Do not brand me a humbug.'

She felt the colour flare in her cheeks at this put-down but, though she knew she deserved it, she was not yet ready to apologise. 'I notice you did not follow my example and give a little money to those beggars.'

'No, because they would spend it all on drink. It is the soldier's panacea for everything. Believe me, I know. It is not charity they need, but work. You said so yourself.' He smiled. 'My dear, if you must indulge in deep debate do, at least, be consistent.'

'Oh, you are the outside of enough!' she exclaimed, proving to his satisfaction that, faced with logic, she reverted to being entirely feminine. He could have told her that whenever a vacancy occurred at any of his grandfather's properties, priority was always given to ex-soldiers, particularly those with families. It had taken him more than a little effort to persuade the Duke to agree, but the policy had paid off with loyal and hard-working staff. He didn't tell her because he did not want to score points over her. And he knew what her reply would be if he did: what he had done was a drop in the ocean compared to what needed doing.

They were interrupted by Lady Howard who felt that her chief guest had been monopolised long enough by Miss Hundon who had no fortune and no

prospects and should never have been encouraged to
share dear Miss Roswell's come-out. It was giving
her ideas above her station.

'Do come and allow me to introduce you to Miss
Greenholme,' she said, dragging him away. 'She is
the Marquis of Bury's granddaughter, you know.'

'And I am the granddaughter of an earl,' Sophie
muttered to Charlotte who had, at that moment, come
to her side.

'Then why not say so and be done with this charade?'

'Charades! What an excellent idea!' Lady Fitzpatrick exclaimed, catching only the last word.

'Charlotte did not mean this evening,' Sophie said,
enunciating carefully. 'It is far too late.'

'Yes, you are right, my dear,' her ladyship agreed
equably. 'We will arrange something for another day.
Now, I think it is time to take our leave.'

The girls dutifully did the rounds of the company,
saying goodbye, but Lord Braybrooke had gone to
play cards in an adjoining room and was nowhere to
be seen. Sophie told herself she was glad; the less she
saw of that pompous young man the better.

Richard spent almost the whole night at the gaming
tables, but his mind was not on the cards; though he
did not lose too heavily, he realised that playing whist
was not the way to take his mind off a certain young
lady. He needed to think. Declining Martin's offer to
accompany him, he returned home just before dawn,
bathed, changed into riding clothes and ordered his

horse to be saddled. A long ride into the country might serve to clear his head.

The sky was shot with pink and mauve as the sun rose slowly in a great orange orb above the horizon as he rode out on to the Hampstead road. The trees were in full leaf and the air was heady with the scent of blossom. The heath, when he reached it, was dotted with grazing cows and goats, and in the clear air, the birds were in full song, greeting the dawn. There was nothing to beat the English countryside in early summer, he decided, breathing deeply. It was something he had dreamed about in the heat and dust of Spain, England's green and pleasant land and his home in Hertfordshire.

He walked his horse, allowing it to have its head and go where it willed, reflecting on those dreams of home and how he had felt when he was told he had become his grandfather's heir. The war had been coming to an end at the time, but he would have been expected to give up his commission in any case, to come back and prepare to take up the responsibilities of administering a vast estate, to learn how to be a landowner, to care for his people, to do his duty.

He was a military man, an officer; he knew the importance of doing one's duty even when it was disagreeable. He had punished men for failing the high standards of courage he expected of them. He could not be any easier on himself. And his duty was clear; he must marry. It was all very well to joke with Martin about his requirements in a wife, but it was a deadly serious business and he would do well to take stock of his situation.

He was thirty years old next birthday, wealthy and titled. He was strong and healthy, not ugly by any means, and he dealt well with almost everyone. He would not make unreasonable demands of his wife, but she must be up to being a duchess and that took breeding. Being cool and level-headed about it, he could see that Miss Hundon was already out of the running. Miss Greenholme was a possible, but she was hardly out of the schoolroom and terrified of him. There were others, but the one who stood out as being the one his grandfather would most likely sanction was Miss Roswell.

Charlotte. If there had been no Miss Hundon, no kiss in the park, he might have been very content with Miss Roswell. Perhaps he still could be. He would stop being frivolous and seriously set about wooing that young lady.

His horse whinnied, reminding him that the sun had climbed high in the sky and food and water were required for both of them. He stopped at an inn on the other side of the heath for refreshment, before riding back to town, his mind made up. Duty before love.

Because Lady Fitzpatrick had her hands full concentrating on Charlotte, Sophie was often left to her own devices, a state of affairs she found very agreeable, even though Charlotte frequently protested. 'You are the heiress, not me,' she said. 'You should be the one to be paraded before all the eligibles.'

'And very glad I am not to be,' she said, watching her cousin change to go out with Lady Fitzpatrick.

'You can sum up their characters for me and weed out the hopeless ones.'

'And how am I to know who they are?'

'You know my criteria.'

'If I am to adhere to that, then every single man I have met so far falls a long way short.' She paused. 'There is Lord Braybrooke, of course.'

'Him! No, he was the first to go. We will not mention him again.'

Charlotte sighed heavily. 'Very well. But if I am to pay calls with Lady Fitz this afternoon, what will you be doing?'

'I am going to see the sights: the Tower and London Bridge, Westminster Abbey, St Paul's, the waxworks and Bullock's Museum. I believe Napoleon's coach is on view there.'

'You cannot do that in a single afternoon, Sophie.'

'Naturally I cannot. Hatchett's is sure to have a guide book to help me find my way about. Shall I find a book for you while I am there?'

'Sophie, I am not given time to read, you know that, nor for sightseeing, though I would dearly love to accompany you, and it is all because of this masquerade you have embroiled me in. It rates more than a scolding and I dread to think what Mama and Papa will say when they find out.'

Sophie felt exactly the same, not so much for herself because she did not care two pins for Society's conventions, but for her cousin, but whenever she thought she could play the part no longer, she thought of Madderlea and why they had come to London. Choosing a husband who would be good for Madderlea was one thing, falling in love quite another. And she had fallen in love, she could not deny it. She had fallen in love with the most unsuitable man in the whole of London, if her list of requirements were to be the yardstick.

He was a dandy, a fortune hunter, a flirt, a man without honour who could take a gently brought-up young lady into the bushes and kiss her without so much as a by-your-leave or any sort of declaration and then accuse her of being a tease! And all that when he was clearly trying to fix Charlotte's attention, believing her to be the heiress. Would he, as soon as he knew the truth, suddenly turn to her? She didn't want him on those terms. No, she did not! She would find herself a husband and then reveal who she really was and that would serve everyone right for engaging in this affectation they called the Season.

'Wait until after our ball, Charlotte, please. I promise I will not prolong it after that.'

Charlotte agreed. In truth, she enjoyed playing the heiress and found it very gratifying to have every eligible young man in London paying her court, but she was not such a goose as to imagine their attentions were sincere and she had a great deal of sympathy for her cousin's predicament. She smiled and picked up her reticule. 'But I will not have you crying off outings to go to staring at old buildings, it is no way to go on if you want to find yourself a husband. Tonight we are invited out to supper and entertainments at Mrs Whitworthy's and you must come.'

Sophie had every intention of going to Hatchett's, but there was something else she wanted to do as well, something she knew perfectly well Lady Fitzpatrick and her cousin would not approve of and it had nothing whatever to do with social engagements and finding a husband. Before she set out, she went to the mews to find their groom who was busy harnessing the greys to the carriage.

'Sorry, Miss Sophie, I was told two o'clock,' he said, finding that mode of address easier than her fictional one of Miss Hundon. What Mr Hundon would make of it all when he heard, Luke dared not think. But he was very fond of both girls and the five guineas would go a long way to allowing him to propose to the young lady he had set his heart on. 'I will have the carriage ready in a shake of a lamb's tail.'

'I am not using the carriage this afternoon, Luke. It is Lady Fitzpatrick and Charlotte who are going out in it and they are not yet ready. I came to ask you a question.'

'Oh, and what would that be, miss?' he queried, his heart in his boots in case it was another outrageous request like pretending she was her cousin.

'There are a great many discharged soldiers in town, begging in the streets…'

He looked startled. 'Yes, miss, there are. But, cravin' your pardon, miss, you should not be bothered by them.'

'But I am bothered. I cannot stop thinking about them. What I wondered…' She stopped and swallowed. 'Do you know where they congregate?'

'I'm sure I don't know, miss, and you shouldn't be asking me such a question.'

'I want to help them.'

He forgot to be subservient and stared at her in astonishment. 'How?'

'I don't know. I need to ask them. Food, lodgings, work. Luke, I am a very rich young lady and it is not fair that I should have so much when they, who have fought so gallantly and achieved such a fine victory, should have so little. So tell me, where can they be found? I saw some in Covent Garden a week or so ago. Is that where they are?'

'Lady Fitzpatrick would never agree to let you go there!'

'I do not intend to tell her.'

'You don't mean to go alone? No, miss, it is not to be thought of. You will be set upon, robbed. Worse. I could not have that on my conscience. I shall be obliged to tell her ladyship.'

'I won't be alone if you are with me, will I? Lady Fitzpatrick's coachman can drive the carriage this afternoon and you can come with me.'

'Oh, Miss Sophie, I dursn't.'

'You are quite right,' she said, realising it was not fair to the young man to bully him so. 'Forget I asked.'

He breathed a sigh of relief and watched her as she left the mews. But she did not go back towards the house, but carried on to the main thoroughfare and he knew she intended to go alone. It wasn't as if she didn't know the answer to her question. His brother had died out in Spain and he had often, when he had an hour or two off duty, gone to drink and chat with the veterans, hoping that he might meet someone who had known and fought alongside Matthew. Hastily he called to Lady Fitzpatrick's coachman to take over and hurried after her.

'There is a soup kitchen I know of, where the men line up for a hot bowl of soup and a hunk of bread,' he told her when he caught up with her. 'It is run by a Mrs Stebbings.'

'Good. Take me there. You will be well rewarded. And I am not Miss Roswell, nor yet Miss Hundon, I shall be Mrs Carter. A widow. An officer's widow, I think. Do you understand?'

He scratched his head in perplexity. 'Yes, miss.'

Mrs Stebbings, thin as a rake and dressed from head to foot in black, except for a huge white apron, was serving the men from the back of a wagon parked in an alley off Covent Garden. She was the widow of an infantry sergeant, she told Sophie, after Luke had introduced her. 'Some of his men came to visit me after the war ended and I was appalled at their condition. The poor things were in rags and almost starving. They were men my husband had lived and fought with and naturally I fed them, but they told me of others, some in even worse straits, so I started a little subscription fund to buy the ingredients for the soup. Most of it is scrag of mutton and vegetables, but it is hot and nourishing.'

'How long have you been doing it?' Sophie asked, taking off her cloak and donning a sacking apron to help.

'Almost a year, but the line of men and their families waiting to be served does not grow any shorter.

Indeed, with the withdrawal of the occupation troops earlier this year, it has become even longer.'

'And you have very little shelter against inclement weather.'

'No, but they take no account of that, though I have noticed that many of them are ill when the weather is bad—some are still suffering from their wounds. What they need is shelter and medical care, but the fund will not stretch to that.'

'Then more money must be found.'

'I have tried, but most people look upon the poor men as a nuisance and want to see them off the streets.'

'The best way to do that, surely, is for them to have work and homes.'

'Oh, if only it were possible.'

'I will undertake to raise enough for one refuge, at least.'

'You can do that?' Mrs Stebbings's astonishment was comical, making Sophie smile.

'I think so. I have some visits to make now, but I will be back.'

She had sounded so positive when talking to Mrs Stebbings, but making good her promise would not be easy, she knew. Her allowance, though more than generous, was not a bottomless purse. Most of London was owned by aristocratic landowners, even the poor districts, and they employed agents to look after their interests. Accompanied by a bemused Luke, she set off to find such a one.

She wanted to rent a house, she told him. It had to be very cheap so it did not have to be in good repair, because she was sure the tenants would be only too pleased to make it habitable, and it ought to be somewhere around Covent Garden.

The poor man did not know what to make of this extraordinary request from someone who was obviously a gentlewoman. Had she run away? Had she been abandoned by a lover and was too frightened to go home?

'I would advise you to return to your parents, miss,' he said. 'You do not know what you are embarking upon. You would never survive living in such a district.'

'I do not intend to live there, sir,' she said, perfectly able to read his mind. 'I am representing an association of philanthropic ladies dedicated to looking after out-of-work soldiers. We wish to make a refuge for them to stay until they find work.'

'Then I think I have the very property,' he said, breathing a huge sigh of relief which made her smile. 'It is in Maiden Lane. I will conduct you there, if you would not object to waiting while I arrange for my clerk to take over in my absence.'

When Sophie saw the house her disappointment was acute. It was in a dreadfully run-down state, with broken windows and doors, tiles missing from the roof and damp everywhere. The agent assured her she would find nothing cheaper, so she paid a deposit and returned to Mrs Stebbings with the good news.

She would write to Uncle William and tell him their expenses had been much higher than they had calculated and she needed an increase in her allow-

ance. He would not refuse her, knowing how important this trip to London was for the future of Madderlea and the lifting of his burden as trustee. Later
she would tell him the truth, along with a confession
about her change of identity with Charlotte. If, by
then, she had secured a husband, he would not be too
angry.

Securing a husband was the main stumbling block.
The Season was already well underway and she had
not done a thing to advance that cause. In fact, she
had been dilatory to the point of standing still. And
the reason for that was a tall, handsome man who set
her nerves tingling and turned her legs to jelly. She
must stop thinking about him, she really must. She
saw him everywhere, expected him round every corner, wanted him to be there, was disappointed when
he was not. She longed for him and knew that whatever her future life held, she would never love anyone
else. Was Madderlea worth the anguish?

Richard had been in Holles Street, intending to pay
his respects to Lady Fitzpatrick, and request Miss
Roswell's company for a carriage ride in the park,
when he saw Sophie leave the house alone. He had
dived, like a thief, into the cover of the nearest bush
and watched her.

She was dressed in that awful grey gown and cloak,
but she walked with a purpose and held her head high,
her red-gold curls peeping out from beneath a small
straw bonnet. Martin had been right, she did have
dignity and presence, but that covered a very pas-
sionate nature as he knew to his cost. He could not

put that kiss and the feel of her body held against his from his mind. It eclipsed everything else, made nonsense of his coldly calculated list of requirements for a wife, turned him from a man of the world into a boy in the throes of first love, and he resented it.

As he watched, the young groom had joined her and they set off together, talking animatedly. He felt an uncontrollable envy of her young escort and had set off after them, intending he knew not what. She had no business going out with no other escort but a servant; he had told her that when he had intervened over those begging soldiers. Did she never listen to advice?

He had followed them, keeping out of sight, while they made their way along Oxford Street and down Charing Cross Road towards Seven Dials. Surely she was not going to venture into that notorious den of iniquity? He had quickened his pace. She must be stopped and that groom called over the coals for taking her anywhere near the place. He smiled grimly, remembering the last set down she had given him for interfering. Well, he would interfere again and chance her wrath.

He had been relieved when she safely negotiated the corner, but the danger was not over and he kept close behind, ready to pounce on anyone who so much as lifted a finger against her. When she turned down Long Acre and into Covent Garden, he guessed it was the discharged soldiers she was thinking of. Her compassion did her credit, but he did not see what good giving them a handful of sovereigns would

do. They would never leave her alone once they realised she was a soft touch.

He watched in amazement as she approached the
soup kitchen where she took off her cloak and donned
an apron to serve food to the line of men. It was
magnificent of her and his annoyance turned to admiration and a burning desire to stand at her side and
do likewise. But he desisted, knowing she would not
welcome him.

He stood, lost in admiration of her cool perfection,
knowing there would never be another woman for
him and, however much his grandfather blustered and
threatened, however often Martin reminded him of his
rash and arrogant list of requirements, he would marry
no other. But how to win her? Was it already too late?

He had been a thorough-going fool and ruined his
chances with his brash conduct and his half-hearted
efforts to engage the attention of other hopefuls, including her very rich, very pretty, but somewhat un-
inspiring cousin, who deserved to have a husband
who loved her. He could not love her, or anyone else,
while Sophie Hundon lived and breathed.

And he had insulted her with that kiss. It had been
intended to hurt for making him feel as he did, to let
her know who was master, not only of her but of his
own emotions. Her response had been unintentional,
a physical reaction down to his own practised ability
and her innocence. And he had called her a tease—
worse, a demi-rep! Would she ever forgive him for
that?

The men to whom she was administering were
rough and unkempt but they treated her with extraor-

dinary courtesy and good humour, and she was in no danger with Luke glued to her side. He waited until she left, assuming she was returning home, then turned and strode away, unaware of the next call she made.

He must see his grandfather, tell him the truth and beg to be allowed a free choice. If the old man met Sophie, he would surely understand. He could put an end to the charade he had been playing and be himself. But first he needed to know how Sophie really felt about him, whether, she held him in complete aversion or whether if he tried to explain, she might understand. It was going to be decidedly tricky, especially as she was so evidently very fond of her cousin and would do nothing to hurt her.

He arrived back at Braybrooke House in the late afternoon. Leaving his horse for a groom to stable he strode indoors, intending to order the tea-tray to be taken to his room, where he could drink it while he changed. He was puzzled to find a mountain of luggage in the hall.

'What's that?' he demanded of the footman who had opened the door to him.

'Lady Braybrooke is here,' the man said. 'She and Miss Braybrooke arrived earlier this afternoon. They are taking tea in the drawing room.'

Aunt Philippa and Emily! They were the last people he wanted to see. 'Tell them I will join them directly I have changed,' he told the servant, before bounding up the stairs two at a time.

Half an hour later he entered the drawing room,

bathed and dressed in a modest kerseymere frockcoat and matching pantaloons. He bowed to his aunt before kissing her hand and then turned to do the same to Emily, noticing the colour flare in her pale cheeks when he asked her how she did.

'We have been hearing such tales, Richard,' his aunt said, when the courtesies had been completed. 'I determined to come at once and scotch them.'

'Rumours, Aunt? About whom?'

'You, of course. Tell me you have not been flirting with every unmarried girl in town, making a cake of yourself…'

He laughed, though the sound was a little cracked. 'Grandfather ordered me to find a wife and that is what I am doing. How I go about it is my affair.'

'And that includes making up to dowds who are no more than paid companions…'

He did not doubt she was referring to Sophie, though how she had found out about her he did not know. He supposed tattle was as easily spread by writing letters as by word of mouth. 'If you mean Miss Hundon, she is far from a dowd.'

'She is highly unsuitable. You know perfectly well what your grandfather's wishes are and acting the park saunterer will not endear him to you. I only wish the estate had not been entailed, then Emily would hold all the cards, not you.'

'Marriage is not a game of cards, ma'am,' he said sombrely. 'Though I own it is a great gamble.'

'Of course it is not. You simply do your duty.'

'Mama…' Emily began. 'Please, you are putting me to the blush.'

'Then go and do your embroidery. I came to speak my mind and I intend to do it.'

'Aunt, you are being unkind to Emily,' he said. 'Given a free choice she would not choose me, I am quite sure.'

'How do you know? You haven't offered for her.'

Emily, overcome with embarrassment, fled from the room in floods of tears.

'There! See what you have done,' his aunt said. 'She will make her face all blotchy with weeping and we are meant to be going out this evening.'

He did not answer. What was the good? His aunt was in no mood to listen. In fact, she continued to scold. 'I think you might at least make a push to be agreeable to your cousin and let the world see that you are not the scapegrace they think you are. A little conduct would not come amiss.

'Escort us both to Mrs Whitworthy's this evening. We were invited to supper, but I was afraid we would not arrive in town in time and undertook only to join the company for the entertainment afterwards. It is just as well because it will take some time to repair the ravages to Emily's complexion.'

He was not aware that he had been disagreeable to Emily. In fact, he had always been scrupulously care-ful in his conduct towards her. He was fond of her in a cousinly sort of way and had done nothing to en-courage her to think of him as a husband. It was her mother who had put the idea into the old duke's head and kept it there with constant nagging.

To save his cousin from any more scolding from her mama, he agreed, but that didn't mean he would

abandon his plan to go to Hertfordshire to see his
grandfather. Escorting his aunt and cousin was simply
an unwelcome diversion.

Sophie and Charlotte, in a whispered exchange,
agreed that the supper party was extremely dull. The
young men were either peacocks, making no secret of
their need for a rich wife, or were already very rich
and looking only for a breeding machine to produce
the mandatory heir. Some were extremely silly. The
young ladies were their counterparts and, in Sophie's
opinion, they deserved each other. It was a bigger
masquerade than ever she and Charlotte were perpe-
trating and she hated it.

'We shall have to do something to liven it up, or I
shall die of boredom,' Charlotte murmured, as they
applauded a very out-of-tune duet. 'Shall you play
and sing for us?'

Mrs Whitworthy, catching the end of what Charlotte had said, turned to Sophie. 'Oh, Miss Hundon,
do entertain us. It is always nice to listen to a new
talent.'

'I am not very talented, ma'am.'

'Oh, she is, she is,' Charlotte put in.

Sophie rose reluctantly and took her seat at the pi-
anoforte, wondering what to play. And then an imp
of mischief jumped into her head and nudged her.
'You wanted to liven things up,' it said. 'Then go on
and do it.'

She struck a chord, then her fingers danced over
the keys and her melodious voice began to sing in
French. It was not until she repeated the chorus that

the assembled company began to fidget. Few of them were able to translate accurately because the song was in patois, but the tune and the rhythm was quick and lively and her manner of delivery was enough to alert them to the fact that this was not a song for the drawing room. After a time she heard a murmur in the room behind her, then the rustle of skirts and a cough or two and then a chuckle. Someone appreciated it.

At the end she turned in her seat, with a smile which could almost have been construed as triumphant, to receive the applause which was more enthusiastic from the young men than the ladies who were present. It was when she rose to go back to her seat she saw Richard standing at the back of the room, an expression of delighted surprise on his face. How long had he been there? Had he understood the words of the song? She could feel the colour burning her cheeks and wished she had not been so lacking in decorum. What must he think of her?

'Viscount Braybrooke, Lady Braybrooke and Miss Emily Braybrooke,' the footman announced.

'His lordship's aunt and cousin,' she heard Lady Fitzpatrick whisper to Charlotte as she returned to sit with them. 'There is talk that the old duke would like to see a liaison there. If the gossip is right, it is a great shame. But I cannot think why else they have come to town. You are going to need your wits about you, my dear, if you are to prise him loose.'

'My lady,' Charlotte returned, 'if that is where his heart lies, I have no wish to detach him from her. In truth, I...'

'Fustian!' her ladyship said, bracingly. 'It is all part of the game. You will see.'

Game! Sophie grimaced. Was that how Lord Braybrooke saw it? Had he simply been amusing himself until his cousin arrived in the capital and put an end to the fun? If so, she had been right to discount him. But it hurt, it hurt so much she didn't know how she was going to keep her composure for the rest of the evening.

Chapter Five

Mrs Whitworthy, who had not seen her new guests arrive, hurried forward to greet them, all a-twitter. 'My lady,' she said, 'please forgive me, I did not see you there. And Miss Braybrooke, how charming you look.' Emily, in a white muslin open gown over a pale pink underskirt, inclined her head at the compliment. Their hostess turned to Richard. 'Lord Braybrooke, I had not expected you to honour our little gathering with your presence. You are welcome.'

'Thank you, ma'am.' He bowed towards her, immaculate in an evening coat of mulberry velvet and dark pantaloons, his cravat a masterpiece of his valet's art.

'I believe you are acquainted with most of the company,' Mrs Whitworthy went on, almost dragging her ladyship round the room, to meet her guests one by one. Stopping opposite Charlotte, she said, 'But I do not think you know Miss Roswell. Allow me to present her.'

Lady Braybrooke, in mauve half-mourning for a

husband lost over three years before, lifted her lorgnette and subjected Charlotte to a thorough inspection. 'Earl of Peterborough's niece, I believe. Inherited the lot when his lordship stuck his spoon in the
wall. Not that it isn't a millstone round your neck, for
I am persuaded it is in a parlous state of repair and
needing a man's hand.'

Charlotte, taken aback by her ladyship's outspo-
kenness, curtsied but could find nothing to say. Richard gave her a wry smile of sympathy as they passed
on to Sophie, who was bubbling with indignation.
'This is Miss Roswell's cousin, my lady, Miss Hundon.'

The quizzing glass went up again and Sophie, unlike her cousin, returned the gaze unwaveringly, looking from a mauve satin turban topped with a tall black
feather, down over a thin face and thin lips to a rake-
like figure which was held very upright. It was meant
to intimidate, but she would not be intimidated, especially as Richard was standing just behind his aunt,
smiling enigmatically. Was he laughing at her or with
her? She could not tell. Her chin went up. 'How do
you do, Lady Braybrooke.'

Her ladyship's answer was almost a snort. Top-
lofty in the extreme, Sophie decided, watching her
move away, followed by her daughter, a tall dark-
haired girl who had not yet rid herself of her puppy
fat. She had her hand on Richard's sleeve in an un-
equivocal gesture of possession. So Lady Fitz had
been right and that was where the wind lay!

'This is Lady Fitzpatrick, Miss Roswell's sponsor.'
'Oh, we have known each other since we were

girls,' Lady Braybrooke said. 'How do you do, Harriet?'

'I am well, thank you, Philippa. What brings you to town?'

'Family affairs, my dear. Must keep the young people up to the mark, must we not?'

'Indeed, we must.'

'I did not realise you were acquainted with the Earl of Peterborough.'

'I was not. Mrs Hundon is a distant cousin and Hundon is Miss Roswell's trustee. I am acting *in loco parentis* for both girls.'

'Oh, so that is the connection.'

Sophie was beginning to worry that somehow other truths might be revealed and the last thing she wanted was for anyone to begin digging deeper. The deception was hard enough to maintain as it was.

Lady Fitzpatrick, equally reluctant to be quizzed, came to her rescue. 'I was about to suggest charades, my lady,' she said, then, turning to Mrs Whitworthy, 'What do you think, Annabel?'

'Capital idea!' their hostess exclaimed. 'Perhaps Miss Braybrooke and his lordship would care to take part.' And without giving the new arrivals time to respond, she added 'I shall select teams of four.'

This took some organising because the good lady was mindful of the main reason for the gathering, to bring hitherto single young men and ladies together and she had already mentally paired everyone off, except Sophie and Charlotte.

Sophie found herself in the same team as Richard and Emily, probably because it was deemed more prudent, in view of Emily's arrival, to keep Richard away from the heiress of Madderlea than from the poor cousin, a situation Sophie might have found amusing, if she had not been worried about the fact that the viscount was standing next to her, his head bent towards her as the group decided on the adage they were going to enact.

He was stirring her insides up in such a froth she could hardly breathe. If his close proximity did this to her, whatever would happen if he touched her? But, remembering that kiss, she knew the answer to that. She would melt, just as if she hadn't a bone in her body and everyone present would see and guess what was the matter with her. She would be a subject for derision; the poor relation who had the temerity to wear the willow for the Season's biggest catch. The fact that she wasn't the poor relation was neither here nor there. Whatever happened, she must remain cool.

They chose 'a bird in the hand is worth two in the bush' at Richard's suggestion. Three chairs were set side by side and a large potted plant placed behind them to represent the bush. Sophie and Emily and one of the young men sat side by side pretending to preen themselves and flutter their wings, oblivious of Richard stalking them. He reached out suddenly and grabbed Sophie by the hand, pulling her to her feet, while the two remaining birds twittered nervously.

They had expected the company to guess the answer at this point, but when they did not Richard cupped Sophie's hand in his, stroking the back of it, as if stroking a nervous bird. She was meant to cheep like a bird, but the sound she made was more a strangled cry of distress. The gentle pressure of his fingers was playing havoc with her resolve. She was shaking and prayed that everyone would assume it was part of the play-acting because she could not stop it. Was he also play-acting when he looked down into her eyes with such gentle concern for the bird he had trapped?

He released her at last and made an effort to catch the two in the bush, but his efforts ended in failure. He spread empty hands to the company and shrugged his shoulders in defeat, as they began murmuring among themselves.

'Have you not guessed it yet?' he enquired, forcing himself to sound normal, though Sophie's little hand trapped in his had had the most disturbing affect. 'Must we do it all again?'

Sophie didn't want a repeat performance, especially as Emily was looking at her with venom in her dark eyes as if it were her fault Richard had chosen to 'capture' her. 'Oh, Charlotte, you surely know,' she said. 'It is a very common truism.'

'They were birds, were they not?' one of the young ladies said. 'And one of them was trapped in Lord Braybrooke's hand.'

Charlotte laughed and clapped her hands. 'Oh, I know what it is. A bird in the hand is worth two in the bush.'

The players bowed and took their place in the audience while the next team, which included Charlotte, began their charade, but Sophie could not concentrate—she was too aware that Richard had chosen to sit beside her, even though he seemed to be concentrating on the players. She hid her hands in the folds of her gown so that he would not see that they were still shaking, and tilted her chin up.

'I enjoyed your little song, Miss Hundon,' he whispered, proving that he was paying no more attention than she was.

'Thank you, my lord.'

'You learned the French accent very well.'

'You understood it?'

'Oh, yes, I understood most of it. The point is, did you? Or did you simply learn it by rote?'

She could not admit that her French was perfect or that she knew the song to be a little *risqué*. She smiled. 'I learned it by rote, my lord. I have a good ear.'

'Indeed you have and a very pretty one,' he said, looking at that organ. He leaned towards it to whisper. 'Miss Hundon, I must speak to you. It is important.'

He had a guilty conscious, she told herself, and all he wanted to do was to excuse himself and explain about his attachment to his cousin and how he had been amusing himself with the young ladies of the *ton* until her arrival. Sophie did not want to hear it. Besides, it was Charlotte who deserved an explanation, not her. 'Shush, my lord,' she whispered. 'You are disturbing the others.'

He sighed and turned his attention back to the charades. It was not the right time to unburden himself to her, he must wait for a more appropriate moment. But no such moment presented itself that evening.

Charlotte's team managed to portray 'too many cooks spoil the broth' and this was followed by 'pride goes before a fall' and then the party broke up. As everyone was saying their goodbyes and arranging to meet at other social occasions, Sophie heard their hostess invite Lord Braybrooke and Miss Braybrooke to a ball and the young lady's enthusiastic acceptance.

She watched his lordship closely. He gave no indication that the arrangement was not acceptable to him. Indeed, he seemed to have lost his light-hearted air of dalliance and though he smiled, it was a smile of serious intent, as if his wings had truly been clipped. And by Miss Braybrooke! Sophie was more sure than ever that was what he had wanted to speak to her about.

She turned away to fetch her pelisse and bonnet, feeling as though her heart were breaking. All her play-acting, her masquerade as her cousin, had been to no purpose. She could not have the man she loved; though there were others eager to become master of Madderlea and her fortune, they thought Charlotte was the heiress, not she. Not that she wanted to marry any of them, so that did not signify.

She could return to Upper Corbury unattached but that would certainly displease her uncle who had been so good to her, giving her a home and looking after Madderlea, but he could not be expected to continue to do so now that she had recovered her health and was of marriageable age. Madderlea was a burden he should not have to bear, especially when he would rather be spending more time with his invalid wife.

Oh, what a coil she had got herself into! And she had embroiled Charlotte. She had not been fair to Charlotte. She was thankful that her cousin had not fallen in love with any of the young bloods she had met, that her mind was as firmly fixed as ever on marrying Frederick Harfield.

The cure for her ills, she decided, during a sleepless night, was to immerse herself in the problems of others and perhaps, in trying to solve those, a solution to her own would present itself to her.

The keys to the house in Maiden Lane had been handed to Mrs Stebbings the day before and she and her helpers were going to start preparing it for its new role. It was not enough to provide the money, Sophie decided, she must become actively involved.

'I would like to go shopping,' she told Lady Fitzpatrick and Charlotte after breakfast the following morning. 'There is a law book Papa was interested in and I thought I would buy it for him. It is quite a rare book and I might have to visit several shops, so do you mind if I take your coach, my lady?'

Charlotte gave her such a look of blank astonishment that Sophie was glad her ladyship was concentrating on her correspondence and did not notice. 'A book for Papa?' she queried.

'Yes,' Sophie said firmly. 'I remember him saying he needed it.'

'Why should she not buy her father a book?' Lady Fitzpatrick put in, proving that her loss of hearing was inconsistent. 'I am sure it is a very daughterly thing to do.'

'And I collect you and Charlotte are taking the carriage out this morning,' Sophie went on. 'So may I borrow the coach? Luke will drive me, I am sure.'

'Very well,' her ladyship agreed. 'But do take care, won't you?'

Sophie went to fetch her cloak and then made her way to the kitchen where she made sure the servants were busy elsewhere before delving in the store cupboards for brooms, scrubbing brushes, dusters and soap. Putting the smaller things into a bucket and carrying the two brooms, she hurried out to the mews and instructed Luke to put the horses to the old coach.

If he was surprised at the strange collection of implements Miss Sophie was carrying he did not express it, nor did he question why she was taking the coach which, in his opinion, was fit only for the dustheap; he was becoming immune to the young lady's little peccadilloes. Ten minutes later they were trotting down the road on their way to Maiden Lane.

Because there was bound to be many more men than they had places for at the refuge, they had decided to limit a stay to one night. The men would be given a bed, a bath and a healthy breakfast before going on their way. Feeling clean and refreshed, they might find it easier to obtain work.

Sophie also intended to try and set up an agency to find employment for them, but that would mean talking to prospective employers and she was not sure if she were the right person to do that. They needed a man to help them, a man of some substance, who would understand what was needed and, more importantly, had a persuasive manner.

The only man who came to mind was Richard Braybrooke, but he came to her mind whatever she was doing, sleeping or waking, so that did not signify anything except that she was not making a very good hand at forgetting him. Asking for his help would only make her shattered emotions worse. And he would very likely refuse on the grounds that what she was doing would not make a scrap of difference.

As soon as she arrived at the house she rolled up her sleeves, donned an apron and worked with a will, sweeping and scrubbing alongside Mrs Stebbings and two other women, while Luke helped some of the soldiers, recruited for the purpose, to assemble beds, put up shelves, fill palliasse covers with straw, chop firewood, put bolts on the doors and generally do everything the women could not. By the middle of the afternoon, the house was beginning to look habitable, if not exactly homely.

Sophie was exhausted, but it was a contented kind of exhaustion. Chatting to the women and the soldiers about their lives while they worked had put her own privileged existence into perspective. She was fortunate she had her health and a roof over her head and was in no danger of starvation and for that she must give thanks.

She was about to suggest they finish for the day and go home, when she heard a crash coming from the adjoining room where Luke was putting up a curtain rail. She dropped the broom she was using and ran into the room to find Luke sitting on the floor, tangled in the steps he had been using, and broken glass everywhere.

'Luke, are you hurt? Oh, my goodness, you are bleeding.' He was holding one hand in the other and blood was pouring down his arm. 'It's nothing, Miss Sophie. The steps gave way an' I put out my hand to save m'self.' He grinned ruefully. 'Straight through the window.'

'We must bandage it up.' She looked round as Mrs Stebbings came in from upstairs where she had been making up beds. The good lady took in the situation at a glance and told one of the men to fetch her basket and a bowl of water. The men had been to the pump several times during the day and there were some buckets of clean water still in the kitchen.

'I always carry ointment and bandages,' she said. 'It's being a soldier's wife, I suppose. When we were out in Spain—' She stopped speaking as the water and basket were brought to her and she set about washing the wound, which was quite deep, and picking out tiny shards of glass, which made Luke bite his lip in pain. 'I preferred to treat my husband's minor wounds myself, rather than let him go to the army sawbones. If I'd been with him at the end instead of coming home ahead of him, he might have survived.'

'I am so sorry,' Sophie murmured, squatting down to support Luke's hand.

'Curtains!' one of the men said, watching her. 'I said we didn't need curtains. Now, we've got a wounded man and a window broke. This ain't Carlton House, nor yet Grillon's Hotel. And it ain't a bit of use pretending it is.'

Sophie was too worried about Luke to argue with the man. It had been her idea to have curtains and rugs on the floor to make it more homely, less like the workhouse which was what the men dreaded most of all.

'Dawkins, you are the most downpin man I ever did meet,' Mrs Stebbings said. 'If Mrs Carter is so good as to provide curtains, then why brangle about it? She did not know the steps would collapse, did she? It was an accident.' She finished bandaging Luke's hand. 'There, it's the best I can do, but perhaps you should see a physician.'

'No, no, I'll mend,' Luke said, trying to move his fingers and grimacing when he discovered it hurt him. 'They be a bit stiff. I'll be right as ninepence tomorrow.'

'Then we'd better get you home,' Sophie said, reaching down to help him to his feet.

Aghast that she should do such a thing, he scrambled up on his own.

'You'll never manage the horses with one hand,' Dawkins said. 'Shall I drive you?'

Sophie looked at Luke, as the realisation dawned that he could not drive and she could not allow anyone else to see where they lived. Her identity was secret and she wanted it to stay that way. Luke caught her eye and gave her an imperceptible nod of understanding. 'I can drive,' he said. ''Tain't nothin' but a scratch.'

Sophie smiled at the sergeant. For no reason that she could explain, he made her nervous. It may have been the scar on one side of his face which gave him a permanent leer, or it may have been that he was constantly finding fault, even when people were trying to help him. To give him his due he had worked

hard during the day and his offer was a kind one—
she ought not to be ungrateful. 'Thank you, Sergeant,'
she said, allowing him the courtesy of his rank,
though he had long since been discharged. 'But if
Luke is incapacitated, I can drive myself.'

'Are you sure?' Mrs Stebbings asked.

'Yes, I often drive, don't I, Luke?'

He could hardly call the young lady a liar and so
he muttered that, yes, Mrs Carter was used to amuse
herself by taking the ribbons occasionally.

He walked beside her to where the old coach had
been left and she climbed up on the driving seat with
Luke beside her. She had driven the new carriage in
the park once or twice, but not this bulky coach and
not in heavy traffic and she was more than a little
nervous. But she had to pretend to be confident because Mrs Stebbings and several of the others had
come out to see them go.

She waved cheerily to them and picked up the
reins, while Luke muttered instructions. It was not as
bad as she feared. The horses were nearly as ancient
as the coach and they were quite content to set off at
a steady plod.

'Keep 'em walkin', Miss Sophie,' Luke said. 'But
keep a tight rein in case they're spooked by the traffic.'

She obeyed and slowly the nervousness left her and
she began to enjoy herself. This was better than sitting
over the teacups listening to the latest *on dit*. In fact,
the whole day had been very rewarding, except for
Luke's accident. She felt responsible for that and very
concerned about him.

'How do you feel?' she asked him, when she had safely negotiated the worst of the traffic around Covent Garden, most of it empty farm carts, which were being driven home after a successful day's trading in the market. 'Is it very painful?'

'It ain't too bad, Miss Sophie,' he said stoically. 'But what are we going to tell Lady Fitzpatrick? If she was to ask me to drive the carriage this evening…'

She hadn't thought of that. 'Goodness, we shall have to think of something. How could you have sustained a cut like that while driving me out shopping?'

'I don't know,' he said gloomily. 'I wish I'd never let you coax me into this humbug, Miss Sophie. It'll get me the bag for sure.'

'You won't be turned off, Luke, you are employed by Mr Hundon, not Lady Fitzpatrick.'

'But we gotta tell 'er something.'

'Yes, we must,' she said, turning into Oxford Street. It was crammed with vehicles of all kinds, from high-perch phaetons to sedan chairs, heavy drays to stage coaches laden with passengers. There were beggars in the gutter, pedestrians on the pavement, hawkers plying their wares from trays and here and there a stationary vehicle to negotiate. It was a minute of two before she felt confident enough to put her mind to other things besides her driving. 'I think you must have done something heroic,' she said, at length. 'Then everyone will be all sympathy and allow you to rest and recover.'

'On my life, Miss Sophie, I ain't no 'ero.'

She had enough to do concentrating on the road

and trying to think of something Luke could have done to sustain his injuries, without further distraction. But there was no mistaking the tall figure of Viscount Braybrooke, standing on the side of the road, watching her with a such a look of amazement on his face, she could not help breaking into a smile. He was elegantly dressed in a dark green superfine frockcoat and biscuit pantaloons, his dark curls peeping beneath a shiny brown beaver. Mischievously she wondered whether to stop and offer him a lift and if he would be too proud to accept it, but before she could pull the horses up she heard shouting ahead of her.

She looked up to see a curricle bearing down on them at great speed. There was no driver but a little boy was clinging to its sides, so terrified he could not even cry out. Everything in its path was being frantically pulled to the side out of its way. Pedestrians were fleeing in all directions, some of them screaming. Lady Fitzpatrick's old coach was too cumbersome and the horses to old to move fast and though Sophie did her best, it seemed a collision was inevitable.

Sophie's only thought was for the poor little boy. She hauled on the reins, helped by a one-handed Luke and the curricle hurtled alongside so close they almost touched. Luke was down like a shot long before they pulled to a halt and made a grab for the reins of the runaway horse, as it passed. He was not alone. Richard had moved equally fast and was on the other side. Sophie watched in horror as the terrified horse dragged them both along the street.

The vehicle was bouncing from side to side and the little boy in danger of being thrown out. Sophie jumped down and ran along the road, desperate to save him, though how she thought she could do it, she did not know. The panicking horse, trying to throw off the two men who impeded its progress, halted suddenly and reared up. The curricle turned over and Sophie heard the little boy scream. Then everything stopped.

The horse stood still; the curricle lay on its side, the uppermost wheel still spinning; Luke and Richard, both battered and bruised, were too winded to move. The bystanders were doing no more than gape. To Sophie, running towards it, the whole thing seemed like a set tableau and she was the only one capable of action.

And then everything started again. The little boy began to cry, proving he was still alive, Richard left Luke calming the horse and ran to the overturned curricle, the bystanders began to crowd round all talking at once, and Sophie reached Richard's side. Without speaking, they lifted the little boy out. He was about six or seven years old, his small face deathly white and his eyes wide with terror.

Sophie picked up one of the seat cushions which had been thrown out and put it on the ground, so that she could sit down and nurse him. He was badly shocked and there was a nasty bruise on the side of his head, but a quick examination by Richard established that no bones were broken.

'Thank heaven for that,' she said, stroking the boy's tumbled curls away from his face and wiping his tears away with her handkerchief, while Richard dispersed the spectators with such an air of authority it did not occur to them to do other than obey. 'He's had a lucky escape. I wonder where his parents are.'

'I don't know,' Richard said grimly, looking back along the street. 'I shall certainly have something to say to them, when I see them. How could they be so irresponsible as to leave a small child alone in a vehicle like that?'

He looked down at Sophie. Her face was dreadfully pale and there were smudges below her eyes. Her gown, visible beneath the grey cloak, was grubby and her hands, tenderly ministering to the child, seemed workworn, her usually well-buffed nails broken. What in heaven's name had she been up to? But the child did not care about that. He was lying in her arms, his head against her soft breast, while she stroked his hair and talked soothingly to him, with an expression of such compassion and love, Richard's heart turned a somersault in his breast.

'What's your name?' Sophie asked him but he looked blankly at her.

'Ne comprends pas.'

Sophie smiled and tried again. *'Qu'est-ce que t'appelle-toi?'*

'Pierre Latour.'

'Je m'appelle Sophie,' she said. 'You are quite safe now. Where are your parents?'

He turned and buried his head in her breast, crying for his mama and talking in rapid French, which Richard found very difficult to follow, punctuated as it was by sobs.

'He says his papa left the carriage to ask directions and the horse bolted. His father tried to stop it but was hit by the wheel,' Sophie translated without even thinking.

'Then he must be lying injured in the road. I'll go and look for him.'

But before he could go, a man limped towards them, his fine clothes torn and muddy and his expression distraught. He rushed up to the child. *'Pierre! Mon pauvre fils!'*

'Papa!' The boy reached out and was enfolded in his father's arms.

'Merci, merci, madame,' the man said to Sophie.

Sophie smiled and, relieved of her burden, stood up. Now it was all over, she felt weak and stiff. She took a step and stumbled, but before she could fall, Richard reached out and pulled her towards him, supporting her with his arm around her. It was comforting there and she did not move away.

Monsieur Latour had been speaking to his son and now he turned to Richard and Sophie to thank them, explaining that he was a diplomat and had come to England as part of a delegation. His wife had never visited England and so he had brought her and their son with him. He had hired the curricle to show them some of London. He had left his wife at the mantua-makers and taken Pierre for a turn about the park before returning for her and they had lost their way.

He had stepped down to ask directions and something had spooked the horse. He was eternally grateful to *monsieur* and *madame* for looking after the child. Now, he must go and find his wife, she would be beside herself with worry. All this was said in rapid French which Richard had great difficulty following. Not so Sophie, who answered so fluently he was astonished.

Luke had calmed the horse and enlisted the help of bystanders to right the vehicle, but it was in a sorry state. 'The wheels might turn, but I wouldn't like to try and drive it,' he said.

Sophie immediately offered to take the Frenchman to his destination, forgetting that Luke could not drive. In fact, his struggle with the horse had set his hand bleeding again and the bandages were stained red with his blood.

'Very tender-hearted of you, my dear,' Richard murmured close to her ear. 'But perhaps the gentleman does not have my confidence in your ability as a whipster.'

'What are we to do then?' she asked. 'We cannot abandon them.'

'Then I had better drive.'

'My lord, I am sure you have other things to do. An appointment perhaps.'

'Nothing of any import,' he said. 'I cannot simply walk away, can I?'

'N…no, but—'

'Your French is unquestionably better than mine,' he went on before she could find any more objections. 'Tell the gentleman I shall be pleased to drive him. Then lead the way back to that bone-breaker you call a coach. The sooner we reunite the boy with his mama, the better. He should see a doctor and so should your groom. We shall take him, after we have discharged our duty to the Frenchman.'

She knew it would do no good arguing with him but, in truth, she was feeling very shaky and very tired and thankful to have someone with an air of authority to take charge. The Frenchman and his son took their places with her inside the coach alongside the brooms and bucket, while Richard hitched the horse from the curricle to the back of the coach. The vehicle itself was abandoned and would have to be fetched by the hire company. Luke managed to climb up to the driver's seat, where Richard joined him.

It took Sophie a few minutes to establish which mantua-maker Madame Latour was visiting, but it was not far away and the little boy was soon reunited with his mother, who had been standing outside the shop looking this way and that in growing panic. When she saw the state of her husband and son, she all but fainted and then burst into tears. It took Monsieur Latour a little time to convince her that he was not hurt and there was nothing to get into hysterics about. Eventually she joined him and their son in the coach and were conveyed to their hotel where a doctor was sent for and the runaway horse was handed over to one of the hotel staff to return to the hire company.

They insisted on Luke, the hero, being administered to after the doctor had treated Pierre and given him a sleeping draught, and it was very late when they took their leave.

'I am afraid Lady Fitz and Charlotte will be wondering what has become of me,' she said, as Richard escorted her back to her coach.

'That, my dear Miss Hundon, is an understatement. The sooner we have you safely home, the better.'

It was then she realised that he intended to continue his mission of mercy. And though half of her wanted him to stay, wanted his support, the other half told her it would be dangerous to her hard-won independence. 'My lord, there is no need to accompany me,' she protested. 'I admit I was a little shaky, but I am fully recovered now and perfectly able to drive.'

He smiled. 'I should be a poor tool, indeed, if I allowed that. And no doubt you will have some explaining to do to your patroness. I should hate to see you roasted, so I shall come to lend you support.' He turned to Luke, who was looking decidedly green after having his old dressing removed and several stitches inserted in the wound to his hand. 'Get inside, old fellow. Miss Hundon can ride on the box with me. It is a position she seems to prefer.'

'Yes, do it, Luke,' Sophie said, as he hesitated. 'I do not want you fainting and falling off.'

Reluctantly he climbed in and Richard helped Sophie up on the driver's seat before taking his place beside her.

'Now,' he said, as he took up the reins and the coach moved. 'I should very much like to know what deep game you are playing.'

'Game, my lord,' she repeated innocently. 'There is no game. I came out shopping and you saw what happened.'

'Shopping for buckets and brooms, I assume.'

So he had noticed them! 'Yes, my lord.'

'What a hum!'

'My lord,' she said, mustering her dignity, 'I am not accustomed to being called a liar.'

'Then you had better become accustomed to it or resolve to tell the truth from now on.' He turned to glance down at her. 'Do you usually go shopping in dirty clothes, with smudges on your face?'

'Have I?' she asked, momentarily diverted and scrubbing at her cheeks with the handkerchief she had used to mop up Pierre's tears, which made her even grubbier.

He laughed, loving her whatever she was wearing and however dishevelled she was. In fact it made her even more appealing. 'You look like an urchin.'

She managed a wan smile. 'It is not to be wondered at, is it? I have been sitting on the ground, comforting a small boy.'

'Oh, it didn't happen then,' he said airily. 'Certainly not all of it.'

It was not a question and so she declined to confirm or deny it. 'And you are no picture of elegance, my lord. In truth, I do not think you are in a fit state to go visiting. Your sleeve is torn and you have lost your hat, not to mention scratches and bruises on your hands.' She glanced down at them as she spoke. Big, tanned, capable hands, hands which had recently been about her waist, hands which had caressed her and comforted her, hands that bore the scars of his efforts to stop the runaway curricle; hands she longed to take in her own and put to her lips.

'*Touché*, my dear,' he said with a smile. 'But the

more determined you are that I shall not take you home, the more determined I become that I shall. I am interested to know what Banbury tale you will tell to explain your tardiness.'

'The overturned curricle, my lord. You can bear witness to that.'

'Oh, I am to compound your mischief by telling half-truths, am I? And I suppose your coachman sustained his injuries stopping the runaway horse.'

'It certainly made his hand worse, it was only a scratch before that.'

'Do you take me for a flat, Miss Hundon? You would hardly put half a yard of bandage on a scratch and you forget I saw it when the doctor stitched it. It is a severe cut. And whatever your activities this afternoon, they were not those usually indulged in by well brought-up young ladies.'

She had to put an end to his questions somehow. 'My lord, you said you would hate to see me roasted and then you proceed to do exactly that. It is very uncivil of you. What I do with my time is my own business; if it had not been for the accident, I would have been home in good time for dinner at five and no explanations would have been necessary. I beg of you to desist from quizzing me.'

'And will you desist from bamming me?'

She did not answer and he turned in his seat to look at her. There were tears glistening on her lashes and he was suddenly filled with compassion. He wanted to stop the carriage, to take her in his arms and tell her that whatever she did made no difference to how he felt about her, that his search for a wife had been no more than a half-hearted effort to appease his grandfather and he had long ago become heartily sick of it. 'Oh, my dear Miss Hundon, forgive me. I had no right to go on so, when you have had such a dreadful day.'

'I have not had a dreadful day,' she contradicted, regaining her spirit suddenly. 'I have had a very good day. It is others who have suffered, not me. That poor little boy and Luke. Even you. You must be in great haste to return home to change your clothes and put some salve on your hands, I am sure they are very painful. Do see if you can put a little life in the horses.'

'I comprehend the game must be played to its end,' he said, as he urged the horses into something resembling a trot. 'I do hope, my dear Miss Hundon, you will not come out the loser.'

It was no comfort at all to her; she was already the loser and though she wanted to tell him that she was not his Miss Hundon, dear or otherwise, she decided she had nothing to gain by confession. She wasn't the only one playing a game; he had been indulging in one himself, pretending to be looking for a wife, setting all the young ladies into a twitter, when his choice had already been made.

The rest of the short journey was made in silence. At its end he saw her safely into the drawing room, paid his respects to her ladyship and withdrew, leaving Sophie to tell the tale in whatever way served her purpose. But it wasn't the end; his curiosity had been aroused and until he had satisfied it, he would not say anything of what was in his heart.

Chapter Six

Lady Fitzpatrick and the girls were taking tea with Lady Gosport and a group of her friends two days later and the talk was all of the accident to the curricle.

'Poor Luke was dreadfully injured,' Lady Fitzpatrick said. 'And Sophie came home covered in blood and dirt and with her hair all falling out of its pins. I never saw the like.'

'I was not hurt, my lady,' Sophie said, squirming uncomfortably. 'I beg you do not refine upon it.'

Her ladyship ignored her. 'And it was so late I had twice put back dinner and then Cook said if she did not serve it at once it would be quite spoiled, so I allowed Tilly to bring it in. But I could not eat a morsel of it, fearing some terrible fate had befallen Sophie. Charlotte was weeping and would not be comforted, not that I had any comfort to offer, for I had not. There are so many villains about, especially with all the soldiers abroad on the streets.'

'The soldiers cannot help it if they have no work

and nowhere to go,' Sophie said. 'It is not right to blame them for every misdemeanour in town. I was in no danger with Luke beside me.'

Her ladyship was intent on telling her tale and would not be sidetracked. 'Monsieur Latour came to call the very next day. Such a fine gentleman and so grateful.' She laughed suddenly. 'He asked for Monsieur Hundon and it was a minute or two before I realised he thought Viscount Braybrooke was Sophie's husband. Can you imagine it? Why, it was a mere coincidence that they were both at the scene of the accident. I own I was glad of it, though, because Luke was so badly hurt he could not drive and his lordship drove the carriage home.'

'Yes, so his lordship told Martin,' Lady Gosport put in, proving that Lord Braybrooke, however much he disapproved, had confirmed that Luke had sustained his injuries at the scene of the accident. Not that Sophie had lied about it; in telling the story, she had simply allowed everyone to make the assumption.

'He was to meet Martin at White's at eight o'clock and did not arrive until nearly ten,' her ladyship went on. 'Martin said he seemed a little bemused. He was surprised, he said, for Dick is not one to make a Cheltenham tragedy of something of so little consequence. He was a soldier after all and, according to Martin, he was always cool in battle. He would not tell Martin what was on his mind but, whatever it was, he did not stay for cards, made his excuses and left.'

'Perhaps he is in love,' Verity Greenholme suggested with a giggle which made Sophie feel like slapping her.

'Who do you suppose can have gained his affection?' Verity's mother asked archly, while smiling at her daughter.

'I think it might be his cousin Emily,' Charlotte said.

'No, my dear,' Lady Fitzpatrick said, patting her hand. 'That is by no means decided. You must not give up as soon as a rival appears on the scene.'

'I heard he was very particular about his requirements,' Lady Gosport said. 'He gave Martin a long list of them.'

'What might they be?' Mrs Greenholme queried.

'Oh, I cannot remember them all, but I know she was to be wealthy—that seemed important, though he is already plump in the pocket. It had something to do with disliking being constantly dunned for lady's fripperies.'

'How mercenary that sounds,' Charlotte said. 'I never would have believed it of him.'

'Was there anything else?' Verity asked. 'Was she to be fair or dark?'

'Martin did not say. But he did say she was to have presence and dignity befitting a future duchess and hoydenish behaviour certainly would not do.'

'There you are, Charlotte,' Lady Fitzpatrick said. 'I am sure you fit the bill exactly.'

This remark served only to make Charlotte blush to the roots of her blonde curls and fumble in her reticule for a handkerchief. Sophie, who had been telling herself that she had been totally mistaken in Viscount Braybrooke who was nothing but a cold-hearted pinchcommons if all that concerned him was not hav-

ing to pay for his wife's clothes, heartily wished the
subject of Lord Braybrooke could be dropped.

It was abandoned the very next minute and in the
last way Sophie could have wished. The door was
flung open and a footman announced, 'Mr Frederick
Harfield, my lady.'

'Freddie!' Sophie and Charlotte exclaimed in uni-
son, looking at each other in dismay as he strode over
to bow before their hostess and exchange civilities
with her.

'What are we to do?' Charlotte whispered. 'We are
undone.'

His greetings done, he turned to survey the company and spotted them on the far side of the room.
'Miss Roswell. Miss Hundon,' he said, hurrying forward, a broad smile on his face. 'What an agreeable
surprise it is to find you here.'

Charlotte had gone very pale and Sophie very pink.
Oh, dear,' Sophie said, rising from her chair and step-
ping forwards. 'It is so hot in here, I do believe I...'
She put a hand to her brow and, timing it to perfection, fainted in Freddie's arms.

He was obliged to gather her up before she reached
the floor and looked round for somewhere to deposit
her.

'Oh, poor Sophie, I do believe she has not fully
recovered from that dreadful accident,' Charlotte
cried, realising what Sophie intended. 'Freddie, do
bring her outside where the air will revive her.' She
pulled urgently on his sleeve and he followed her
through the door which led onto the terrace, with the
whole company trooping out behind them.

'Get rid of them, Freddie,' Sophie whispered. 'We must speak to you alone.'

Startled, he looked down at her, but her eyes were closed and she gave every appearance of being in a deep swoon.

'There is a seat down the garden a little way,' Lady Gosport said, while Lady Fitzpatrick clucked around like a worried hen. 'She will recover there.'

'My lady, we do not need to trespass on your kindness. Do, please, take your guests back indoors and drink your tea before it becomes cold,' Freddie said. Sophie was becoming very heavy and he would have to put her down soon or drop her. 'I am sure Miss Roswell...'

'Of course I shall stay with her,' Charlotte interposed quickly. 'All she needs is a little air.' Then in an undertone to Lady Gosport. 'Lady Fitzpatrick fusses so and she is really no help at all, though she means to be, I know. Please persuade her to go back indoors with you.'

While she was speaking, Freddie had gained the seat and thankfully lowered Sophie onto it, took off his coat and folded it beneath her head, as Charlotte joined them and sat on the bench beside Sophie.

'Now, you may put an end to the dramatics, Miss Roswell' he said. 'I ain't such a cake as to think you would swoon at the sight of me, even though I was the last person you might expect to see.'

'That's true,' Charlotte said. 'What *are* you doing here, Freddie?'

'M'father sent me to get a little town bronze and find me a rich wife.'

'Oh, Freddie,' Charlotte cried. 'You didn't agree?'

'No choice in the matter, my dear, besides, I couldn't see it would do the least harm. I wanted to come, had a great fear you might take a liking to one of the *ton* and accept his offer. Couldn't allow that.'

'Oh, Freddie, you are absurd!' Charlotte said, delighted by this statement. 'As if I would! But that doesn't explain why you came to this house.'

'My father asked me to pay his respects. Lord Gosport is a particular friend of his. They were at school together. Didn't expect to find you here, though.' He paused, looking from one to the other. 'And it's plain as a pikestaff you didn't expect me.'

'No. Oh, Freddie, are your parents in town too?'

'No, they ain't. Came up alone, staying in lodgings. Now, are you going to tell me why you staged this little charade? Miss Roswell is no more unconscious than I am.'

'We had to stop you letting the cat out of the bag, Mr Harfield,' Sophie murmured, still pretending to be feeling ill because, although everyone else had gone back to the house, they were undoubtedly watching from the window.

'I told you we should never have embarked on this masquerade, Sophie,' Charlotte said in a voice which was certainly not one of solicitude for an invalid, although she was waving her open fan over her cousin's face. 'Someone was sure to put the cat among the pigeons. What are we to do?'

'Cats, bags, pigeons,' Freddie exclaimed. 'Be so good as to explain. If you have got yourselves into a scrape...'

'Oh, you will have to know, though what you will think of it, I dare not imagine,' Charlotte said. 'You see, we changed identities. I am known in town as Miss Roswell and Sophie is Miss Hundon.'

He stared from one to the other for several seconds, taking in the fact that Charlotte, in pale blue muslin with a ruched frill of silk decorating its neckline, was far more modishly dressed than Sophie in a dove-grey cambric round gown. 'In the name of heaven, why?'

'It will take too long to explain,' Sophie said. 'And Lady Gosport is coming out again. But whatever you do, do not address me as Miss Roswell or Charlotte as Miss Hundon.'

'But we have kept our own given names,' Charlotte put in quickly. 'It would have been too easy to make a slip if we had not. But you must not be too familiar with me, because I am the heiress and…'

She stopped as Lady Gosport approached. 'I see you have come round, Miss Hundon,' her ladyship said. 'Please do come indoors again, it is becoming much cooler and you will catch a chill. If you wish, you may rest in my boudoir and I will have a restorative sent up to you.'

'It is very kind of you, my lady,' Sophie said, standing up. 'I am perfectly recovered.'

'I think we should go home,' Charlotte said decisively, while Freddie retrieved his coat and stood looking with dismay at the creases in it. 'I am persuaded that the accident knocked you up more than you will admit, Sophie, and you ought not to have come out today.'

'Yes, that must be it,' her ladyship agreed. 'Perhaps

you should fetch a doctor to your cousin, Miss Roswell.'

To which Freddie said he would call on the young ladies the following day to see how they did, but he was hard put not to laugh aloud and his eyes were twinkling mischievously.

During the flurry of solicitous enquiries when they rejoined the other guests before taking their leave, he managed to whisper to Charlotte, 'I shall expect a full account tomorrow.'

The carriage was called for and Lady Fitzpatrick hustled the girls into it. She was not at all pleased with Sophie making a scene just when she was in full flow over the fascinating Monsieur Latour. It was her opinion that the lowly Miss Hundon was trying to steal Miss Roswell's thunder with her antics and that could not be borne. And if, as she had been led to believe, Sophie had an understanding with Mr Harfield, it was not to be wondered at that she had fainted at the sight of him.

It was her bounden duty to warn that young man to make his offer as soon as maybe and secure the young lady's hand before she could cause any more mayhem. It was her ladyship's aim to attach Miss Roswell to Viscount Braybrooke and she would not be thwarted. After all, she had been paid to find a suitable match for the heiress and she was determined to discharge her obligation.

Freddie, in his best superfine coat and grey check pantaloons, arrived in Holles Street soon after noon the following day and was ushered into the drawing room, expecting to find the two girls alone with Lady Fitzpatrick, but it seemed half the *haute monde* was there, sitting over the teacups, continuing the gossip started the day before, much to Lady Fitzpatrick's satisfaction.

He made his bow and turned to discover Miss Hundon and Miss Roswell deep in conversation with Martin Gosport, whom he knew slightly, and another gentleman, whose easy manner, superbly tailored coat and pristine neckcloth proclaimed him a pink of the *ton*.

'Lord Braybrooke, may I present Mr Frederick Harfield,' Charlotte said, after Freddie had stood before them to make his bow.

The two men bowed slightly, eyeing each other warily. 'And this is Mr Martin Gosport,' she went on. 'But perhaps you are already acquainted?'

'We met when we were boys, before the war, when Sir Mortimer brought him to London on a visit,' Martin said. 'How d'you do, Harfield? Sorry I was not at home when you called yesterday.'

'You are from Miss Hundon's home town?' Richard enquired of Freddie.

'Indeed, yes.' Suddenly remembering it was Sophie the viscount meant, Freddie tore his gaze from Charlotte and smiled at Sophie. 'We have known each other since we were in leading strings.'

'And we have so much to tell you, Freddie,' Sophie said, eyes brimming with laughter. 'I know it has only been a few weeks since we came to London, but we have met so many people and seen so much, it is difficult to know where to begin. I shall carry you off to talk in private, if his lordship will excuse us.'

Richard nodded and watched with growing alarm as she took Freddie's arm in a very proprietorial way and led him to a quiet corner of the room, sat down beside him and began an animated conversation with him.

'Miss Hundon seems to have recovered her spirits remarkably since the accident,' he commented drily.

'Oh, yes,' Charlotte said, as a sudden idea occurred to her. 'Yesterday she was in the dismals and then, lo and behold, Mr Harfield arrived and put the blue devils to flight.'

'My mother said she fainted at the sight of him,' Martin put in. 'Now, I would not have said she was the swooning sort.'

'Nor I,' Richard agreed. 'But she did have a very nasty experience three days ago, and the effects were, perhaps, delayed. That sometimes happens, I believe.'

'And you, my lord?' Charlotte queried, keeping one eye on the two people in the corner and wondering what Sophie was saying to Freddie. 'Have you sustained any ill effects?'

'No, only to my jacket and a little to my pride to think that your groom was there before me. Nothing of consequence.'

'We are very grateful to you, my lord. Sophie is sometimes a little headstrong and perhaps it was unwise of her to go out with only Luke for company, but she is used to being independent, you know.' She smiled disarmingly. 'I am afraid Freddie will have his hands full with her.'

'Has she fixed on Mr Harfield, then?' He tried to make the question sound casual, but was obliged to admit to himself that the answer was of considerable interest to him.

'No, not exactly. You see, Sir Mortimer is determined that his son shall marry money and Miss Hundon has no fortune, as you must know. How they will contrive, I do not know.'

Richard assimilated this piece of information with mixed feelings. If Sir Mortimer had his way and forbade the marriage, would Miss Hundon be consoled by another suitor? And did he want to be second best? 'But Miss Hundon has scarcely been out of Leicestershire,' he said. 'She can have little experience of the world. Do you think it is possible that she might find she was mistaken in him? After all, he is little more than a green boy and if he cannot stand up to his father...'

'He is not a green boy,' she contradicted hotly. 'Freddie is...' She stopped suddenly, her face on fire. She had so nearly given the game away, when all she had wanted to do was make Lord Braybrooke just a tiny bit jealous, so that he would see Sophie's merits. Sophie might deny she had a *tendre* for the viscount until she was purple, but Charlotte knew better.

If only Sophie had not been so particular about the man she wanted for a husband and looked into her heart instead, she might be happier and they could call off this subterfuge. 'I believe he is at a stand, that is all.'

Richard smiled. So the heiress was jealous of her own country cousin! Sir Mortimer might be gratified to know it, but it did Miss Roswell credit that she was prepared to stand back for her cousin's sake. Or was there more to it than that? He glanced over to where Mr Harfield and Miss Hundon were still deep in conversation and decided it was time to intervene.

He strolled over to them, catching the end of the conversation before they became aware of him.

'Freddie, we shall neither of us speak to you again, if you breathe a word,' Sophie was saying. 'You must wait until after our come-out ball. It is only three weeks away.'

'Three weeks!' It was an exclamation of anguish. 'I shall never manage it.'

'Of course you will.'

Richard coughed lightly, making them both look up at him. He was intrigued to see that both faces bore unmistakable signs of guilt. 'Mr Harfield,' he said smoothly. 'We cannot allow you to have Miss Hundon all to yourself, you know.'

Freddie rose with alacrity. 'No, beg pardon, thoughtless of me. We had so much to impart, but the rest can wait. Come Sophie, let us rejoin the others.'

Sophie rose and they moved across the room to where Charlotte and Martin were in conversation with Lady Fitzpatrick. Her ladyship was regaling Martin with a colourful account of Monsieur Latour's visit and saying she intended to invite him and his wife to the girls' ball, if they were still in England when it took place. Seeing Freddie, she lifted her quizzing glass to peer at him.

'Ah, Mr Harfield. So glad you have come. I may count on you to be Miss Hundon's escort to the ball,

may I not?' Without waiting for an answer, she turned
to Richard. 'And Lord Braybrooke, you will honour
us, will you not?'

'It promises to be the event of the Season and I
would not miss it for worlds,' he said. 'I shall be
honoured if Miss Roswell will stand up with me for
a waltz.'

'Of course,' Charlotte said, ignoring Freddie's
black looks.

Lady Gosport was trying to escape from Verity
Greenholme and her mother, who had been quizzing
her about Miss Roswell's supposed wealth and wondering why the young lady did not put it about a little
more. 'Not a bit like an heiress,' Mrs Greenholme
said. 'No different from the country cousin. Why, it
is sometimes hard to tell one from the other. You
would think someone with the blunt she is supposed
to have would have a little more style.

'If you ask me, it is all hum and what Lord Braybrooke will say when he finds he has been taken for
a flat, I dare not think. Let us hope someone opens
his eyes before he discovers the truth for himself.'

'I am sure I do not know what you mean,' her
ladyship said miffily. 'Miss Roswell is a charming
young lady and it is to her credit she don't advertise
her prospects.'

'I am persuaded his lordship would be well advised
to enquire into the details of her inheritance.' She
looked round suddenly when she realised the room
had gone very quiet and everyone except Lady Fitzpatrick had heard her last remark. Unable to back
down, she laughed shakily. 'Lord Gower is making a

cake of himself over Miss Thomson, you know. And
no one knows the least thing about her, except what
that silly woman who says she is her aunt spreads
about. Can't take people on face value, can you? Not
that I ain't sure everything is right and tight as a
drum.'

'Oh, dear,' Charlotte murmured. 'What am I to
say?'

'I should not dignify it with a reply,' Richard said,
bowing towards Mrs Greenholme and smiling silkily.
'Indeed, ma'am, one would be very unwise to play
one's hand unseen.'

Sophie was put in mind of a tiger, sleek, muscled
and dangerous. But what if his lordship were to take
the lady's advice and make enquiries about Miss Roswell? What could he discover? Nothing but the truth,
she told herself, as long as no one was able to identify
her. Freddie could, but Freddie was sworn to secrecy.

'Is Lord Braybrooke going to play cards?' Lady
Fitzpatrick enquired, gazing about her short-sightedly.
'Is it not a little early in the day for that?'

'Much too early,' Richard said, with heavy emphasis which could have been for her ladyship's benefit,
but which seemed to Sophie to be loaded with another
meaning and she felt her heart lurch uncomfortably.

'I have been thinking of arranging a little outing to
Vauxhall Gardens on Saturday,' Lady Gosport put in
before the conversation became even more fraught.
'Would you care to join us, Miss Roswell? And Miss
Hundon? I believe there are to be tableaux represent-
ing the Battle of Waterloo and fireworks afterwards.

Lord Braybrooke, would you consent to be one of our escorts?'

'Delighted, ma'am,' he said bowing. Then, to Lady Fitzpatrick, 'Regretfully, I must take my leave.' He bowed over her hand, then took Charlotte's and raised it to his lips. 'Miss Roswell. Until Saturday.'

'I shall look forward to it, my lord.'

'Miss Hundon.' He turned to Sophie. 'I am glad to see you recovered. But I beg of you, be more careful in future.' In spite of her efforts to hide her hands in the folds of her skirt, he managed to possess himself of one of them and raise it to his lips. The gentle pressure was enough to set her tingling with sensations she could not control; a warmth spread from the top of her head to the tips of her toes and her stomach churned itself into knots. The smile on his face told her all too clearly that he knew what he was doing to her and it angered her.

'My lord, I am always careful and it was hardly my fault the curricle overturned. Indeed, it might very well have collided with us if it were not for my...' She stopped, gulped and went on, 'Luke's quick thinking.'

'Yes, the inestimable Luke,' he murmured. 'How is he? I think I shall have to ask him how he hurt himself so badly.'

'No, my lord.' It was out before she could stop it. She flushed, but forced herself to face him out. 'He hates a fuss and becomes quite irritable if anyone makes a to-do over him. He will be bound to say he was only doing his duty.'

'Then I must not embarrass him,' he said, eyes twinkling. 'Good-day, Miss Hundon.'

There was something havey-cavey going on, he was sure of it. Both young ladies were behaving in a most unnatural manner, answering for each other and threatening that pup, Harfield, who seemed not to know where his interests lay, either with the heiress or the country cousin. As for Sophie, she was playing the deepest game of all and he would not rest until he knew all. And if that meant allowing himself to be inveigled into escorting Miss Roswell, then he would do it. Miss Roswell, he felt, was the weak link in the chain.

He was riding down Oxford Street towards home after a canter in the park the following morning when he saw Sophie come out of the end of Holles Street. She was on foot and dressed very plainly in dove grey and wore sturdy half-boots and a small straw bonnet with no brim to speak of. Luke, walking half a pace behind her, looked decidedly uneasy.

Richard reined in and watched as she set off at a fair pace in an easterly direction. Walking his horse, he followed, though he could make a good guess at her destination. Would she never learn! Only four days ago she had been in a fair way to being run down and though she had eschewed that monstrosity of a chariot on this occasion, she was still courting danger and flying in the face of convention.

True, she was not high-bred, but she was a gentle-woman and should not be allowed to wander all over London at will. London was not Leicestershire, where perhaps things were done differently, it was a great cosmopolitan city full of strange characters, footpads, cut-throats, pickpockets and worse. Even some who appeared the height of respectability were nothing of the sort.

He had a good mind to speak to Lady Fitzpatrick about it. But the thought of the scolding Sophie would receive and his own curiosity prevented him. He would see she came to no harm, even if it meant following her everywhere she went.

Sophie, unaware of her second escort, continued on her way to Maiden Lane, where they were to open the house to their first lodgers. Determined to be there, she had told Lady Fitzpatrick that because of the accident and having to take the Latour family back to their lodgings, she had not been able to purchase the book she had set out to buy. Her ladyship, deep in discussions about food and flowers and musicians for their ball, hardly raised an eyebrow.

Charlotte was expecting Freddie to call and was all on edge, even though Sophie had assured her Freddie would not let them down, and had not wanted to accompany her. It was only Luke who raised any sort of objection and she had been obliged to order him to do as he was told in her best Mistress-of-Madderlea manner.

She saw the long line of men waiting to be admitted to the house long before she reached it. She hurried past them to join Mrs Stebbings and her helpers.

'What are we to do?' the good lady asked when

Sophie had taken off her cloak and donned an apron. 'We cannot look after them all.'

'Then it will have to be first come first served and those admitted today must be barred tomorrow.'

'There will be arguments.'

'Then we will enlist those who helped us prepare the house to keep discipline. The men are used to obeying orders, they will not cause trouble if they see we are being fair. In the meantime we can feed as many of them as we can. I shall send Luke to the market for more supplies.'

Sophie was so busy serving the men with the food cooked by Mrs Stebbings's helpers, she did not notice the passage of time. It was only when she heard the church clock strike noon that she remembered she had promised to be back at Holles Street for nuncheon. She hurriedly took off her apron and left, promising to return as soon as she could, though how it was to be achieved, she did not know. She could hardly use the excuse of going to the bookshop again.

Richard had walked his horse up and down the street for what seemed an age and, tiring of that, had purchased a news sheet from a vendor on the corner of the road and was sitting on a wall opposite the house, reading it. The Luddites were busy in the north again, wreaking destruction, and he wondered how long it would be before their activities manifested themselves in the south. Already there were rumblings of discontent. If there were riots in London, the unemployed soldiers were bound to join in and Sophie would be in even more danger.

He folded the paper when he saw her depart with Luke at her elbow, but instead of following immediately, he crossed the road and entered the refuge where he introduced himself to Mrs Stebbings as Major Richard Braybrooke and expressed an interest in the work she was doing.

Flustered, she apologised for not being able to offer him proper refreshment, or even a comfortable chair. 'We have been rushed off our feet, Major,' she said. 'We did not expect so many.'

'Good news travels fast, ma'am,' he said, smiling. 'But tell me, how have you been able to accomplish so much? You must have a very generous benefactor.'

'Yes, indeed, though we do not know who she is. Mrs Carter is acting for her, but she dare not reveal her identity, being sworn to secrecy.'

'Mrs Carter?' he enquired, raising a well-defined eyebrow. 'Who is she?'

'A war widow, my lord. She is companion to the lady in question but that is all I know.'

'Could it be the lady I passed on my way in? She was wearing a grey cloak and a small bonnet. Red-gold curls, I recall.'

'Yes, that would be Mrs Carter. A lovely lady, so compassionate and not afraid of getting her hands dirty.'

'So, I collect,' Richard murmured under his breath, then pulling a purse from his pocket, he laid it on the table beside the dirty plates and beakers. 'Please accept this towards your expenses. It is all I have on me, but I will arrange for a larger donation to be sent to you.'

She thanked him effusively and he left, mounted his horse and set off after Sophie.

Companion to the lady in question, he mused. That could only be Miss Roswell. So, the heiress of Madderlea was also a philanthropist, which was to her credit, but it was Sophie who was doing all the donkey work, while she cavorted about town in her new carriage, making calls and gossiping over the teacups. It was easy to be generous when you had a great deal of blunt; Sophie gave something more precious than money, she gave her time. Oh, how he loved her for that, misguided as she was.

Did Harfield know what she was about? Yesterday she had been swearing him to secrecy, so undoubtedly he did know, but why was he not escorting her instead of going sparring with Martin? It was a dashed ungentlemanly way of going on and he might very well find an opportunity of telling him so.

Sophie, late back for nuncheon and still unable to produce the book she went out to buy, told Lady Fitzpatrick that it was out of print and she must needs give up on it, to which the good lady replied, 'Well, your papa cannot say you did not do your best for him. Now, perhaps you will settle down with Charlotte to discuss the arrangements for the ball and your costumes. Rattling around town on your own is not the thing, you know, not the thing at all. Why did Mr Harfield not accompany you this morning?'

'I believe he was otherwise engaged, my lady,' Sophie said demurely. 'His father has given him endless commissions.'

'He does have to find a rich wife too,' Charlotte put in with a giggle.

'And so does Braybrooke,' her ladyship retorted. 'You would do better, miss, to make a push to engage his attention instead of worrying about what don't concern you. I shall be very disappointed if you have not brought him to an offer by the time your ball is over. And so will Mr Hundon.'

'I cannot make him want me, if he has set his sights elsewhere.'

'Of course you can. You know, my dear, you are too modest for an heiress and the future mistress of Madderlea. You must assert yourself more or you will be despised.'

'If modesty is to be despised, then I scorn those who despise it,' Charlotte said with some heat. 'I am who I am and cannot change.'

At this point Sophie could stand no more and was obliged to excuse herself on the pretext of having to change for their carriage ride in the park. Once in her room, she burst into laughter.

Charlotte, following her, did not share her amusement. 'Sophie, it is all very well for you to laugh, but you have not been looking for a book for Papa, that I know. It is all a hum. And you are not making the smallest effort to find a husband.'

'I have not met anyone I would even consider.'

'And that's a whisker. You are wearing the willow for Lord Braybrooke, I know that.'

'And Lord Braybrooke is looking for a rich, complacent wife who will allow him to continue his bachelor existence unhampered by considerations of faith-fulness,' Sophie snapped.

'Wherever did you come by that idea?'

'Mr Gosport said so. He seemed to think that being a duchess would be enough to compensate for any shortcomings in his lordship.'

'And that has sunk you in the suds and why you have been going out all alone to brood. Oh, Sophie, I am so sorry. Perhaps if he knew you were really a considerable heiress…'

'Do you think I would want him on those terms? He is the very opposite of the man I want for a husband. He is arrogant and vain and unfeeling and…' She stopped, remembering that kiss and how she had melted into his arms and enjoyed every delicious second, and how her whole body tingled with excitement when he so much as took her hand or looked at her with those liquid brown eyes.

'And what?' Sophie asked, curious.

'He thinks he has only to snap his fingers and every young lady in town will prostrate herself before him. Did you ever hear such a conceited recital as that list of requirements he wants in a wife? Beauty. Wealth. Deportment. And what is he prepared to offer in return? The dubious pleasure of one day becoming a duchess.'

'And Lady Fitz exhorts me to set my cap at him,' Charlotte put in. 'I am no more likely to acquiesce to such Turkish treatment than you are and so I shall tell him if he deigns to make an offer. Not that I would accept him, even if he behaved like an angel, because I am already engaged.'

Sophie, diverted, stared at her cousin. 'Engaged?'

'Yes. Freddie called while you were out and we contrived to have a few moments alone when Lady Fitz left the room to speak to Cook about something she had forgot about the ball—something to do with poached salmon, I think.'

'Never mind about the fish, tell me what happened.'

'Nothing happened. Freddie said he was not going to make any sort of push to make the acquaintance of this year's debutantes and unless I agreed to marry him then and there, he would reveal all to Lady Fitzpatrick the minute she came back into the room.'

'And you agreed.'

'Of course I agreed, it is what I have always wanted, though it will have to remain a secret until he has been home and confronted his father. He has already spoken to Papa.' She giggled suddenly. 'He even promised to pretend to pay particular attention to you.'

'Me?'

'Well, he has been dangling after Miss Hundon ever since he came down from Cambridge, everyone knows that. What more natural that he should be seen often in her presence?'

'Oh, I see. I thought you were tired of our masquerade?'

'So, I was, but now Freddie is part of it, it might be fun. And besides, I have not yet brought Lord Braybrooke to an understanding.'

'You can't have them both!'

'I don't want them both. I mean to make him un-

derstand the error of his ways and realise what a treasure he will have in Miss Sophie Hundon and when
I speak of treasure, I do not mean anything so vulgar
as money. Nor will it hurt him to become just a little
jealous of Freddie.'

'Charlotte, I beg you to do no such thing. He will
be so angry.'

'Then you must contrive to turn it to your advantage. He is to escort me to Vauxhall Gardens on Saturday and Freddie is to escort you. We shall see what
transpires. And please, Sophie, do not dress in the
unbecoming fashion you have adopted since we came
to London. It is enough to put Freddie off, not to
mention Lord Braybrooke.'

Sophie sighed, knowing she had lost control of the
situation. She had been almost ready to agree with
Charlotte that they must reveal their true identities
and take the consequences when Charlotte changed
from being an unwilling accomplice to an enthusiastic
accessory. And what she was planning was even more
hazardous. Well, she would go down fighting.

She dressed for the visit to Vauxhall Gardens with
particular care in a gown of amber crepe over a cream
satin slip. The short bodice had a round neck and tiny
puff sleeves and was caught under the bust with a
posy of silk flowers from which floated long satin
ribbons in amber. Her hair was dressed *à la Grecque*
and threaded with more ribbon. Her accessories were
a single strand of pearls around her neck, long white
gloves, white satin slippers, a small satin drawstring
bag and a fan which had once been her mother's.

'Beautiful,' Charlotte said when Sophie came to her room to see if she was ready.

'You too. That rose pink is exactly right for your complexion. Freddie will fall in love with you all over again.'

'I hope he may, but it would be fatal to show it. I do believe I heard the front-door knocker. Are you ready?' Sophie took a deep breath and together they descended to the hall where Lady Fitzpatrick was greeting their escorts.

Richard, who had himself risen to the occasion and clad himself in a lilac evening coat of impeccable tailoring and dove grey pantaloons, looked up when he heard the rustle of their gowns and his breath caught in his throat as he beheld Sophie.

Here was no dowdy country cousin, here was a young lady with the face and figure of a goddess, who came down the stairs as if she were floating. If he had had any doubts about his choice of a wife, they fled at the sight of her.

What he most wanted to do was take her away somewhere private and declare his intentions before taking her in his arms once more and kissing her. He needed to feel her soft lips on his, her pliable body close to his so that he could enjoy her heart beating against his as he had done once before. But would she have him? Apart from her response to that kiss she had never given any indication she would welcome an offer from him.

It was neither the time nor the place and Freddie was hurrying forward to take her hand and claim her, showering her with compliments which were a little too effusive to be sincere. There was nothing for it but to make his bow to Charlotte and offer his arm to escort her to the waiting carriage.

Chapter Seven

The tableaux of Waterloo were impressive for the uniforms of the protagonists, for the simulated noise of the wooden guns and the smoke which threatened to obscure the whole thing. The actor who played Wellington sat impassively upon his horse doing nothing at all except look superior and Napoleon, short and stout and wearing his cockaded hat sideways, strutted about waving his arms ineffectually, while the armies rushed about pretending to fire muskets and stabbing each other with their bayonets. The English died stoically, while the French screamed and flung themselves about. The audience, standing in the darkness beyond the flambeaux-lit stage, were convulsed with laughter.

'Such realism! Such heroics!' Richard laughed, as the whole thing came to an end with Napoleon fleeing in his coach and the English soldiers cheering. 'If that is how the general populace see our hard-won victories, it is no wonder they have so little sympathy for our returning soldiers.'

'You would have everyone frightened to death by the truth?' Sophie asked him. 'The blood and the stench and the screaming of wounded horses, men torn limb from limb and dying in agony? It is supposed to be an entertainment, not a history lesson and it does no harm to remind people how brave our soldiers were. They might be a little more generous towards them.'

That she could describe such things, he put down to her taste in reading and a vivid imagination, not experience. She had spoken with spirit, her eyes glowing in the darkness, so vividly alive that he was obliged to clench his fists at his sides to stop him from pulling her into his arms. The tension he felt clamped his jaw, so that he could not trust himself to speak.

'You are silent,' she went on. 'Do you not agree?'

'Oh, you are right,' he said, forcing himself to respond. 'I can find no fault with your argument.'

'There is nothing more to see,' Charlotte said, laying her fingers lightly on his arm. 'Shall we walk a little? The coloured lanterns in the trees are so romantic, don't you think?'

'Miss Roswell, forgive me,' he said, turning to smile down at her and leading the way along one of the many pathways which wound around the gardens, many of them ending in little arbours. 'I am persuaded you share Miss Hundon's particular concern for the destitute soldiers.'

'Oh, I cannot believe they are destitute,' she said. 'Surely they have been given pensions?' She looked up at him coquettishly. 'You do not look like a man who is impoverished. I do believe you must outdo Mr Brummell, though I have never met that gentleman.'

'It is different for Lord Braybrooke,' Sophie said from behind them where she was walking with Freddie and Lady Fitzpatrick. 'He is an officer and a gentleman of independent means.'

'Of course he is,' Charlotte said. 'Did I say he was not?'

'Miss Roswell, you are putting Lord Braybrooke to the blush,' Freddie put in, annoyed with Charlotte for playing up to the viscount. 'Pray desist.'

'I was only bamming.' She turned to walk backwards in order to face him and Sophie. 'And I do not know what he means when he says I share your particular concerns, Sophie. Have you voiced concerns to his lordship?'

'I expect his lordship was referring to our conversation the first time he was so good as to take us to the park in his carriage,' Sophie said.

'Fancy him remembering that. I had quite forgot it.'

Either Miss Roswell was very good at dissembling or she was not the benefactress he had supposed her to be, Richard decided. Then who was it? Not Miss Hundon herself, for she had no money with which to be munificent. Lady Fitzpatrick, perhaps? It might account for her allowing Miss Hundon to go out alone, but her ladyship did not give the impression of being a philanthropist, or plump in the pocket. Ten to one she had been paid to chaperone the young ladies.

The mystery occupied his mind to such an extent that he lost the thread of the conversation going on about him. Charlotte, who had resumed walking at his side, had to speak to him twice to bring him back in line. 'I beg your pardon, Miss Roswell.'

'I said the fireworks are not to be let off until midnight and I suggested we might go to the bandstand and listen to the orchestra. I believe we might buy refreshments from a tent nearby.'

'By all means.'

They had barely taken their seats when Charlotte nudged Sophie. 'Is that not Monsieur Latour over there, Sophie?'

'Goodness, so it is. He is with his wife and little boy.'

'Oh, do introduce me to Madame Latour and the little boy, Sophie. I do not think I have ever met a real live French family.'

'Of course you have. London is full of *emigrés*, has been ever since the Terror. Why, the French king was exiled here until he returned to France at the end of the war.'

'Well, I never met him, did I? Oh, he has seen us and is coming over.'

Monsieur Latour was indeed making his way over to them, his wife on his arm. Pierre skipped ahead and made a formal bow before Sophie. 'Ma'amselle Hundon. Papa has brought us to see the sights. It is past my bedtime but he says it does not matter for I may sleep late tomorrow. Did you see the battle?' All this was said in breathless French.

Sophie smiled. 'Yes, and I am sorry for it.'

'Why?' He turned as his parents came up behind him. 'Ma'amselle did not like the tableaux, Mama.'

'Did she not?' Monsieur Latour smiled and bowed. 'Miss Hundon. Viscount Braybrooke. It is a pleasure to meet you again.'

Sophie left her seat to shake hands with Madame Latour and introduce her to Lady Fitzpatrick, Charlotte and Freddie. It was only when they sat down they realised the language would be a barrier to conversation. Monsieur Latour spoke a little English, but his wife and son none at all.

Richard tried manfully to keep up with them, but it was left to Sophie to translate, which she did without hesitation, moving fluently from one language to the other. It was only when the Frenchman commented on it that she realised she had probably made a dreadful mistake. 'I had a French governess,' she said, trying to retrieve the situation.

'She is to be congratulated,' he said. 'I could almost take you for a native, though the accent is not Parisian.'

'I believe Madame Cartier came from Brussels,' Sophie said, wishing the ground would open and swallow her because Richard was looking at her with a strange gleam in his eye.

'Miss Roswell did not share your teacher?' Madame Latour asked.

'No. We have not always lived together. My cousin did not come to live with us until her guardians died in a tragic accident two years ago.'

'*Pauvre fille.*' Madame Latour patted Charlotte's hand sympathetically. 'Lady Fitzpatrick is not your guardian, then?'

Because Charlotte had not understood the question,

it was left to Sophie to reply. 'No, only while we are in London for the Season. We are to come out into Society at a masked ball in three weeks' time.'

'Ah, yes, the invitation we 'ave received. Lady Fitzpatrick is very agreeable to ask us. *Malheureusement*, we expect to return to France the week before.'

Sophie hoped fervently that her relief did not show as she expressed her regret.

The conversation was interrupted when the first of the fireworks burst upon the sky and Pierre cried out with excitement. Richard hoisted him on his shoulders and pushed his way through the crowd to be near the front and the little boy sat perched on his vantage point, his eyes round with wonder as, one after the other, the fireworks fizzed skywards and fanned out in brilliant colours of red, yellow and green before dropping to earth.

Sophie's heart contracted as she watched them. What had she said to Charlotte all those weeks ago when they walked in the woods at Upper Corbury? He must be good with children. Viscount Braybrooke was giving every appearance of enjoying the company of the little boy and was not at all concerned about Pierre's boots dirtying his lilac coat.

She found herself with an image of Richard at Madderlea, playing in the garden with several children. Their children. Oh, if only... But being good with children was not the only requisite she had expounded. There had been a whole list of them. How vain and top-lofty she had been! But he had been no less arrogant in his requirements and she must remind herself of that when she felt herself weakening.

The endpiece of the display was a huge wheel which spun round emitting brilliant sparks and illuminating a huge set-piece of Saint George slaying the dragon, which breathed fire and smoke. Richard, who had explained the story to Pierre, set him down and took his hand to return him to his parents; soon afterwards the Latours took their leave. It was very late for Pierre to be out, Monsieur Latour explained, and now he had seen the fireworks, he must be taken home to bed.

'I think it is time we went too,' Freddie said, looking daggers at Charlotte who was hanging on to Richard's sleeve and looking up at him for all the world as if she adored him. It was all very well to say she was pretending for Sophie's sake, but she was doing it too brown. And he didn't see that it would do a pennyworth of good. 'Lady Fitzpatrick is already slumbering.'

They turned to look for the dowager and discovered her sitting on a bench with her head dropped on her chest and her bonnet all askew. 'As a chaperon, she is hardly to be recommended,' Richard laughed. 'Why, we could have carried you off and she none the wiser.'

'One must suppose she took you both for gentlemen,' Sophie said, though he could not tell if she were indulging in sarcasm or not.

'I suggest you wake her and bring her to the entrance, while I call up the carriage, before the temptation to prove otherwise overwhelms me,' he said.

She looked up at him, eyes glittering. 'Again, my lord?' The words were said in an undertone and not heard by Charlotte and Freddie who were gently shaking her ladyship awake.

Furiously he turned and strode away to find the carriage among the long line waiting for their owners to tire of the entertainment and ask to be taken home. Some would still be there at dawn, he well knew. It was a place for secret assignations and declarations and stolen kisses in the dark, but all he had managed was a stringent exchange of words which told him nothing except that she had not forgiven him.

But he had learned something. He had learned that she spoke fluent French and Miss Roswell did not. Miss Roswell professed never to have met a French family and yet, according to the *on dits* which were current about town, she had spent her childhood in Belgium. He was beginning to wonder if she had ever been abroad. But if not, where had she lived the first fifteen years of her life?

And had Miss Hundon really had a Belgian governess? And one called Cartier, a very similar name to the one adopted by her at the refuge. Tonight she had not looked or behaved like a country cousin; her clothes had not been flamboyant but elegantly understated. She had a presence, a stature which demanded attention. And lips that asked to be kissed, too. And he had not even managed one private word with her! He had wanted to ask for her forgiveness for the kiss he had stolen and to try and explain himself, but all he had done was to confirm her disgust of him.

The only way he would succeed in returning himself to favour, if he had ever held that exalted position, was to forget all about that embarrassing list of requirements and begin again, as if he had only just met her, to take this business of courtship seriously. But was it already too late?

'Richard!' He looked up at the sound of his name and was appalled to see his aunt and cousin bearing down on him.

'Richard,' his aunt said, tapping him with her fan. 'We did not know you were to be here. Why did you not say? We could have come together.'

'I am in company, Aunt.' He made his bow to both ladies. 'Good evening, Emily.'

'Whose company? Shall we join forces for supper?'

'We are on the point of leaving. The ladies are fatigued.'

'Ladies, eh?' She laughed. 'Barques of frailty. Oh, well, sow your wild oats, if you must, but do remember what is expected of you before the Season is out.'

'How could I forget?' He was on the point of explaining that his companions were not barques of frailty, when Frederick hove into view with Sophie on one arm and Charlotte on the other, followed by a somewhat sleepy and dishevelled Lady Fitzpatrick.

Lady Braybrooke laughed, making the tall plume on her turban nod. 'My goodness, what a handful you have there, Richard. I do hope you can manage them.' She gave Charlotte an unctuous smile, while ignoring Sophie. 'Good evening, Miss Roswell. Lady Fitzpatrick. I was about to suggest supper, but my nephew tells me you are fatigued and are going home.'

'Yes, my lady,' Charlotte said. 'The night is well advanced.'

'Oh, I had forgot, in the country you go to bed at sunset and rise at dawn. You must find town hours very irksome.'

'Not irksome, my lady,' Sophie said sweetly. 'Unhealthy perhaps. I have heard it said that rest taken before midnight is more efficacious than that taken during the morning. It makes for a smoother complexion and a better temper.'

Richard laughed aloud and earned a swift look of annoyance from his aunt. 'You live in the country three parts of the year yourself, Aunt Philippa, so you must have heard the expression.'

'Of course I have heard it, it is not meant for the *haute monde*, but the labouring classes. Take the ladies home, Richard, but I shall expect you to escort Emily and me in the park tomorrow afternoon.'

'Ma'am, I am...'

'Oh, please do,' Emily said. 'We have been in town nearly a week and you have not taken me out once.'

Richard's inbred good manners would not let him give his cousin a set down. He bowed to her and to his aunt in acquiescence and turned to offer his arm to Sophie, only to find she had taken Freddie's arm and was strolling towards the carriage with him, her bonnet so close to his cheek they were almost touching. He gave his arm to Charlotte.

Sophie could not sleep. Plagued with visions of Richard, she went over every conversation they had ever had, every look they had exchanged, remembered the taste of his lips on hers, the vibrant masculinity of his body when he held her in his arms. She argued with herself that it meant nothing except that she was a total innocent when it came to men and was no more to him than a mild flirtation. It must be so, for he seemed to be able to turn to Charlotte, his cousin Emily or Miss Greenholme with perfect ease of manners.

She tossed about so much the bedclothes were heaped around her, the pillows flattened. She sat up and pummelled them angrily. It was nearly dawn; she could see the light through the curtains, the outlines of the furniture and the reflection of the bed in the long mirror. She rose and went to the window to draw the curtains back and sat on the window seat to watch the pink light come up over the roof tops.

Was Lord Braybrooke still out on the town, playing cards at his club perhaps, or had he gone home to bed? Why was she so obsessed by him? The lamp lighter went down the street extinguishing the lamps; a cat padded along the street with a mouse in its mouth; a milkmaid led a cow to the back door of the house across the other side of the road, its udder heavy with milk. A chimney sweep, black as the soot he shifted, walked down the road, a sleepy-eyed young boy in his wake. A hackney stopped on the corner to set down a late-night reveller. Another day had begun, another day to live through.

She turned, slipped on a house robe, and went downstairs. A skivvy was clearing out the grate in the dining room, humming tunelessly under her breath.

'Oh, miss, you startled me,' she said. 'Did you want something?'

'No, Hetty, you carry on.'

She wandered all over the ground-floor rooms, her legs as heavy as lead. She desperately wanted to sleep, but she could not. It was all her own fault, this mull she had made of her life. She had been so sure of herself, so sure of what she wanted, so determined to put Madderlea first, she had embroiled not only herself but Charlotte, too, in a game of make-believe without considering what the consequences might be. It had all been intended to find the husband of her dreams, but it had turned into a nightmare. Only she was wide awake!

She went back to her room and sat on the rumpled bed. Lady Fitzpatrick and Charlotte would not be awake for hours. Suddenly making up her mind, she flung open her wardrobe door and pulled out her riding habit. She would go riding and blow the blue devils away in a gallop.

Luke, who had a room above the stables at the mews, was still fast asleep when she made her way there. Rather than wake him, she saddled Pewter herself with a man's saddle and set off alone, trotting through the quiet streets towards Hyde Park.

It was going to be a warm day, but now the air was pleasant with a slight breeze which lifted her red-gold curls as she set her horse to canter along the almost-deserted ride. But cantering was not enough. She turned off the path and spurred Pewter to a gallop across the grass.

It reminded her of the rides she had taken with her

Uncle Henry around the estate at Madderlea. She had not been back since that dreadful accident because Aunt Madeleine considered it would be too upsetting for her. But she ought to go back. She should know what was going on there even if she was debarred by law from having control of it. She ought to test her memory, find out if it really was worth all the heartache she was suffering. Supposing when she saw it again, she discovered it was no more than bricks and mortar, a millstone, as Lady Braybrooke had suggested? Then what?

She drew up and jumped down to rest her horse, sitting with her back against a tree trunk while he cropped the grass close by. Bricks and mortar. What did Richard think of bricks and mortar? But it was a heritage too and there were people involved, flesh and blood like she was, people who worked and ate and drank and loved. Love. What exactly was it? Her eyelids drooped as her thoughts went round and round, going nowhere.

Richard found her there, under the spreading branches, fast asleep.

After he left the ladies at Holles Street, he had felt too restless to go home, knowing his aunt and cousin would be waiting for him, fussing over him, questioning him. He had sent the carriage back to Bedford Row with the coachman and walked about for hours, so deep in thought he had no idea where his steps had taken him, except that just before dawn he had found himself back at Holles Street as if he had been drawn to it like a magnet.

All the contradictory aspects of Miss Hundon and

Miss Roswell's characters had been going round and round in his head until he was dizzy. He was almost to the point of believing they were not Miss Hundon and Miss Roswell at all, but two imposters, out to trap him. But why?

Was there anything in his past which might account for it? Had he ever done anything to cause two apparently innocent young ladies to want to play games with him? He was no greenhorn and there had been several ladies in his life, little bits of muslin, barques of frailty, as his aunt had so succinctly put it, but he had never knowingly hurt any of them. And he had never met Miss Hundon before; he would certainly have remembered her if he had.

He had stood outside the house, staring up at the windows, wondering which one was Sophie's. He had been answered when he saw the curtains being drawn and just managed to duck out of sight as the subject of his contemplation looked out. He was not the only one who was sleepless.

A few minutes later she had come out and darted down the lane to the mews, the skirt of her riding habit bunched up in her hands. Keeping hidden, he followed and saw her mount and trot away towards the park. His doubts were forgotten and he hurried after her, but by the time he reached the ride she was nowhere to be seen.

The first thing that came to his mind was that she had an assignation. Why else creep out alone at so early an hour? Angry with himself for being such a sousecrown, he had turned to leave but, hearing hoof-beats some way off, turned in the direction of the sound and saw the rump of her horse as she galloped towards the centre of the park and disappeared into a copse. He went after her, but being on foot it was some time before he came upon her, seated on the ground with her back against a tree. So, it was an assignation!

Curious, he had stayed out of sight and watched. Fifteen minutes went by. She did not seem to be anxious or looking about her as if expecting her lover. He had been both relieved and horrified when her eyes closed and he realised she was slumbering like a child.

He came out from his hiding place and stood for a moment, watching the gentle rise and fall of her breast, wondering how to wake her without startling her. Sitting on the grass at her side, he leaned on his elbow and allowed himself the luxury of studying every inch of her face. He noted the arched brows, the straight nose, the perfectly shaped lips, slightly parted now, even the dimple in her chin and the light sprinkling of freckles on her cheeks and the soft curve of her throat as it disappeared into the frill of the blouse which peeped above the collar of her habit.

He picked a stem of grass and tickled her chin with it. She twitched like a sleeping puppy but did not wake. Slowly he bent his head and put his lips to her forehead. She did not stir. Becoming bolder, he kissed her lips very, very gently. Her eyes flew open. He leaned back as she came fully awake, sat up and stared at him as if she could not believe what she was seeing. 'It's you!'

He inclined his head, smiling. 'As you see.'

She had been asleep. And dreaming. She had dreamed he was bending over her, kissing her, a look of such tenderness in his eyes, she had been in ecstasy. And then she woke to find him sitting beside her, laughing at her. And still wearing the lilac coat and the dove-grey pantaloons of the evening before. Was she awake or still asleep? 'Where am I? What are you doing here?'

He smiled. 'I am sitting on the ground in the middle of Hyde Park, the same as you.'

'I know that. What I meant was, why, for what reason? I'll take my oath you have not been home to bed. You are still wearing your evening coat and you have not shaved.'

'If I had known I might meet Sleeping Beauty, I might have attired myself as Prince Charming.'

'I was not asleep, I was merely resting my eyes.'

He did not bother to contradict her; they both knew the truth. 'I was out walking. What reason can you give?'

'I could not sleep. I decided to take a ride.'

'All alone?'

'Why not? I did not want to wake the rest of the household.'

'And so you came here, to one of the loneliest parts of the park, and fell asleep like the Babes in the Wood. What do you think might have happened if someone other than me had found you? Unless you were expecting someone else. If so, you must be sadly disappointed he did not arrive.'

'An assignation? Whatever gave you that idea?' She was so genuinely astonished, he realised he had been mistaken. 'Sir, I think it very uncivil of you to suggest that I would meet up with someone secretly, and at this hour. But then, I collect, you have no great opinion of me...'

'Miss Hundon, that hit is below the belt. And unworthy of you.'

'I told you before I know nothing of pugilism, but how clever of you to turn the tables and put me in the wrong. You would have me apologising to you next for discommoding you.'

'That was certainly not my intention and I beg your pardon if I mistook the matter, but I was, and am, concerned for your safety. What madness possessed you to come out at this hour? Good God, you might have been robbed or your horse stolen. Worse, you might have been attacked.'

'But I wasn't, was I?' She sounded a great deal more spirited than she felt.

'It was your good fortune that I was on hand.'

'How did you come to be on hand? Have you been following me?'

'I saw you leave the house; it behoved me to make sure you came to no harm.'

'And what, pray, were you doing outside our house at so early an hour?'

He laughed. 'Now, you are turning the tables. Let us say I was on my way home after a night out.'

'And you saw me and immediately jumped to the conclusion I was meeting a lover—not that it is any concern of yours. You are not my keeper.'

'No, I am not, but if this morning is a yardstick,

you are certainly in need of one. The sooner you find a husband to take you in hand, the better.'

'Do you think I might not find one willing to undertake the task?' she asked mischievously.

'He would certainly have his hands full. A greater hoyden I have yet to meet.'

'And I collect you dislike hoydens excessively.' She scrambled to her feet and began dusting down her skirt. The conversation was so barbed, she could not bear to continue it. 'I must go.'

'Then allow me to escort you.'

'Oh, please do not trouble yourself, my lord, I am sure you must be in some haste to be elsewhere.' She looked about for Pewter, who was nibbling a dandelion a few yards away.

'It would be very disobliging of me to be in a hurry when I meet a young lady who so obviously does not know how to go on and needs assistance.'

'I need no assistance,' she said, catching Pewter's reins and preparing to mount by herself. The horse stepped sideways and she found herself hopping after him with one foot in the stirrup.

He strode up to her and grabbed the bridle, making the horse stand still. 'Allow me.' He bent to offer his cupped hands for her foot. 'Do you ever observe the proprieties?' he asked, noting the man's saddle. 'Who taught you to ride astride?'

'Papa,' she said without thinking.

'Really? You surprise me. Lawyers always seem to me to be rather stuffy gentlemen.'

'That just shows one should not jump to conclusions,' she retorted, spreading her skirt.

He smiled a little grimly. She was the most infuriating chit imaginable. And the loveliest. 'Yes, you would have thought I would have learned that by now, would you not? Nothing is ever what it seems.'

She was feeling tired and confused and did not know how to answer that and so she clicked her tongue at Pewter and set off at a walk, back towards the Stanhope Gate.

He took hold of the horse's bridle to lead him. 'Miss Hundon,' he said, walking purposefully beside her. 'I want you to promise me you will not go out riding alone again. If you feel like early morning exercise, will you tell me? I shall be happy to accompany you.'

'Oh, I do not think that would be at all the thing, my lord. We shall have the tattlers talking and that would certainly not please Lady Braybrooke. And besides, this morning's ride was not premeditated. It was a whim and unlikely to be repeated. You need not concern yourself with my eccentricities.'

She had given him a disgust of her and instead of meekly accepting his scolding and thanking him for seeing her safely home, she had snubbed him. He was angry, she could tell by the set of his jaw as he strode beside her horse, looking straight ahead.

When they reached the mews, he turned to help her dismount, putting his hands about her waist and lifting her to the ground as if she weighed no more than thistledown. They stood together looking into each other's faces, trying to read thoughts that were hidden, desires which could not be expressed, hope where there was none. Or so it seemed.

'Miss Hundon…' His voice was soft and gentle, making her heart jump into her throat.

'My lord?'

'We have made a poor start, you and I, have we not? I should like to…' He got no further because Luke came hurrying out of the stable towards them.

'Miss Rosw—' He stopped, his mouth a round O of dismay at his mistake.

Sophie, turning to face him, said the first thing that came into her head. 'What about Miss Roswell, Luke? Has she been looking for me?'

'Yes, miss.' His relief was obvious. 'She couldn't find you in the house. I didn't know where you were, but Pewter were gone and…'

'I went for a ride to see the sun come up,' she said. 'I am sorry if I worried anyone. I'll go in and see Charlotte straight away.' She turned to Richard. 'Thank you, my lord, for seeing me safe.'

Dismissed, there was nothing to do but take his leave.

Lady Fitzpatrick and Charlotte were still abed and Sophie was not required to explain her absence. She hurried to her room and dressed in a striped cambric morning dress with a high neck and straight sleeves, one of those Charlotte had decried as being dowdy, and was brushing her hair before the mirror when Anne came in with her morning chocolate.

'I thought I heard you moving about, Miss Sophie, and Hetty said you were downstairs before it was even light.'

'Too much excitement, Anne. I could not sleep.'

'That's just what I thought, so I've brought your chocolate early. Shall I do your hair?'

'Please.'

Anne took over the brush. 'Goodness, this is in a tangle. What shall I put out for you to wear today, miss?'

'This will do for this morning. I am going out. As for the afternoon, I shall have to see what Lady Fitzpatrick has arranged.'

'I doubt she will stir before noon. Nor Miss Charlotte neither.'

'Good. Let them sleep as long as possible, Anne. I have some business to see to.'

'I ain't so sure you should be rushing about on your own, Miss Roswell. And pretendin' to be Miss Hundon. What Miss Charlotte's mama would say if she knew…'

'But she doesn't know, does she? And we shall all come to rights before the Season ends. If anyone asks for me this morning, I have gone to Pantheon's Bazaar because I have been told they have some new lace come in and I need to buy some for my costume for the ball. It's a secret, so I do not want anyone to come with me.'

'Very well, miss.'

Putting on a light pelisse and a plain bonnet, she picked up her reticule and left the house again, ignoring the fact that less than an hour before Richard had scolded her for going out alone. She could not see that she was in any more danger on the streets of the metropolis than she had been in Upper Corbury.

And as for the conventions, she had already flouted them too often to worry about conforming now.

His lordship had said it would be a good thing when she found a husband, but he had no more thought of offering for her himself than he would of offering for her maid. She was beneath his notice, except as a sparring partner, a nuisance who was forever inconveniencing him, a hoyden who sometimes amused him; it was too late to turn herself into the kind of genteel young lady he would take as a wife. Nor did she want to. If he did not like her as she was, then there was no point at all in sighing after him.

Remembering the last time she had said she was going shopping, when she had returned without the book she had expressly set out to buy, she called first at Pantheon's Bazaar and selected several yards of lace to be put on Miss Roswell's account and delivered to Holles Street, then went on to Maiden Lane.

The refuge was busy as always. Mrs Stebbings and her helpers were serving what could be called either a late breakfast or an early nuncheon. Sophie took off her cloak, donned an apron and stood beside the giant stewpot, ladling out food on to plates, smiling at each recipient as she did so. They passed by so quickly that all she really saw of them was a hand and an arm and perhaps a grubby coat.

'Thank you, miss.'

She raised her head at the sound of the voice and almost fell over in surprise as she found herself looking into the laughing eyes of Richard Braybrooke. He was wearing a very dirty uniform coat with a torn sleeve. He had still not shaved and his hair was unkempt.

'Go away!' she hissed at him. 'You have no right to come here, pretending to be poor. This food is for the sick and needy and you are neither.' She reached out to take the dish from him, but he held it out of her reach.

'No, but then this is not for me. It's for poor Davy, over there.' He nodded towards a legless, one-armed man who sat on the floor in a corner. 'He can't stand in line like everyone else.'

'Oh.' She was chagrined, but quickly recovered. 'Then why dress like that?'

He smiled. 'Do you suppose they would welcome me if I came in a coat tailored by Scott and Hoby's tasselled hessians?'

'No, but why come at all?'

'You have come. And you dress the part.'

'That's different.'

'Why? You are not the only one to feel compassion for those less fortunate.'

'Compassion?' She did not try to conceal her surprise.

'Do you find that idea so very difficult to grasp, Miss…Mrs Carter?'

'Hey, will you stop your jabberin' and move on,' the man behind him grumbled.

Richard apologised gruffly and moved away. 'I should like to speak to you when you are free,' he murmured to Sophie.

She went on with her task, but part of her was watching Lord Braybrooke as he knelt beside the legless man and helped him to eat. There was nothing arrogant about him now; he was considerate and caring.

'Who would have believed it?' Mrs Stebbings said beside her. 'It just goes to show, don't it?'

'Goes to show what?'

'That a true gentleman don't need fancy clothes and there's more to compassion than handing out money.'

'You know who he is?' she asked, doling out potatoes on to the next plate.

'Yes, he is Major Richard Braybrooke. He was an aide to Wellington, you know, and a fine officer, so I have been told, though very strict on discipline. He came here a few days ago and asked who our sponsor was.'

'What did you tell him?'

'Only what you yourself said we might say, that the benefactress wished to remain anonymous and you were acting for her. He seemed exceedingly interested and promised a further donation himself, though I shouldn't tell you that. He wishes to be incognito, but there can be no harm in you knowing, I am sure, if you are known to him.'

'He is an acquaintance of my employer.'

'Then he will have guessed the name of our benefactress?'

'Very possibly,' she said, realising he would conclude that it was the heiress of Madderlea, which was all very well, but now she would have to tell Charlotte and her little secret would be out. Unless she could persuade his lordship to say nothing to her cousin.

The legless man had finished his meal and Richard was helping him on to a kind of platform on wheels which he used to propel himself about the streets, paddling it with his one hand. As soon as he had gone, Richard brought the empty plate back to Sophie, who had just served the last of the long line of men. There would be another batch of supplicants later but others would serve them. She had been absent from home long enough and she was nearly asleep on her feet.

'When you are ready, I will take you home,' he said. 'I left my curricle round the corner.'

She was too tired to argue. Taking off her apron, she allowed him to help her into her pelisse and, saying goodbye to Mrs Stebbings and the other ladies, she stepped outside and took the arm he offered. Neither noticed Sergeant Dawkins ambling up the street towards the refuge.

He stopped when he saw them. 'Well, well, well,' he muttered. 'If it ain't Major Braybrooke. And with the little filly, too. Now there's a turn up.' He forgot all about his rumbling stomach and set off after them, keeping well to the rear. The last thing he wanted was to be seen and recognised.

When they climbed into a carriage and trotted away too fast for him to follow, he cursed under his breath. But it did not matter; the chit would return and, unless he missed his guess, so would the Major.

He had forgotten all about his threat of revenge made three years before in the heat of Lisbon where his court martial had been held, but seeing and recognising Major Braybrooke had brought it all back:

the stifling heat of the prison, the humiliation of being flogged before his men, the loss of pay and the fact that he had lost the only job he had ever had. He was a good soldier and loved the life now denied to him. And, on top of that, he had been obliged to find his own way back to England. And all because of a few tawdry ornaments and a silver brooch.

His resentment rekindled, he determined to have his revenge.

Major Braybrooke, who always knew where his next meal was coming from, who could throw coins to beggars with gay abandonment, would die a slow and painful death. And he would know why he was dying too. He, George Dawkins, would make sure of it. He grinned and went back to the refuge to stand in line for a meal and try his luck for a bed for the night.

Chapter Eight

The tiger, in his yellow and black striped waistcoat, had been walking his lordship's equipage up and down the street for the best part of two hours and was relieved to see his employer appear.

Sophie watched as Richard stripped off the ragged coat and donned a frockcoat of brown superfine which he had left on the seat and, running his hand through his hair, found his tall beaver hat and set it upon his dark curls. 'Behold, the transformation,' he said. 'It would not be at all the thing for a tramp to be seen escorting a lady in the Braybrooke curricle.' He handed her up and climbed in beside her; the tiger jumped on to the back step and they set off at a brisk trot.

She was still annoyed with him for appearing at the refuge as he had and she was determined not to soften towards him. That way lay more heartache than she thought she could bear. 'In the absence of the husband you spoke of, have you appointed yourself my keeper?' she asked.

He was unsmiling as he guided the carriage through the traffic. 'Someone has to watch out for you.'

'So you followed me again.'

'No, for I was sure you were safe home in bed and making up for lost sleep.'

'It was too late to go back to bed and I had promised Mrs Stebbings I would help her this morning, not that I think it is the least necessary to explain myself to you.'

'Such stamina fills me with admiration.'

'You have not been to bed either.'

'No, but I am—was—a soldier, accustomed to remaining alert for two days without sleep.'

'If you did not follow me, how did you know about the house?'

'Oh, I came upon it quite by chance about a week ago. It seemed to me to be a very worthy cause and one I could support.'

'Do you mean that?'

'I am not in the habit of saying things I do not mean.'

'I was thinking that besides a place to eat and sleep, what the men need most is work. I had thought of setting up an employment agency, but that would mean finding out what the men could do and talking to employers and persuading them to take them on. It would need to be done by a man who knew what he was about. Do you know of such a one?'

'You thought of that yourself?'

'Why, has it been done before?'

'There are agencies…'

'Yes, for domestic workers and people like that,

not specifically for ex-soldiers and ex-sailors. I am sure it will help them, especially if you sponsor it.'

'Because you ask it of me, I will give it some thought.'

'Thank you.'

'I make no promises—there are many aspects to be considered before a decision is made. It would have to be done in a businesslike way, not by a chit of a girl who has more compassion than sense.'

'That is unfair, my lord, I am not without sense.'

'You have shown little evidence of it in the short time I have known you. It is certainly not sensible to walk about the streets of London alone. I cannot allow it to continue.'

'You cannot allow it!' She was so incensed she turned towards him, her face flushed with anger. 'And, pray, what gives you the right to dictate to me, Lord Braybrooke?'

'Someone must. Lady Fitzpatrick has obviously failed to have the correct influence upon you and though Mr Harfield has but lately come to town, I would have expected him to have more care of you. Such a ramshackle way of going on, I never did know.'

'Then I am surprised you allow yourself to be seen with me,' she said. It was easier to be angry with him than to sit in silent misery. 'I can do your reputation no good. I am not in the running for the next Duchess of Rathbone and that must surely be your first consideration. Countenance and elegance and presence, I am informed, are requisites, along with a fortune and turning a blind eye to infidelity. My goodness, I fail in every respect.'

'Where did you learn that tarradiddle?'

'*On dits*, my lord. Your list of requirements is the talk of the town and all the mamas are busy trying to make their daughters conform in order to please you.'

He cursed Martin, who must have told his mother—that inveterate gossip had tongue enough for two sets of teeth. 'Which just goes to show how silly they are,' he said. 'Do you think I cannot tell false from true?'

Her little gasp of shock amused him, but he let the remark hang in the air, waiting for her to find a response. 'Then it is true, you have made a list of your requirements and are busy ticking them off, one by one against all the possibles. I never met such a top-lofty, conceited man in all my life.'

'Then you have not met many men, for I am the soul of modesty.'

It was said in such a light-hearted way, she found herself laughing. 'And that boast itself is proof of the contrary.'

'You have a very caustic tongue for a young lady brought up in the seclusion of the country.'

'I do not see why I should sit meekly saying nothing while you scold me, my lord, especially as I do not, nor ever will, attempt to conform to your list.'

'I would be disappointed in you if you did.'

'Nor will Charlotte.'

'No, but we were not talking about your cousin, were we? Charlotte is a delightful young lady, pretty as a picture and as mild as you are sharp, but I have no intention of earning Mr Harfield's undying enmity by making an offer for her.'

'Mr Harfield?'

'I am not blind, you know. I have seen the way they look at each other and two people more in love I have yet to see. I wish them well. They will deal famously with each other.'

'If his father allows it.'

'Why should he not?' he asked, testing her. 'Miss Roswell has a fortune, does she not? And a large estate. Sir Mortimer could hardly quarrel with that.'

Oh, how she wished she did not feel so tired. She might know how to answer that without giving the game away, except it was not a game but a deception of terrifying magnitude. How was she going to endure staying in London a moment longer, knowing he was ticking off those attributes in every other eligible young lady he knew and had discounted her right from the start. But Charlotte, at least, would be glad to know she was not being considered.

'No cutting response?' he queried after a moment or two of silence. 'No set down to put me in my place? No turning of the tables? No denying the truth?'

'My lord, I am too tired to bandy words.'

'Yes, my poor Sophie, I know you are and it is unkind in me to tease you. You will soon be home and then you may rest.'

'What are you going to do?'

'Do?' he queried, as they turned into the end of Holles Street. 'Why, I think I shall go home to Bedford Row, have a bath and a shave and then I might well take to my bed for an hour or two.'

'No, I meant what are you going to do about my secret. Will you tell Lady Fitzpatrick?'

He turned to grin at her. 'Which secret?'

'My work with the veterans, of course—what other secret would there be?'

'Now, do you know, I thought there might be something else.'

'I cannot think what you mean. I was always taught that good should be done by stealth and that is why I have said nothing about the enterprise to anyone, not because I am ashamed of it. Besides, I doubt Lady Fitzpatrick would understand.'

'Then she is not the unknown benefactress?'

'No.'

'Who is?'

'Would you have me betray a confidence?' she queried evasively.

She was good at being evasive, he mused. 'No, I am sure you would never do that.'

'Then are you going to tell her ladyship?'

'No, but there is one condition.' He brought the curricle to a stop outside Lady Fitzpatrick's front door. 'You will not go to Maiden Lane alone again. It is a most unsavoury district.'

'I have seen worse,' she said, referring to her journey through war-torn Europe.

'I wonder where?' he mused.

'Every city and town in the land has it slums,' she said, though she wondered how much longer she could keep thinking of answers to his awkward questions.

'True, but that does not make it acceptable for you to wander about the streets alone. If you must indulge in philanthropy, then we will go together.'

'But, my lord, if we are seen too much in each other's company, there will be gossip…'

'There is one way to silence it,' he said slowly, turning in his seat to face her. He was feeling reckless. Sitting there, wanting to take her in his arms, wanting to confess his love for her, it was immaterial to him whether it was Miss Hundon or Miss Roswell he was proposing to; names meant nothing. It was the person she was that drew him to her; rich or poor, it was all one to him. But she was also a clever prevaricator. He did not want to believe it was anything reprehensible, but a woman who could keep a secret was a rare specimen. Until he knew the reason for it, oughtn't he to hold his horses?

'How?' she asked.

He reached out and touched her cheek. 'My lovely Sophie, I do believe you are too fagged to continue sparring with me and I am not one to take advantage of an opponent's weakness. We will leave it for another day. I believe you are to be at Almack's on Wednesday?'

'Yes, Lady Fitzpatrick obtained vouchers two days ago. Do you go?'

'I have to leave town for a day or two, I have pressing business in Hertfordshire, but I hope to return in time to be there. If I am not, rest assured I will call on you the next day.'

'Why?' she demanded bluntly.

He laughed. 'Why, for the next round, of course. I shall expect you to be in fine fettle again and leading with your chin as always.'

'It is all very well to amuse yourself roasting me,' she said. 'but if there are paragons who fit your criteria, they will surely all have been snapped up by the time you come to realise that bamming me is not the way to find yourself a wife.'

'I am not looking for a wife, much less a paragon. How dull life would be leg-shackled to such a one.' He jumped down and held out his hand to help her down. 'Come, allow me to escort you indoors.'

She put her hand in his and let him to lead her to the door, so weary that she was almost stumbling. 'My lord, I beg you, do not stay. You are as tired as I am and you cannot go into Lady Fitzpatrick's drawing room unshaven as you are.'

'Do not fret so, little one, her ladyship is too shortsighted to notice, you know that.'

'But Charlotte will notice.'

'She will be too polite to mention it.'

They reached the door as a footman opened it but he was too well trained to show any sign of shock or disapproval.

'Where is Lady Fitzpatrick?' Sophie asked him.

'I believe she has gone shopping with Miss Roswell, Miss Hundon. The Pantheon Bazaar, if I understood correctly.'

'Oh, then I must have missed her.' Relieved, she turned to Richard, who obviously could not stay under the circumstances. 'Thank you for your escort, my lord.'

'My pleasure, ma'am.' He swept her an elegant bow and ran lightly down the steps and back to his curricle, fired with determination to see his grandfather.

He did not need to go to Hertfordshire to do so, for when he arrived home he found Lady Braybrooke hurrying upstairs behind a chambermaid who was carrying a pile of bedlinen. She caught sight of him as he came in and handed the footman his hat.

'Richard, where have you been?' she demanded, returning downstairs. 'The Duke is here and asking for you.' She looked at his dishevelled appearance and the stubble on his chin in disgust. 'Really, Richard, you look like a vagrant. Have you been out all night?'

He smiled and bowed. 'As you see.'

'Then you had better go upstairs to change and be shaved before seeing His Grace. I will tell him you are home.'

'Why has he come to town? He hates London.'

'I have no doubt he will tell you. He is in the library.'

Richard hurried to make himself respectable and presented himself in the library twenty minutes later, a picture of studied elegance in a frockcoat of green superfine, biscuit-coloured pantaloons, yellow kerseymere waistcoat and a neat but not flamboyant cravat. His chin was smooth and his hair carefully arranged.

His grandfather was sitting in an armchair by the hearth, fortifying himself with a glass of brandy. The tragedy of losing both his sons had taken their toll on him and he seemed to have shrunk a little, so that his dark brown nankeen coat hung loosely on his shoulders. His own, very white hair was covered by a dark wig, but for all that he was upright and alert and his knowing brown eyes missed nothing.

Richard stood before him and bowed from the waist. 'Your Grace, I did not expect you or I would have been here to greet you.'

'Didn't expect to be here. Don't like the Smoke above half. Sit down, boy, sit down.'

Richard obediently sat in the chair opposite him. 'I am pleased to see you, sir, but why are you here?'

'Your aunt asked me to come. Seems you have been making a cake of yourself, rattling round town, playing fast and loose with every unmarried wench…'

'Your Grace, I have simply been doing as you asked and looking for a wife.'

'With an impossible list of requirements which has the whole *haute monde* buzzing with conjecture.' He smiled suddenly. 'I cannot blame you for that, but why make it so public?'

'It was only a jest between Martin Gosport and me, not meant to be taken seriously, but he must have told his mother…'

'That gadabout. Tell her and you tell the world.'

'Yes, I should have known. But it has certainly had some revealing consequences…'

His Grace held out his glass. 'Fill that again, will you? And have one yourself. I must speak bluntly and you may have need of it.'

Richard, who had never known his grandfather to be anything else but blunt, went to obey.

With the newly replenished glass in his hand, His Grace leaned back in his chair and surveyed his grandson for fully a minute before speaking. 'Well, what have you got to say for yourself?'

'In what respect, Your Grace?'

'In respect of finding a wife. Though why you should feel the need when I have already made known my thoughts on the subject, I do not know.'

'You mean Emily?'

'Yes, whom did you think I meant?'

'But, sir, Emily is my cousin; we grew up together as children. She is little more than a child now. She needs more time and you have told me to make haste…'

'Marriage will soon mature her.'

'Grandfather, you are being unfair to her. Given a year or two more and a free hand, I am sure she would not choose me.'

'And what would happen to the noble families of England if their daughters were allowed to pick and choose? Why, they would be so diluted they would die out, the estates would be broken up and, before you know where you are the proletariat would be running the country. Your Aunt Philippa understands that, if you do not.'

'You did give me an alternative.'

'So I did. And what have you done about it, except earn yourself the reputation of being a rakeshame?'

'I have met someone…'

'Ah, if my information is correct, you mean the

Roswell filly, niece of the late Earl of Peterborough. Coming out with her cousin Miss Hundon, under the wing of that antidote widow of an Irishman, are they not? She's as queer as Dick's hatband. If Miss Roswell is as high in the instep as rumour says, why could her guardian not find someone more *au fait* with Society to bring her out?'

'Lady Fitzpatrick is short-sighted and a little deaf, but good-hearted enough.'

'So good-hearted the chits are allowed to do as they please. You have not made an offer, I hope.'

'No. There are complications...'

'Indeed, there are. There is Philippa, for one. Not that I can't deal with her, if I have to. But Emily is also my grandchild and I am fond of her.'

'As I am, Your Grace. That does not mean we should suit.'

'You know your aunt is bringing forward Emily's come-out and giving a ball for her next week? I am persuaded she means to steal a march on Miss Roswell and bring you to the mark before that young lady's own come-out.'

Richard sighed. 'I was afraid of that.'

'I have told her she must invite Miss Roswell. I want to look her over.'

'And Miss Hundon, I hope.'

The Duke, in the act of setting down his empty glass, looked up at him sharply. 'Miss Hundon? The country cousin? I thought it was Peterborough's niece you were dangling after?'

'She will not come without her cousin. They are

inseparable.' He smiled. 'Sometimes it is difficult to tell one from the other.'

'Then invite them both. Invite the whole *ton*. Let me see them all at once. The sooner I meet them all, the sooner I may return to the country.'

'You may see them before the ball, if you wish. They will be at Almack's on Wednesday and I have said I will meet them there.'

'You want me to dress up in evening clothes and sit around drinking lemon cordial all evening?'

'You need not stay the whole evening.'

'No, I should not do so in any case.' He sighed heavily. 'Oh, well, we might as well get it over with. But if I have come on a wild goose chase and you change your mind, I shall not be pleased.'

He would never change his mind about Sophie, he told himself as his grandfather released him; the thought of marrying anyone else was abhorrent, but he knew instinctively that she would never agree to marry him if he had to defy his grandfather to do it. But how to bring about the metamorphosis from country cousin to Madderlea heiress without upsetting the whole applecart, he did not know. He could not humiliate her by revealing her secret, but on the other hand, if she could not bring herself to confide in him, then could he trust her at all?

'Well?' His aunt accosted him in the hall. 'What did he say?'

'Nothing of import. Where is Emily?'

She gave a smile of unconcealed relief. 'Why, I do believe she is in the garden. Go and find her, Richard. She will be so pleased to see you.'

He bowed and hurried away to find his cousin. She was sitting on a swing in a little arbour at the end of the garden, dreamily pushing herself with her toe. She looked like a gangly child, all arms and long legs. Her dark hair had been fastened back with a ribbon, but it had come undone and her tresses were spread across her shoulders.

'Emily.'

She looked up and he noticed she had been crying. 'Oh, it's you.'

He went over to her and put his hand under her chin to lift her face to his. 'What is wrong?'

'Nothing.'

'I do not believe you are the sort to weep for nothing.'

'I am not weeping.'

'That is a whisker. Has your mama been scolding you?'

'Not exactly.'

'No, for you never do anything to invite a scolding, do you? Do you not sometimes feel like rebelling?'

'Oh, no.'

'So, if you were told to marry someone you hold in aversion, you would do it, simply because your mama says you must.'

She looked up at him with startled green eyes. 'I do not hold you in aversion.'

'But you do not love me.'

'Of course I do.'

'Yes, but as your big cousin who carried you on his shoulders when you were very small, who taught you to ride and fish and fall into scrapes, not as a husband.'

'Mama says…'

'I do not want to know what your mother says. I want to know what you think. If I was to offer for you, would you throw yourself into my arms in delight or run away and hide and wish you could die rather than share my bed?'

'Richard!' she exclaimed, shocked by his bluntness, as he knew she would be.

'Marriage is for life, my dear,' he said. 'You may please your mother, you may even please Grandfather, but you would certainly not be storing up happiness for yourself in marrying me.'

'I wish you would not roast me so. I have had enough of that already.'

'I am under pressure too, you know.'

She raised pleading eyes to his. 'Yes, but you will not give way to it, will you?'

'You do not wish me to? You would refuse me if I did?'

'Oh, Richard, please do not ask me, then Mama cannot blame me if it does not come to pass.'

'Then I won't. We will remain friends and cousins.'

She jumped off the swing and threw her arms about his neck. 'Oh, thank you, Richard, thank you. But, you know, Mama will fly into the boughs over it.'

'Then we shall not tell her of this conversation,' he said, gently disengaging her. 'Wait until after your come-out ball because I am sure there will be other young men there more to your liking. Aunt Philippa will come about.'

'Oh, I do hope so. You see, there is someone…' He smiled indulgently at her. 'Is there, now? And am I to be taken into your confidence?'

'You will not laugh?'

'Now, why should I do that?'

'Because he is older than me and has told everyone he is not in the petticoat line, which is a good thing because I must grow up first. But I have known him for years and years…'

'My dear Emily, you intrigue me. I cannot, for the life of me, think who it might be.'

'Can you not? You have known him for years and years too. You introduced us the day before you both left for the war…'

'Martin! Do you mean you have set your cap at Martin Gosport? The sly old dog!'

'I knew you would laugh.'

'I am not laughing, my little one. I wish you happy. He will inherit his father's title one day and, though he is not so wealthy as I shall be, his income is certainly not to be disdained. Your mama can have no objection to him.'

'You must not say anything to her. It is a secret.'

He took her hand and linked his arm with hers. 'Then a secret it shall remain until you give me leave to felicitate you. Now, let us go back inside and no more tears, eh?'

Lady Braybrooke, watching them approach the house arm in arm, smiling at each other, felt thoroughly pleased with herself and returned to her es-

critoire to add the names of Lady Fitzpatrick, Miss
Roswell and Miss Hundon to her guest list, as her
father-in-law had instructed. It did not matter now and
the downfall of those two young ladies would give
her immense satisfaction.

Sophie was woken by Anne coming into the room.
She had been dreaming of Madderlea, but instead of
the usual peace and calm it was the centre of a pitched
battle. Guns had been going off and there had been
smoke and men falling and screams and she was trying to find someone, moving about in the mêlée,
searching faces. The nightmare had been brought on
by her conversation with Lord Braybrooke and the
talk of fighting and soldiers and memories of her
flight from Europe. She shook off the dream and
looked at the clock. It was gone six.

'Her ladyship put off dinner to give you longer to
sleep, Miss Sophie, but Cook won't keep it back
above another quarter of an hour, so I came to wake
you and help you dress.'

Sophie scrambled off the bed. 'Goodness, have I
slept all afternoon? Whatever will they think of me?'

'Nothing, why should they?' She was busy pouring
hot water into the washbasin. 'Her ladyship and Miss
Charlotte slept most of the afternoon themselves. It's
what happens when you stay up most of the night.
Now, you have a wash while I lay out your clothes.
What shall you wear?'

'The brown striped jaconet, I think. We are not
going out and there is to be no company tonight.'

Fifteen minutes later she was dressed and went downstairs.

She had reached the hall and walked across to the dining room door when she heard Lady Fitzpatrick's voice. She paused with her hand on the doorknob.

'I hope your cousin is not ailing,' her ladyship was saying. 'Why, when I was your age I could stay up all night and think nothing of it.'

'I believe she did not sleep well, my lady. Anne said she was wandering round the house in the early hours. She took her some hot chocolate.'

'So she went out shopping as a cure for insomnia. My dear, I know you are very fond of your cousin, but she is not doing you any favours, behaving as she does. She seems to flout every convention. I fear I shall have to write to her papa about it.'

'Oh, no, my lady, I beg of you not to do that. He will be so displeased.'

'Displeased with me, I shouldn't wonder. Not that I haven't done my best...'

'And so you have, my dear Lady Fitzpatrick. You have been the very best sponsor we could have had— I should hate having him make us return home with the Season only halfway through. It would be such a waste of time and money and nothing to show for it.'

'You are right, I cannot let you go back unspoken for. I fully expect Lord Braybrooke to declare himself at your ball. We will contrive to keep your cousin on a tighter rein until then. Do you think Mr Harfield will offer for her? I should like to think I had discharged my duty to you both.'

Sophie went into the room before Charlotte could

reply and smiled at them both. 'Why did you not wake me?'

'You looked so peaceful,' Charlotte said, as Lady Fitzpatrick rang the bell for the first course to be served. 'Anne told us you had not been able to sleep. It was probably all to do with that accident and meeting Monsieur Latour again and Mr Harfield turning up so unexpectedly. And we have no engagements this evening, so we decided to let you sleep. Do you feel refreshed now?'

'Yes, thank you.'

'Did you find what you wanted at Pantheon's? We went there ourselves, you know, expecting to find you, but there was no sign of you.'

'I expect we passed each other on the way. I bought some lace and a few yards of muslin. It is being delivered tomorrow.'

'Sophie, I have told you before about going out alone,' Lady Fitzpatrick said. 'It is not the thing, you know. Please don't do it again.'

'I came to no harm, my lady.'

'But you might have. And supposing someone saw you…'

Sophie smiled. 'Someone did. Lord Braybrooke met me in the street and brought me home in his curricle.'

'Lord Braybrooke!' exclaimed Lady Fitzpatrick. 'And Charlotte not here to receive him. Oh, how mortifying! Did he leave a message?'

'No, except to say that he had business in Hertfordshire which would keep him out of town for a day or two. He said he hoped to be back in time to join us at Almack's on Wednesday. And if he did not return in time, he would call on us the next day.'

'There you are!' her ladyship exclaimed in triumph. 'He has gone to visit his grandfather to tell him of his intention to offer for Charlotte and ask his blessing. I knew he was coming to the point, I told you so. Ten to one he will go on to Leicestershire and speak to Mr Hundon too.'

'Oh, no!' Both girls spoke together.

'Why not? You must surely know he must ask your trustee, Charlotte, though I am surprised he has not spoken to me of it first, for I am your sponsor while you are in town.'

'Perhaps you mistake the matter,' Charlotte said, 'for I am convinced he means to offer for his cousin.'

'That chit! She is no more than a schoolroom miss. No, no, my dear, that is only a wish of her mama, not realistic at all.'

'But, my lady, I do not want to marry him.'

'Fustian! Of course you do. Any girl would.'

'Ma'am, I do not love him and I am sure he does not love me.'

'Oh, that is of no consequence. Love will come later, if you are lucky. You must remember you are not like other young ladies who have nothing more than their dowries to recommend them. You have a fortune and a large estate as your portion. You must leave falling in love and such frivolity to your cousin who has no such assets.'

'I begin to think I am unmarriageable,' Sophie said, as a servant brought in a tureen of mulligatawny soup.

'So you will be if you insist on cavorting about

town on your own,' Lady Fitzpatrick retorted. 'Such behaviour is eccentric and gentlemen of any standing do not like eccentricity in the least. I beg you to conform or you will spoil your cousin's chances, for they will say it runs in the family.'

'The last thing I want is to be the cause of Charlotte's unhappiness, my lady.' She dare not look at Charlotte for fear of bursting into laughter.

'Then oblige me by observing the proprieties in future. You may go out with me or with Charlotte, escorted by gentlemen of whom I approve and always chaperoned.'

'Yes, my lady,' she said meekly, wondering how she was going to be able to go to Maiden Lane again. Mrs Stebbings could manage the work with her helpers, but when the next month's rent was due, she would have to be there or arrange for someone else to pay it on her behalf.

Lord Braybrooke sprang immediately to mind. He had said he wanted to help, had offered her his escort and, though he sent her emotions into a wild spin whenever she was near him, she must put her feelings aside and ask him. She would try to behave in a businesslike manner and refuse to let him bait her. But what of the gossip? He had said there was a way to deal with it, though he had not answered when she asked him how.

Oh, if only he had meant that he wanted to marry her. Once the engagement had been announced, the tattlers would lose interest and he could come and go as he pleased. But that was an idle dream. Men of consequence did not like eccentrics and, if Lady Fitz-

patrick was right, she was on the way to becoming
one. And he had called her a hoyden, a tease, a demi-
rep, someone to amuse him, not to be taken seriously.
And when the truth about the switch in identities became known, he would know he had been right in his
conjecture. Her spirits were as low as they could possibly be.

Satisfied that she had made her point, Lady Fitzpatrick picked up her spoon and began on the soup.
The rest of the meal was eaten with little conversation
and afterwards they retired to the drawing room.
Charlotte picked up her crewel work, Sophie idly
turned the pages of the latest *Lady's Magazine* without taking in a word and Lady Fitzpatrick sat reading
Miss Austen's latest novel with the aid of a large
magnifying glass. Before long the hand holding the
glass dropped and then the book fell to the floor. Her
head fell on her chest and light snores told that she
was fast asleep.

'What are we going to do?' Charlotte whispered.

'Leave her, she looks comfortable enough.'

'No, I meant about Lord Braybrooke. You don't
think he means to go to Leicestershire, do you? Papa
will think he is offering for you when he speaks of
Miss Roswell and he would mean me. Oh, Sophie,
what a coil we have got ourselves into.'

'He isn't going to Upper Corbury, Charlotte. He
told me he knew you and Freddie were in love and
he has no intention of coming between you.'

'Oh, thank goodness. But what about you?'

'We should not suit. Charlotte, we may both forget
all about Viscount Braybrooke.'

'Why, what else has he said? Oh, Sophie, I am quite sure if he knew the truth, he would offer for you.'

'If he did that, then I should hold him in contempt, changing his mind just because he has discovered I have a fortune, when he would not dream of having me without it. You remember Lady Gosport telling us about his list of requirements for a wife? I taxed him with it and he did not deny it and when I said I failed in every respect, he did not repudiate that either.'

'Poor Sophie! But you made a list too, I recollect.'

'Yes, but that was meant as a jest...'

'No, it was not, you were in deadly earnest. And as far as I can see, his lordship qualifies perfectly. And you are not so far off a good match for his.'

'He does not know I have the fortune he requires, nor would I tell him, simply to make him offer for me. Neither would I agree to shut my eyes to infidelity.'

'I do not believe he is the kind of man to play fast and loose with a lady's affections. Once married, I dare say he will become a paragon of virtue.'

'Charlotte, I am beginning to think you are not so averse to him as you pretend.'

'I never said I was averse to him. He has many qualities I admire, but that does not mean I would marry him.' She reached out put her hand on Sophie's arm. 'Do not give up hope, my love, Lord Braybrooke is being very short-sighted, but he must surely see your worth soon and then all will be well.'

'How can it be, when we have deceived everyone

about who we are? It seemed such a good notion at the time, especially when fate seemed to be on our side with Lady Fitz making the mistake of thinking you were me, but now I realise that it was not only foolish, but really dangerous. I tried to play God and must be punished.'

'Fustian!'

'You are forgetting something, Charlotte. You are forgetting that whether he offered for you or for me, he would have to speak to your papa first and as he thinks Uncle William is my father and not yours...'

'Then the sooner we confess the better.'

'Yes, but to whom? Do we make an announcement? Do we put a notice in the *Gazette* or the *Morning Post*?'

Charlotte suddenly giggled. 'Tell Lady Gosport, that should do it. Much cheaper and quicker too.'

'I am glad you can laugh about it.'

Charlotte became serious. 'Oh, Sophie, I am so sorry. What shall you do?'

'There is nothing I can do. We shall return to Upper Corbury and the engagement of Miss Hundon to Mr Frederick Harfield will be gazetted and no one will be the wiser. As for Miss Roswell, she will live quietly in retirement, an ape leader and eccentric. If Uncle William does not want to remain my trustee, he will have to appoint someone else. Or sell Madderlea. I shall be able to live in comfort on the proceeds and leave what is left to your children, for they will be as close to me as my own.'

'Sell Madderlea! Oh, Sophie, you cannot.' Charlotte's voice rose in protest and Sophie looked at Lady Fitzpatrick in alarm. She slumbered on.

'It is that, or accept the first man who offers for me,' she whispered.

'I will not let you do it. Something must be done. There are other men, considerate, kindly men who would make good husbands. Lord Braybrooke is not the only fish in the sea.'

'He is for me.' And that was the last word she would say on the subject.

A few minutes later Lady Fitzpatrick woke up with a start and straightened her cap. 'Goodness, how late it is! I think I shall retire and I advise you to do the same. We are out tomorrow evening and at Almack's on Wednesday and it would never do for you to be seen with dark circles under your eyes. Come along, both of you.'

They rose and followed her upstairs.

Chapter Nine

Almack's was a disappointment. Everything was so stiff and formal and there was nothing to drink but tea and lemonade. And, what was worse as far as Sophie was concerned, Richard, in black coat, white knee breeches and dazzling white shirt, arrived with Emily clinging to his arm and Lady Braybrooke looking like a cat in a cream bowl.

They were accompanied by an elderly gentleman who, in spite of his outmoded satin breeches, high-collared brocade coat and the black wig covering his white hair, had a very formidable presence and the patronesses buzzed round him like bees round a honey pot.

Both girls' dance cards were soon full, but Sophie perversely kept a dance free in case Richard should ask her to stand up with him. She had been dancing with Sir Peter Somersham and he was escorting her back to her seat when she overheard one of the matrons saying, 'Yes, I have it from Augusta Green-holme who had it from Philippa Braybrooke herself.

He has already offered for his cousin and the announcement is to be made at her come-out ball. It is why His Grace has come to London.'

So that was the reason for his visit to Hertfordshire. He had been summoned by the Duke to account for his tardiness and told to make his cousin an offer and, by the look of her, Viscount Braybrooke had obeyed. Was he so faint-hearted? She did not believe that for a minute. No one would make him do anything he did not want to do and she was forced to conclude that it had been his wish all along.

'His Grace is still a fine figure of a man, don't you think?' Lady Fitzpatrick said, as Sophie and Charlotte joined her between dances. 'But I never thought to see him here. We must contrive to be presented.'

'Oh, no, my lady, that would be too presumptuous,' Charlotte said, while Sophie remained silent. She had supposed that sooner or later Viscount Braybrooke would make an announcement, but however much she had prepared herself for it, she could not stop herself feeling thoroughly downcast.

'I do not see why that should be. No doubt he has come to bring Lord Braybrooke up to the mark and look over the possibles. I would be failing in my duty if I did not see that you were introduced. There! The viscount is looking this way. He is coming over.' She gave a little squeal. 'And His Grace is coming with him.'

Sophie's heart began to pound when she realised her ladyship was right and Richard and his grandfather were walking purposefully towards them. All three ladies stood up.

'Your Grace.' Her ladyship attempted a wobbly curtsy, as he stopped before her. 'May I present Miss Roswell.'

Charlotte executed a deep curtsey. 'Your Grace.'

'I am pleased to make your acquaintance again, Miss Roswell,' he said. 'I believe we have met. It was before the war. I was on a diplomatic mission to Belgium and your father and mother were so kind as to offer me hospitality. You were very small and naturally will not remember me. I was sorry to hear Captain Roswell perished in the fighting in Spain. A gallant soldier. You will be proud of him.'

Charlotte, her face crimson with embarrassment, could find nothing to say but 'Yes, Your Grace.'

'We will talk again later. Richard bring her to me at supper.'

Sophie, consumed by guilt and the dreadful fear that she was about to be found out in the worst possible way, wished she could cut and run, but there was no hope of that as Richard turned to present her to his grandfather. 'And this is Miss Hundon, sir.'

'How do you do, Miss Hundon.' The Duke lifted his quizzing glass and subjected her to a close inspection, while the musicians struck up for the next dance. She could not recall having met him and, if she had been a baby at the time, he would not remember what she looked like, would he? 'Miss Roswell's cousin, I collect.'

Refusing to be overawed, she met his gaze unflinchingly. 'Yes, Your Grace.'

'Close, are you?'

'Indeed, yes, Your Grace. I am very fond of Charlotte and I think she is of me. For the last two years we have done everything together.'

'Nothing much to choose between you, I dare say.'

'No.' She smiled, mischievously. 'Except a fortune, Your Grace, which makes deciding on a husband very difficult for her.'

'No doubt you are urging her to caution, but her trustees will no doubt make sure she don't make a ninny of herself. Her fortune or otherwise shouldn't trouble you.'

'Oh, it does not.' She was taken aback by her own temerity at hinting that the problems facing an heiress who must marry were as daunting as those of a nobleman. If Richard was going to marry Emily, it hardly mattered and she might as well go down fighting.

'Pert article, ain't you?' He smiled suddenly, making her realise how much alike he and Richard were. They had the same masculine good looks, the sharp nose and humorous eyes. 'Oh, you do not need to answer that. I shall sit here and talk to Lady Fitzpatrick.' He sat down on the seat Sophie had vacated and waved her away. 'Go and follow your cousin's example and dance.'

The ladies of Almack's had, at last, given up their opposition to the waltz and Freddie was whirling Charlotte round, his hand about her waist. Sophie, who had no partner for the dance, turned to find Richard at her elbow.

'Miss Hundon, please do me the honour of waltzing with me.'

She was about to point out that the dance was almost finished, but decided that she would be the loser if she refused. Even in they only managed one turn about the floor, it would be something to savour in the long, lonely years ahead of her. She curtsied and he slid his arm about her and turned her into the dance.

She felt light-headed, almost in a trance as they moved together in tune with the music. In tune with each other as well. Unwilling to believe that it was the end of everything for her, she tried pretending that it was only the beginning and that they had just been introduced: Miss Sophie Roswell and Viscount Richard Braybrooke, eminently suitable and about to fall in love.

'You are quiet,' he said.

'Was I? I am sorry.'

'Did your papa teach you to waltz as well as to ride astride?'

'No, the waltz was not considered quite proper when…' She stopped suddenly, realising she had almost given herself away by referring to her time in Belgium. 'Freddie—Mr Harfield—taught us both, Charlotte and me, when we knew we would be coming to London for the Season.'

'Oh, then he is a good teacher. Or you were a gifted pupil. I must congratulate you.'

'Thank you.' She paused, unable to bear not knowing for sure. 'May I offer my felicitations on your engagement?'

'Engagement? Where did you hear that?'

'It is the talk of the *ton*.'

He smiled. 'And who, according to the tabbies, am I engaged to?'

'Your cousin, of course.'

'Then the gossips are ahead of themselves as usual.'

'It is not true?'

'Does it matter?'

'No, of course not.'

'Liar!' he said softly.

She felt the colour flood her face. 'My lord, I am not accustomed to having my veracity doubted.'

'Then you must learn to be honest. I collect I have said that before.'

The pleasure of dancing with him was spoiled and she fell silent. He watched the fleeting expressions cross her face; guilt, perhaps, sadness, yes, and he longed to banish both. 'Miss Hundon. Sophie, I must speak to you.'

Her heart was beating almost in her throat and her voice came out as a croak. 'You are speaking to me.'

'Not here. When are you going to Maiden Lane again?'

Maiden Lane. Oh, then all he wanted to talk about was the refuge. Perhaps he had found someone to help with the employment agency. Her heart resumed its steady beat and she allowed herself to breathe again. 'I have promised Lady Fitz I will not go out unless I am escorted.'

'Then I will undertake to escort you.'

'I doubt her ladyship will agree. If she realises you are not affianced to your cousin, she will expect you to escort Charlotte, not me. She will not give up hope that you will decide your future happiness lies with my cousin.'

'And do you also subscribe to that view?'

If he was hoping she would let her guard drop, he was to be disappointed. Her expressive grey-green eyes met his in what could only be construed as indignation. 'My opinion is of no consequence, my lord. You said you knew she was in love with Mr Harfield and you would not come between them.'

'Did I?' he said blandly. 'Then just to be sure on that point, I shall ask Mr Harfield to come too. A sightseeing tour perhaps, taking in Westminster and the Tower and St Paul's.'

'Oh, no, that would mean telling them about Maiden Lane…'

He smiled down at her as the music came to an end and they stood facing each other. 'Oh, I think we can contrive to become separated, don't you?' He bowed low as she curtsied to him, then he offered his arm to escort her back to her seat.

She never felt so confused in all her life. He was so insufferably cheerful, as if life had suddenly dealt him a winning hand. And why, oh, why had he changed his mind about Charlotte? Was it his grandfather's doing? When he said they would contrive to become separated, did he mean he expected her to draw Freddie away, so that he could talk to her cousin alone? Did he intend to put pressure on Freddie to withdraw his suit? She would have to warn Charlotte.

Lady Fitzpatrick did not rise before noon and the girls breakfasted together. Usually they had much to talk about—their social engagements, the latest fashions, what so-and-so had said to such-and-such, who might offer for whom, the latest *on dit* about the Regent, news from Upper Corbury contained in Mrs Hundon's letters—but the morning after the visit to Almack's, Sophie was silent.

'Are you not well?' Charlotte enquired after she had twice spoken and received no response.

'What? Oh, I'm sorry, Charlotte. I have something on my mind.'

'I should just think you have! It is that dreadful hum we have been practising. Has someone found out about it?'

'No. At least, I do not think so, but Lord Braybrooke told me last evening that the rumour that he has already offered for his cousin is not true and he has not given up hope of marrying you.'

'He was gammoning you. He has been no more attentive to me than to any of the other young ladies in Society.'

'He was not teasing. He has involved me in contriving a way of speaking to you alone.'

'I shall reject him.' She laughed suddenly. 'I think that might be a new experience for him, so high in the instep as he is.'

'Oh, Charlotte, I think you do him an injustice. Whatever he is, he is not arrogant.'

'You said he was.'

'I have changed my mind.'

'Does he have no idea that you love him?'

'Certainly not! Do you suppose I wear my heart on my sleeve?'

'Perhaps you should.'

'Oh, Charlotte, please listen, for I have something else to tell you and we haven't much time. The viscount will be here at any moment.'

'Here? This morning? I shall refuse to see him. He must speak to Lady Fitzpatrick first and she is still abed. Sophie, we must tell the footman to say we are not at home.'

'No. His lordship is bringing Freddie with him and we are all to go on a sightseeing tour in the Braybrooke barouche.'

'Why is he bringing Freddie? They have not known each other above five minutes.'

'Freddie is supposed to be dangling after Miss Hundon and, as far as his lordship is concerned, that is me. So, it is not so strange. Some time during the morning, I am supposed to draw Freddie away so that his lordship may speak to you alone. At least that is what I think he meant. He was not at all clear.'

'We do not have to go.'

'But we must. I have an errand of my own and you know I promised Lady Fitz I would not go out unaccompanied.'

'What errand? Sophie, you are being very mysterious.'

Sophie took a deep breath and explained to her cousin about the soldiers and the house in Maiden Lane and how Viscount Braybrooke had found out about it and had offered to help. Charlotte listened with eyes growing wider and wider in astonishment.

'So that was where you were the morning after we went to Vauxhall Gardens? I knew Pewter had been out because I went to the mews to ask Luke if he had seen you. And later Anne told us you had gone to the Pantheon Bazaar. No wonder we could not find you there.'

'I did go there, you know I did, because the stuff I ordered was delivered the next day. But then Luke cut himself helping make the house ready and could not drive the carriage home. I was driving when Monsieur Latour's horse bolted with his little boy in the curricle and Lord Braybrooke suddenly turned up. I think he had been following me, though he denied it. He seems to have appointed himself my guardian.'

'There you are, then! It is you he favours or he would not take such good care of you.'

'Oh, Charlotte, he is only doing it to refine upon my faults, which he points out at every opportunity. I should not ride alone, nor walk unescorted, nor speak to beggars. He cannot allow it, he said, as if I would take a jot of notice of what he says.'

'But he is right, you know that very well.'

'That does not mean I enjoy having him ring a peal over me.'

'But if he had not been close by when that horse bolted… Oh, Sophie, you might have been killed. We are indebted to his lordship.'

'Yes, I know, but now he insists on escorting me when I go to Maiden Lane and I must go this morning to see how everything is and pay the rent. And if we are seen, the tattlemongers will have a field day, so you must come too. Oh, Charlotte, it is all such a mull…'

'But where has the money come from to pay for it all?'

'Donations from well-wishers. And my allowance. I wrote to Uncle William and told him I needed extra because our ball was going to be far more expensive than we had at first supposed. He sent me a draft for more, but most of it has been spent.'

'Then I am glad you insisted I had the same allowance as you because I have hardly touched mine. That is no problem. And neither is Lord Braybrooke. I can deal with any overtures from him.' Charlotte, who usually followed where Sophie led, had suddenly taken over the role of leader. Sophie smiled wanly, recognising that it stemmed from a new confidence brought on by the arrival of Freddie and his commitment to her, and a wish to have her cousin as happy as she was herself. 'Now, we had better go and change so that we are ready when the gentlemen come.'

Reluctantly Sophie agreed and followed her cousin upstairs. She dressed in the grey cambric round gown as she always did for a visit to Maiden Lane. The day was too warm for a cloak and instead she tied a fringed shawl about her shoulders. She was just leaving her room when she heard the front door knocker. Charlotte came out of her room at almost the same time. They smiled at each other in mutual reassurance and descended the stairs together.

The two men were waiting for them in the vestibule. Richard was dressed in a frockcoat of brown Bath cloth and buckskin breeches, his neckcloth was plain white muslin, not top of the trees in elegance.

Sophie understood the reason for this and so did Charlotte, but Freddie, not wishing to be outdone by a man whose sartorial reputation was of the highest order, had taken great pains with his appearance and now found himself considerably overdressed in a blue superfine tailcoat, white pantaloons and an elaborately tied cravat about a shirt collar whose points scratched his cheeks whenever he moved his head.

Charlotte, seeing this, hurried upstairs to change her cape for a pink sarcenet pelisse and to replace her plain bonnet for one with pink ruching below the brim and tied with a large satin bow. 'Now we are ready,' she said, rejoining the others who had waited in the hall.

Sophie might have been interested in the sights—Westminster Hall, Horse Guards, the Tower and its ravens, St Paul's, which was more impressive outside than in—if she had not been so aware of the viscount and her own rapidly beating heart. He was at his charming best to both young ladies, and very knowledgeable.

Freddie found a great many questions to ask him about the history and the architecture of the many buildings they looked at which he answered easily. At no time did his lordship suggest Charlotte might like to view something Sophie and Freddie did not.

When they came out of St Paul's, they crossed Covent Garden and though there were few stallholders so late in the day, the area was swarming with urchins, who scrambled in the piles of discarded fruit and vegetables for something edible.

'Poor things,' Charlotte said, throwing them a few

coins from her reticule which they pounced on with cries of delight. 'Is that how they live?'

'Yes. Scavenging in the mud of the river for flotsam and jetsam and begging.' Richard smiled. 'But now you have given them money, they will not leave you alone.'

He was proved right when the few were joined by many more, dancing round them, holding out grubby hands, calling, 'Me! Me too!' Charlotte, who had no more money in her purse, showed every appearance of being frightened to death and even Sophie, who was used to dealing with the soldiers, felt a frisson of alarm.

Richard showed them a guinea and then threw it as far as he could in the direction of a pile of garbage. The urchins raced after it. 'Come,' he said, taking Sophie's arm as rubbish flew in all directions and the children began to squabble. 'Let us make our escape while they are occupied.'

'I have to go to Maiden Lane,' she told him in an undertone as they made for the barouche which had been left in a side street. Freddie and Charlotte were close behind.

'Then I suggest you find some way of parting us from our chaperons.'

She looked at him quizzically, wondering if she had misheard him or whether he was being jocular but his expression told her nothing.

'Charlotte knows about the house in Maiden Lane.'

'Then you do not need to make excuses. Your cousin and Mr Harfield may take the barouche. We can make our own way home.' He smiled down at her. 'We have done it before, have we not?'

She was puzzled. 'But I thought you wanted to speak to Miss Roswell…'

'So I do. Later. Mrs Stebbings first.'

'Then we will all go.'

Richard was convinced that Sophie was deliberately avoiding being alone with him, probably because she guessed he was going to tax her with her deception and demand a reason for it. He sincerely hoped that the young ladies would not let the world know about the switch in their identities before he succeeded in speaking to Sophie. If it became the subject of gossip, then he would never persuade her he had not changed his allegiance as soon as he heard she was the one with the legacy and not Charlotte. If only he had spoken sooner! Now, there was nothing he could do but postpone his confrontation with her and agree.

The visit was not a success. The deputation was too big for Mrs Stebbings to handle calmly and the ex-servicemen looked on with undisguised suspicion. Freddie, in his finery, stuck out like a sore thumb, and Charlotte was so obviously repelled by the ragged men, some of whom had dreadful disfigurements, that she could do nothing but stand just inside the door with a wooden smile on her face, which deceived no one. Freddie, seeing this, took her out to wait in the barouche.

Sophie tried to behave as she usually did, helping serve food and listen to the men's woes, but she felt constrained and her previous natural compassion

seemed forced. She was sure Charlotte was deliberately making it difficult for Richard to speak to her,
and Freddie was not going to help, for which he could
not be blamed.

She gave Mrs Stebbings the rent and Richard escorted her to join the other two, his hand lightly under
her elbow, making her want to howl with misery,
knowing it was no more than a gesture of chivalry,
when she wanted so much more.

Sergeant Dawkins, who had been sitting unseen in
a corner of the dining room, apparently tucking into
meat pudding and potatoes, watched them go. An idea
was forming in his mind. An idea based on the Major's obvious fancy for Mrs Carter; it was evident in
the way his eyes followed her round the room and
the way his features softened when he spoke to her.
'Fine feathers make fine birds,' he murmured to himself. 'And this one's ready for the plucking.'

Charlotte, taking off her bonnet in Sophie's room
where they had gone as soon as the gentlemen had
paid their respects to Lady Fitzpatrick and left, was
thoroughly satisfied with their morning.

'There! You were worrying for nothing, Sophie, the
viscount made no attempt to speak to me privately,
nor even to part me from Freddie. He must know it
would be a waste of time. Though how you can go
near those filthy men, I do not know.' She shuddered.
'I feel dirty myself now and shall have to have a bath
brought up and change every stitch. I cannot understand Lord Braybrooke encouraging you.'

'He feels as I do about the need to help the men.'

'Which only goes to prove how well suited you are. He is blind if he cannot see it.'

'He is guided by that ridiculous list of requirements and the only one I conform to is that I have a fortune, which he knows nothing about. It is a vicious circle, Charlie, without an end.'

'Then the circle must be broken. The first thing is to tell Lady Fitz and throw ourselves on her mercy. She might see a way out.'

'You are no doubt right, but I must be the one to do it. I won't have her giving you a jobation over it.'

But that was easier said than accomplished, as they soon discovered when they returned to the drawing room. The invitation to Lady Braybrooke's ball had come while they had been changing and her ladyship was in high dudgeon.

'She thinks she has stolen a march on us,' she said, tapping it furiously against her chin. 'Putting Emily's come-out before yours and the chit barely out of the schoolroom. Well, she will come home by weeping cross, for it is such short notice that no one will go.'

'Oh, I don't know,' Sophie said. 'I fancy a summons to attend the Duke of Rathbone's mansion will be a huge inducement to cancel all other engagements. It is sure to be the event of the Season.'

'But your ball was meant to be that,' her ladyship wailed. 'We had it all arranged, the musicians, the food, the flowers and everything.'

'I cannot see that anything has changed,' Charlotte said. 'Does it matter which comes first?'

'Of course it does. Philippa Braybrooke will have her nephew shackled to her daughter before they ever get to our ball. They will come together. Or not come at all.'

'But the invitations went out before Lady Braybrooke came to town, did they not? And Lord Braybrooke accepted.'

'Yes, but I was obliged to include Philippa and Emily as soon as I knew they were here.'

'Well, I do not think it is anything to get into a quake over,' Sophie said. 'I do not think Lord Braybrooke will allow himself to be bullied into offering for his cousin if he does not want her.'

'You are a goose if you think that,' her ladyship said. 'He is no different from any other man. He will give in if he is nagged enough.'

'Then I should hope that Charlotte would be glad of her escape,' Sophie said. 'I know I should not want to be married to a man who is so weak that he can be persuaded into something he knows is wrong.'

'And you, young lady, have not the first idea what you are talking about. Pray, keep your thoughts to yourself. Now, Charlotte, we must devise a way…'

'No, my lady,' Charlotte said, very loudly and very firmly.

'No? How can you say no?'

'Easily. My lady, I beg of you to forget all about Viscount Braybrooke. We should not suit.'

'But he is the catch of the Season.'

'I do not think so.'

'How can you say that? He will be a duke one day and the Rathbone estates are vast. Even Madderlea pales into insignificance beside them.'

'Wealth does not guarantee happiness, my lady. I

would rather have a poor man who loved me that a rich one who treated me like a chattel. Sophie agrees with me, don't you, Sophie?'

'Naturally, she would,' her ladyship put in before Sophie could speak. 'But she is not required to put it to the test.'

'Neither am I. I am determined on another.'

Her ladyship looked startled. 'Who is that?'

Charlotte looked at Sophie and received a small nod before answering. 'Mr Harfield.'

'Mr Harty? I never heard of him. And no title either. Has he prospects of one? A fortune? When did you meet him? Oh, Mr Hundon will be so displeased.'

Charlotte tried again, louder. 'Mr Frederick Harfield, ma'am.'

'Harfield! But I thought he was dangling after Miss Hundon. Everyone said he was. She fainted at the sight of him. And he has been much in her company.' She turned to Sophie. 'Did you know about this?'

'Yes, my lady.' She took a deep breath and went on. 'You see, we have been engaging in a ruse.'

'Engaging a what?'

'In a deception, my lady.' It was so difficult to confess while shouting; Sophie would rather have whispered her guilt. 'We have been pretending to be each other, making believe that Miss Hundon is the heiress.'

'Miss Hundon an heiress? I do not understand. Everyone knows who you are and certainly Mr Harfield must, for he comes from your own part of the country. If you have been putting it about that you

are the heiress, Sophie, then you have been very foolish indeed.'

'I know that, my lady,' Sophie said. 'But you have
not understood…'

'As if anyone would believe such a Banbury tale!
The Roswells are a well-known aristocratic family
and the Hundons, respectable though they may be, are
certainly not one of the *ton*. And if Mr Harfield is
such a cake as to believe such tarradiddle, more fool
he.'

Sophie tried again. 'You misunderstand, my lady.
I am…'

'Not another word. You are supposed to be young
ladies with a modicum of good sense and I find you
have been indulging in schoolgirl pranks. I shall make
quite certain that any rumours that Miss Hundon is
an heiress are quashed. No wonder Viscount Braybrooke is confused.'

'Is he confused?' Sophie asked, diverted for the
moment from her task of trying to tell her ladyship
something she did not want to hear.

'Indeed he is. Why, he has been paying as much
attention to you as to Charlotte, as if he could not
make up his mind.'

'But you said his mind would be made up for him
by his grandfather.'

'Oh, that is enough, you are confusing me now.
There is nothing for it, but we shall have to work on
the Duke.'

'To what purpose, my lady?' Charlotte asked. 'Do
you think he would condone Sophie?'

'Oh, you are talking in riddles, both of you,' her

ladyship said in exasperation. 'I can only pray you will come to your senses by the time we attend the Braybrooke ball.'

The girls looked at each other and gave up.

The morning of the ball came in wet and windy and Lady Fitzpatrick was gleeful. 'She will not be able to have the musicians on the terrace and lanterns in the garden,' she said. 'We shall be cooped up in the ballroom and it will be a dreadful crush.'

'I thought that was a good thing,' Sophie said, watching the raindrops sliding down the windows of her ladyship's boudoir where they were drinking their morning coffee. She had been planning a visit to Maiden Lane, but could find no excuse for going out in the rain. 'The greater the crush, the greater the success.'

'Yes, but there are crushes and crushes. One must be able to breathe and converse and dance.'

'But you said you did not think many would attend.'

'Perhaps they won't,' Lady Fitzpatrick said perversely.

Her ladyship was wrong on all counts. The ballroom at Rathbone House was large enough to contain a hundred guests in comfort and a hundred was about the number who had accepted. Whatever the tattlers' private opinions of her ladyship, she was known as a first-rate hostess and it was worth going for the food alone. Add to that the chance of a juicy snippet of gossip, such as the announcement of a betrothal or, more telling, the lack of an expected announcement, and the invitation was impossible to refuse.

Sophie had dressed in what she considered her plainest evening gown. It was made of a filmy pale green gauze which floated over a silk slip of a slightly darker green. It had a round neck, ruched with dark green and little puff sleeves, slotted with ribbon. Another ribbon was threaded through the high waist and was caught up under the bust, from which the ends floated free. More of the same ribbon and a few pearls were strung through her red-gold hair, which was drawn up and back into a Grecian knot that emphasised the long curve of her neck where a single string of pearls nestled against her creamy skin. The Madderlea family jewels, too ostentatious for a young lady not yet in Society, had been locked away by her uncle until such time as her engagement was announced.

This understatement had the opposite effect from the one she had intended. Instead of being dismissed as too plain, she was revealed as a young lady of stunning beauty. And Richard was stunned. She was poised and elegant and that bright hair shone in the light from the chandeliers so that he saw her as a flame of unmatched brilliance, drawing him like a moth. He was consumed with a desire so strong, he could hardly wait to have her to himself. But that was not possible until he had finished greeting their guests.

'Miss Hundon,' he said, bowing as she reached where he stood with his grandfather, his cousin and his aunt.

'My lord.' She was vaguely aware of a black satin

evening coat and muscular legs clad in black kersey-mere trousers strapped under the instep, a white shirt and an elaborately tied cravat as he bowed over her hand. It was not his clothes which took her breath away, but the touch of his hand as he raised it to his lips and the look in his brown eyes which were scanning every inch of her face as if trying to commit every tiny feature to memory.

'I hope I see you well?'

'Yes, thank you, my lord.' So formal, so unnatural, when they had shared so much—the work at Maiden Lane, the accident with the curricle, the dawn encounter in Hyde Park, that kiss, the memory of which still sent shivers of desire through her. But he was being very correct and she supposed the ball marked the end of that easy relationship. Now he meant to keep his distance. Was that what his eyes were telling her?

He took her card from her and scribbled his name against two dances, before she followed Lady Fitzpatrick and Charlotte into the ballroom which was ablaze with light and colour. The air was heavy with perfume and the scent of hothouse flowers which stood in bowls in the window recesses.

Dowagers sat in chairs surrounding the floor, peering through quizzing glasses at everyone else's charges, comparing notes, their tongues as sharp as razors. Young men, dressed like peacocks, stood in groups, eyeing the young ladies in their flimsy gowns, deciding which to choose, as the musicians, on a dais at one end of the room, struck up the first dance.

As soon as Sophie and Charlotte appeared they

were besieged by young men wanting to mark their cards, including Martin Gosport and Freddie Harfield, who whirled Charlotte away before she even had time to draw breath or smile at her other admirers, all of whom believed she was Miss Roswell. Sophie found herself facing Martin Gosport.

He swept her an elaborate bow and held out his hand. 'Will you do me the honour?'

She allowed him to lead her into the country dance, noticing as she did so that Richard had come into the room with his cousin and was dancing with her. Emily was beginning to look more mature, more assured and she was smiling. Did she know Richard's intentions? If she did, she did not seem too unhappy about it.

'May I congratulate you, Miss Hundon?' Martin said, after they had taken their places and were moving down the room in step with the other dancers. 'I do believe you will break every young man's heart tonight. There is no one to hold a candle to you.'

'Mr Gosport, what a hum!'

'I mean it. If it were not for your lack of a fortune, you could have any man in the room.'

'Now you are being very foolish, Mr Gosport. Have you not been told that compliments should be more subtle than that?'

'I have always believed in being direct, Miss Hundon. It saves a deal of misunderstanding.'

'How right you are! But supposing it is not compliments you wish to impart, would you still be so outspoken?'

He smiled, circling round her. 'I think I might remain silent.'

She laughed. 'I shall remember that if you become mute.'

'Miss Roswell is in fine form, too,' he went on, having seen Charlotte in the next set, laughing into the face of Freddie Harfield, who was grinning happily. 'If I were Richard I think I would nail my colours to the mast before Harfield steals a march on him.'

Sophie forced herself to sound light-hearted. 'You think it is Charlotte his lordship has fixed upon then?'

'Who else fits his criteria?'

'Oh, that list. We have all heard of it. Tell me, is it true she must have a fortune?'

'Oh, I do not think that is of prime importance. He said it so that he would not be besieged by penniless fortune hunters. Why do you ask?' He looked down at her suddenly. 'Oh, surely you do not have aspirations in that direction yourself?'

'Certainly not!' she retorted. 'I was merely curious to know how a man can be so cold-blooded as to set out his requirements in so exacting a fashion.'

'Oh, it was only a joke. He did not mean any of it. A more warm-hearted and sensitive man I have yet to meet. Why, he has stood buff for me many a time.'

'Then you think he is capable of falling in love?'

'Oh, I am sure of it, given the right lady.'

'And would he be a faithful husband?'

'There would be none more constant and true. If you are worrying about your cousin, Miss Hundon, then do not. If he offers for her, she could not marry a finer man.'

Sophie was glad the dance ended at that point because she wanted to run away and hide. If what Mr Gosport said was true, Richard Braybrooke would not be proposing to Charlotte because he thought she had a fortune, but because he loved her. As soon as Martin had returned her to Lady Fitzpatrick, she excused herself and left the ballroom to find the ladies' retiring room.

Richard, who had been doing his duty by dancing with the most important of the young ladies, including Emily, Verity Greenholme and Martin's sister, as well as Charlotte who was pretty as a picture in rosebud pink Italian crepe, could hardly wait to claim Sophie for the next dance. He escorted his last partner back to her mama, bowed low to them both and turned to see the object of his desire disappearing from the room.

Now, what deep game was she playing? He went over to Lady Fitzpatrick, who was looking after Sophie with an expression of exasperation on her face. 'My lady, is Miss Hundon not feeling up to snuff?'

'Oh, my lord, I did not see you there.'

'I was expecting to have the next dance with her.'

'Were you?' Her ladyship sounded vague. 'I dare say she will be back soon. Why don't you stand up with Miss Roswell instead?'

'It would give me the greatest pleasure, my lady, but I believe Miss Roswell's card is already full. Please excuse me.'

As he hurried after Sophie, he found himself wondering if Lady Fitzpatrick knew about the deception. Was she part of it? It was a new thought and one which puzzled him. What had she to gain by it? What had anyone? Was it Charlotte's idea or Sophie's? Did they think it would increase Charlotte's chances of finding a husband? But that did not ring true, for that young lady had set her cap at Freddie Harfield.

He did not believe Sophie was capable of harming anyone, but surely a hoax of this magnitude was doing a great deal of harm. Had she been forced into it? Had it been conjured up specifically to test him? Did the whole *ton* know he was being gulled? Why? Why? Why?

Chapter Ten

The music faded behind Sophie as she made her way up to the next floor. The corridor in which she found herself was thickly carpeted and lined with doors. Which one had been set aside for the lady guests to recuperate, she did not know.

She wandered along its length, hoping to hear female voices which would help her, but everywhere was silent. She pushed open one of the doors, to reveal a bedroom, sumptuously furnished with a bed draped in muslin and lace, striped silk curtains, mahogany wardrobes and chests, a striped upholstered sofa and a long cheval mirror. Afraid to be caught prying, she withdrew.

'Looking for a place to sleep, Miss Hundon?'

She swung round guiltily. Richard was standing so close to her she could feel the warmth of him. 'Oh, you startled me.'

'Obviously. Are you unwell? Did you wish to rest?'

'Not at all. I did not mean to pry. I was looking

for the ladies' room. My hair needs attention. I...' She stopped because he had put a hand on each of her shoulders and was looking down at her with an expression on his face she could not fathom. Concern? Tenderness? No, that could not be. It must be annoyance.

'Your hair looks perfect as it is.' He reached out and touched a tendril which was too short to be included in the Grecian knot. 'You are in superb looks tonight.' The touch of his fingers on the soft flesh of her neck was devastating; she felt as if her whole body had become boneless and was a quivering jelly of desire. Her breathing became fast and shallow as if she was being deprived of air. She wanted to grab the hand away in order to stop the torment, but like someone mesmerised she could not move.

'Don't you know the effect you have on me?' His voice was hardly more than a whisper.

'Oh, yes,' she said, forcing herself to react as he expected her to. 'I exasperate you.'

He threw back his head and laughed. 'You never said a truer word. Just when I think I have your measure, you confound me again.'

'I don't know what you mean.'

'Oh, I am sure you do. Tell me you are not at playing cat and mouse with me.'

'I would not dream of doing such a thing.'

'Then why do your eyes say one thing and your words another? I could have sworn...' He stopped. 'No matter. Why did you run away just when it was my turn to dance with you? Am I so repugnant to you?'

'No, no, I had forgotten it was our dance.'

'You find it so easy to forget me?' He put his hand on his heart in a melodramatic gesture. 'I am deeply wounded.'

'Now who is teasing?'

'This is no tease.' He put his forefinger under her chin and lifted her face to his. Taken by surprise, Sophie opened her mouth slightly and then his lips were on hers, gently at first and then with more urgency, as his arms went round her and he held her fast against his body. She was helpless. Caught in the trap of her own desire, she responded with every fibre, putting her hands about his neck and pulling him towards her, wanting the kiss to go on and on, uncaring that she was betraying her innermost longings to this man who held her in thrall and who had every intention of marrying someone else.

He lifted his mouth from hers at last, but did not release her. He leaned back and looked into her face without speaking, as if he were trying to interpret something her eyes were saying. 'Perhaps you will not find it so easy to forget me another time.'

Furious at her own weakness and anxious to regain some of her composure, she put her hands on his chest and pushed him with all her strength. He remained rock solid.

'Is this how you go about courting a wife, my lord? Poor Charlotte. I thought you loved her, wanted her for a wife. I hope she has the good sense to see you for what you are, a philanderer who will take advantage of her cousin when her back is turned and expect that same cousin to succumb like a serving wench. I may not be out of the top drawer, not one of the *ton*, but that does not mean I will allow any Tom, Dick or Harry to take liberties…' She stopped suddenly, too breathless to continue and because he was looking at her with amusement in his dark eyes.

'I would strongly object to Tom and Harry, my dear, but Dick is another matter.'

In spite of her fury, she found herself laughing. 'Oh, you are impossible!'

'Impossible? I do hope not.'

'Let me go, please.'

'Not yet. I have something to say to you. Something I want to ask you. But you know that, don't you?'

'No, how should I?'

'Because every time I say I want to speak to you, you find a way of avoiding me.' He put his hands on the wall either side of her head, trapping her. 'Now, you will listen.'

'Very well, my lord, but make haste because if anyone should come along…'

'I do not give a damn.' He paused to marshal his thoughts. He must make her see that what she was doing was wrong, make her confess, but the memory of the way she had responded to his kiss made it doubly difficult. 'Sophie, I have no intention of offering for your cousin.'

'Good, it will save you the disappointment of being rejected.'

He ignored her retort. 'Do you not know that I have lost my heart to you?'

'No, I do not believe it. It is impossible.'

'Why impossible? Do you think I have not a heart to lose?' When she did not answer, he repeated, 'Do you?'

'No, my lord. I believe you to be compassionate to those less fortunate but…'

'At least, I have that in my favour, but it was not compassion I meant. I was speaking of love.' The words were said very softly, causing her heart to beat faster than ever.

'You fill my thoughts, day and night, wondering what you are doing, if you are thinking of me, until I am in purgatory.' He paused to find a way of shocking her into realising the seriousness of her deception. 'But offering for Miss Hundon would be a travesty. You must see that…'

'Indeed, I can, my lord.' She cut him off before he could finish. 'But if you think I am such a ninny as to consent to such a proposition, my lord, you are gravely mistaken. I would rather die.' She ducked under his arm to try and escape but he grabbed her hand. She stood still facing away from him, her breast heaving.

He gave a despairing laugh. 'You think I am so lacking in honour? Oh, dear, then what did that kiss tell me about you? That you are prepared to be opportuned by a rakeshame?'

It was all too much. She wrenched herself away and ran down the corridor, away from him, away from the torment which she had brought upon herself. Pulling open a door, she found herself in a room where ladies' cloaks and pelisses were heaped upon a bed and there were comfortable chairs and sofas and pots of powder and phials of perfume on a dressing chest. She had found the ladies' retiring room and it was empty. She went in and slammed the door behind her.

He stood outside for a moment, wondering whether to follow her, but then decided against it and turned to go slowly downstairs and back to the ballroom.

The dance he should have had with Sophie had just ended and the couples were returning to their seats. Lady Fitzpatrick was sitting with Lady Gosport, her round face even rosier than usual. She was fanning herself vigorously and looking around her, while appearing to be listening to her companion's chatter. Charlotte was returning to her on her partner's arm.

He crossed the room to them. 'Miss Roswell, I must speak to you.'

She looked startled and turned to Freddie for support but he was grinning knowingly and Lady Fitzpatrick was actually smirking. 'Go along, my dear, you may take a turn about the room with his lordship.'

'Miss Roswell,' he said, walking towards the door and not round the room in full view as he should have done. 'I do not want to alarm you, but I think your cousin is not feeling at all the thing.'

'Sophie, ill? Then I must go to her at once. Why did you not say straight away?'

'I did not think she would want a fuss and telling Lady Fitzpatrick would surely have that effect. Come, I'll take you to her.'

They left the room watched by almost everyone present, who assumed his lordship was taking her off to propose to her. Lady Fitzpatrick was gleeful, Lady

Braybrooke furious and Emily placidly content, her arm tucked through that of Martin Gosport as they perambulated round the room after dancing together.

'I hope, my lord, you have said nothing to upset Sophie,' Charlotte said, as they climbed the stairs.

'Not unless asking her to marry me is upsetting to her.'

She stopped and turned towards him. 'You proposed?'

'I tried to. But she deliberately chose to misunderstand.'

'Why?'

'I thought perhaps you might know the answer to that.'

'Only she can tell you that, my lord.'

'I thought she had some fondness for me, but it seems I was wrong. Unless she is holding back for your sake. She is so close to you, she might deny her real wishes if she thought it would help you.'

'Yes, I know she would, but in this case, you are mistaken. Sophie knows where my affections lie.'

They resumed their climb and stopped just short of the door which had been so recently slammed in his face. 'With Freddie Harfield?'

'Yes.'

'And Sophie knows this?'

'Of course she does. We have no secrets from each other.'

'Then you will know if your cousin has fixed her heart on someone else. Is there some secret love she dare not speak of? She is not affianced already? Or being coerced?'

'No.'

'Then we are at a stand unless you can persuade her to open her heart to me.'

'But the talk is that you are looking for an aristocrat with her own fortune.'

'Oh, that nonsense! Pay it no heed. It is your cousin I want, if only she will have me. But she would not even listen. Please persuade her that nothing will make me change my mind.' He opened the door to usher her inside, but there was no Sophie to be seen.

'Where can she have gone?' she asked.

'Perhaps she returned downstairs while we were in the ballroom,' he suggested. 'You do not think she would be so foolish as to leave the house alone?'

'I do hope not.' She turned and hurried downstairs but he passed her and was the first to question the footman on duty.

'Miss Hundon? You know Miss Hundon?'

'No, my lord.'

'A young lady in a green gown. Red-gold hair.'

'A young lady such as you describe did leave about fifteen minutes ago, my lord.'

'Was she alone?'

'Yes. I saw her into her carriage. She said she was feeling unwell and would send it back for the rest of her party. Her groom was with her, so I thought no more of it.'

Richard turned to Charlotte. 'I'm going after her. I mean to get to the bottom of this.'

'My lord, is that wise? She can hardly admit you with no chaperon in the house. And Lady Fitz and I cannot come until our coach returns.'

'I must see that she has arrived home safely, even if she will not see me. Please return to the ballroom, Miss Roswell. I do not want the rest of the company disturbed. There is enough gossip as it is.' He was tight-lipped and she was afraid his anger would spill over if he forced the truth from Sophie.

'Please, my lord, do not be unkind to her…'

'I? Unkind? All I want to do is marry her—is that unkind? Now, please try and behave as if nothing has happened. I shall be back before you know it.'

Sophie was in her room lying face down on the bed, sobbing uncontrollably. Richard Braybrooke had confessed to loving her in the same breath as saying he could not marry her. Martin Gosport had been wrong about him being a faithful husband and so had Charlotte. It had never been his intention. And though she tried to fuel her anger, it was diluted by misery.

She did not think she could bear watching him courting someone else, knowing he would never touch her again, never put his arms round her, never kiss her. It was time to leave London, to put this disastrous summer behind her, to pretend it had never happened.

An urgent hammering on the street door made her lift her head and listen. She could hear the footman on duty in the hall and the voice of the caller, and then Anne protesting that Miss Sophie had retired. The next minute the maid rushed into the room.

'Miss Sophie, it's Lord Braybrooke and he won't go away. He says he must see you, only he asked for Miss Hundon. He do mean you, don't he? It ain't right to bully me so. I told him you was abed and he said I must fetch you down or he'll come up.' She looked round as if half expecting him to be behind her. 'Oh, miss, he's surely up in the boughs and won't be denied.'

'Very well, go and show him into the drawing room. Tell him I will be with him directly.'

As soon as the maid had gone, she roused herself and went to the mirror. Her face was swollen and blotched from weeping. She washed it and dabbed it dry, gulping back more tears. But what did it matter? She was destined to lose the love of her life and all because of her own vanity. It had been nothing more nor less than vanity, she was ready to admit that, and he had squashed that very efficiently by suggesting she become his mistress! If he had known she was the Roswell heiress, would that offer have been one of marriage?

Well, she was glad, she told herself firmly but untruthfully; it had shown him in his true colours and she had had a lucky escape. She had stripped off her ballgown when she came home and was in her petticoat. She covered it with an undress gown of blue silk, brushed out her hair, picked up a fan so that she might have something to do with her hands and could possibly hide her face with it, then went downstairs to the drawing room.

He stood by the hearth, one hand on the mantelshelf, a foot on the fender, gazing down into the empty grate. He turned when he heard her. She was looking very pale and was obviously distressed, or she would never have come down in that flimsy *demi-*

toilette with her beautiful hair hanging loose about her shoulders. He longed to comfort her, to tell her it did not matter what she had done or why, but she stood just inside the door and looked ready to bolt if he were so foolish as to try and approach her. He spoke softly. 'Sophie.'

'My lord.' It took every bit of self-control to speak normally. 'It was very unwise of you to come. If you had not frightened Anne quite out of her wits, I should have refused to see you. Now you have seen me, please leave.'

'When you have answered my question.'

'And what question is that?'

'Why you will not consent to be my wife.'

'Your wife!'

'What did you think I meant?' He paused, wishing she would lower that silly fan and let him see her eyes. Her eyes gave her away every time. 'Good God! You surely did not think I was offering you *carte blanche*?'

She did not answer.

'You did, didn't you? You must think me the worst kind of coxcomb, if you thought I would do anything so contemptible.'

'We have already established that I do not meet your requirements in a wife, my lord, which is why I thought…'

'Oh, yes, you do. In every respect.'

She forgot her resolve to be cool. 'How can you say that?'

'Easily. You are beautiful and compassionate and good with children and those less fortunate; you ride as if you had been born in the saddle and you have a neat pair of hands with the ribbons. And you have courage. The only flaw that I can see is that you are too independent for your own good, but I can believe that has been forced on you by circumstances. And, in spite of what you say, I do think you have a little regard for me.'

'My lord, I never said that.'

'Your eyes speak more truly than your words, my dear, but if it was the manner of my address which displeased you, then I humbly beg pardon. Only say you will marry me and my whole life shall be devoted to pleasing you; there is nothing I wish for more. I love you.'

She could not make herself believe he was really saying what she had always hoped he would say. But it was too late, too late to come out of the affair with any honour. When he learned the truth, he would be very angry and not amused, as she had so confidently told Charlotte he should be. 'My lord, please do not go on.'

'Why not? I must know what your answer will be before I speak to Mr Hundon.'

'Oh, no!' she cried in desperation. 'You must say nothing to him, you really must not.'

'But I must.' He took a step towards her, but paused when she stepped back. 'Sophie, I am asking you to be my wife and that requires the consent of your guardian…'

She was too distressed to notice his deliberate use of the word guardian and not father or papa. She took a deep breath. 'Lord Braybrooke, I am sensible of the honour you have done me, but the answer is no. I cannot consent to be your wife…'

'Why not?' Fearing she would run away again, he strode forward and grabbed her wrist. She turned away from him but he held her fast. 'Do you find me repulsive? Despicable? Ugly?'

At each question, she mutely shook her head, refusing to turn to face him.

'Then why, Sophie? Are you worried by a lack of a dowry? That is of no consequence at all. And neither is your family background. None of it matters.'

Oh, if only she could believe that! But even now, she was not ready to admit her deceit. She clung to it as if she were drowning and it was her only lifeline. 'It matters to your grandfather.'

Having given her ample opportunity to tell him the truth, it was hardly the response he had hoped for. He took her shoulders and turned her to face him. 'Then let us throw ourselves on his mercy. When he knows how things stand he will not deny us. And even if he did, it would make no difference. If you will have me, I would stand against the world. There is no reason in the world for you to refuse me.'

'I am not obliged to give you reasons.'

He was angry now. 'You little ninny, do you think I am so easily given the right about? You are having a game with me and it goes ill with me, I can tell you.'

'Then I am sorry for it.'

'Why can't you confide in me?' His anger faded as quickly as it had come. 'I know there is something troubling you and unless you tell me what it is, I cannot help you.'

She looked up at him and found herself looking into brown eyes which held nothing but gentle compassion and she knew she did not deserve it. It was all going to come out in the end and it would be better if she told him herself and did not let him hear it from tattlemongers. She took a deep breath and opened her mouth, but before she could utter a word, they heard the door knocker and Anne had burst into the room.

'Oh, Miss Sophie, Mr Hundon is here. What are we to do? He will so angry…'

'Oh, no!' Sophie gasped. 'My lord, he must not find you here. He would not understand.'

'But I must speak to him, explain…'

'Not tonight. He will be tired from his journey and not in a mood to listen. Please go.' She grabbed hold of his arm and pulled him towards the window, which was a low one and gave out on to the terrace. 'Go that way. Quickly. Quickly.' She tugged at the catch and flung the window open.

Reluctantly he disappeared into the rain, just as her uncle came into the room. Anne busied herself securing the window and shutting the curtain.

'What was that clunch of a footman talking about, Sophie?' William demanded. Although he had given his greatcoat and hat to the servant, he looked very wet. 'First he says Lady Fitzpatrick and Miss Roswell are out and then he tells me Miss Sophie is at home.'

'Uncle William, what a surprise to see you,' Sophie said, trying to sound normal and not quite succeeding;

her voice was a pitch higher than it usually was. 'I hope there is nothing wrong at home?'

'At home, no. Your aunt is as well as she can be, considering her affliction. Where are Lady Fitzpatrick and Charlotte and why are you at home alone?'

'They are at the Braybrooke ball, Uncle.'

'Did you not go?'

'Yes, but I felt a little unwell and came home early.'

'I must say, you don't look at all the thing. But surely her ladyship did not allow you to come home alone?'

'I did not want to spoil their enjoyment. I brought the carriage and Luke was with me as well as the driver, so I was in no danger.'

'But why did you not go straight to bed? And surely standing half-dressed by an open window is not a sensible thing to do, especially as it is raining quite hard. You will catch a chill.'

'I came down to ask Anne to heat up some milk for me and while I was waiting for it I felt a little faint and opened the window to get some air.'

William turned to the maid, who still stood by the window, her mouth open. 'Don't stand there gaping, girl, go and heat up the milk and take it to Miss Roswell's room. And then make a bed up for me.'

Anne scuttled away and he turned to Sophie. 'Now, you had better go up to bed. I shall wait for Charlotte and Lady Fitzpatrick.'

She could not let Charlotte bear the brunt of his anger, just because she had pretended to feel unwell.

'Uncle, why don't you retire too. There will be plenty of time to talk in the morning. It is very late.'

'So it is. I had intended to be here earlier, but the coach broke down miles from anywhere and the passengers were left stranded while the guard rode on with the mail.' He smiled wryly. 'His Majesty's mail takes precedence at all times, never mind that people are left wet and hungry in a hedge tavern which was no better than a pig-sty.'

'Then you must be very fatigued. Why not go to bed?'

'You seem to be very anxious to see the back of me, Sophie. I am beginning to think His Grace might be right.'

'His Grace?'

'The Duke of Rathbone. He wrote to me, told me there was something havey-cavey going on and if I didn't want my daughter and my niece to make complete fools of themselves and me too, I had better come and see what was afoot.'

His Grace had recognised her! 'But how—'

'Oh, so there is something. What is it, Sophie?'

She sank into a chair and put her head in her hands, unable to meet his gaze. 'I have been very foolish, Uncle William, and ruined my life.'

'Oh, come, it cannot be as bad as that.' He sat beside her and patted her hand. 'You had better tell me all about it.'

It was some time before she could begin, but then it all poured out, the fear of being married for her money, the need for Madderlea to have a benign master, her own longing to be loved and Lady Fitzpatrick's mistake.

'It seemed as though fate was offering me a way out,' she said. 'I didn't realise how complicated it was all going to be, nor how much gossip there would be among the *haute monde*, watching and speculating…'

'I can hardly believe my ears,' he said. 'Sophie, this is dreadful. How did you suppose it would all end? You could not have allowed it to go on if either of you had an offer…'

'At first I thought I could tell whoever offered for me and he would not mind finding out I had a fortune when all he expected was a small dowry, but then when I realised I would not receive an offer, not from the man I wanted at any rate, I decided we need not tell anyone, because when we returned home, I should live in seclusion. I thought if Madderlea was too much for you, then you could find another trustee, or sell it.'

'Good Lord! I never heard such a fribble. I have a duty to you and your late uncle to do my best for you and I shall discharge that duty until you are married. Though how that is to be brought about after this I do not know. This piece of mischief has done untold damage to your prospects.'

'I know, Uncle, I know.'

'And what about Charlotte? I suppose she followed where you led, as usual. As for Lady Fitzpatrick, she must have lost whatever sense she was born with to be so easily gulled. I do not know who is the more to blame.'

'It was all my fault, Uncle, truly it was. Do not blame Charlotte, or Lady Fitzpatrick.'

'How in heaven's name did you manage to carry it off for a single day, let alone several weeks?'

'It became harder and harder, especially with Viscount Braybrooke a constant visitor and Freddie…'

'Of course, Frederick Harfield is in Town, I had forgot Sir Mortimer sent him to get a little town bronze. How did you silence him? No, you do not need to tell me—he would do anything Charlotte asked of him.'

'You know?'

'Of course I know. He came to see me before he left. I have no objection to a liaison if that is what Charlotte wants, but he has to deal with his father himself. And he will find it doubly difficult after this.'

They were interrupted by the return home of Lady Fitzpatrick and Charlotte who stood just inside the door, staring at him, her eyes wide with shock.

'Papa! What are you doing here? How did you get here? It is nearly dawn…'

'You may well ask. I sent you to have a Season, to learn how to go on in Society, perhaps to find a husband. Certainly I hoped Sophie would do so. Instead I find you indulging in a masquerade which is set to make us all a laughing stock.'

'You know?'

'Your cousin has seen fit to take me into her confidence,' he said laconically.

'Oh, Papa, I am so relieved you know. Poor Sophie…'

'Papa?' queried Lady Fitzpatrick. 'But surely…'
She looked from one to the other in puzzlement.

'We did try to tell you we had been hoaxing every-one,' Sophie said, standing up to take her hand and lead her to a seat. 'I am afraid you misunderstood.'

It took some time to explain everything to Lady Fitzpatrick, who was so distressed she had to be calmed with several glasses of brandy.

'Lord Braybrooke must be told,' William said. 'I shall go and call on him after I have had a few hours' sleep. Now, off to bed, both of you.' He looked down at Lady Fitzpatrick who was sprawled across a sofa, moaning. 'Tell her ladyship's maid to come down and help her. I fear the brandy has taken its toll. Tomor-row we will decide what is to be done. I sincerely hope the Duke and Lord Braybrooke will agree to keep silent and we may avoid a scandal.'

It was also Richard's wish, though how he could obtain his heart's desire without everything being made public he did not know. He walked home in the rain, still pondering on the reason for Sophie's mas-querade. He felt sure she had been going to tell him when Mr Hundon arrived and thrown her into a spin. Her uncle was obviously not party to the deception and he wondered what he would have to say about it. Was it all about to come out? It would be the story of the year, of several years.

It was almost dawn and the last of the guests were leaving as he arrived, wet and bedraggled from the rain. Rather than be seen, he slipped in at a side door and went up to his room, where he stripped off his wet clothes without calling for his valet and climbed into bed. If there was to be a scandal, then it would be better if his grandfather knew of it before it broke.

He would seek an interview in the morning, tell him everything and see what they could contrive. He was as determined as ever to marry Sophie. He smiled to himself, remembering how beautiful she had looked, how spirited, not in the least overawed and able to give him as good as he gave. He fell asleep, reliving the feel of her lips on his, her body pressed close to his.

He woke in the middle of the morning to a room flooded with light. His valet had drawn back the curtains and was busying himself about the room, laying out shaving tackle and towels beside the bowl of hot water he had brought into the room. Richard yawned and stretched and climbed out of bed.

'Good morning, my lord.' The valet turned from the washstand. 'It is a fine day. The rain has gone and I believe it may turn out warm. What will you wear today?'

'Oh, anything, it's of no consequence. I shall be making calls later so perhaps the blue superfine. And trousers, yes, trousers. The light kerseymere, I think.'

The valet smiled; his master knew that trousers were more flattering than pantaloons and made his legs seem longer. Not that he needed to look taller— he was over six feet in his stockings. 'Very good, my lord.'

'Is His Grace up?' He knew his grandfather had only put in a token appearance at the ball and retired early as he would have done in the country and, as in the country, he would also rise early.

'I believe so, my lord.'

An hour later, shaved, dressed and with his hunger alleviated by a good breakfast, he presented himself in the library where his grandfather was reading the *Morning Chronicle*. He put it down when Richard entered.

'Ah, Richard, my boy, come in. Ball go according to plan, did it?'

Richard smiled. 'No, not exactly.'

'Philippa cut up rough, did she?'

'No, surprisingly she did not. Perhaps Emily managed to turn her up sweet.'

'So, it is to be Miss Roswell.' He peered into his grandson's eyes. 'Miss *Sophie* Roswell.'

The emphasis on Sophie's given name was not lost on Richard. 'You know?'

'There is not much escapes me.'

'But how do you know?'

'She is the image of her mother. The same features and the same colour hair, almost impossible to describe, but unforgettable.'

'Gold with red highlights, as if streaked with fire.'

His Grace smiled. 'Very poetic, Richard, but what have you done about her?'

'I have asked her to marry me.'

'An offer she had no hesitation in refusing, I'll wager.'

'Yes, but I am sure it was only because she has been playing this game of make-believe and it has gone wrong.'

'So I conjectured, which is why I alerted Mr Hundon.'

'He arrived this evening, but she would not let me speak to him…'

'Of course she would not. It would have meant her secret was out.'

'But you and I had guessed it, so did it matter?'

'I fancy she would like to come out of it with some remnant of dignity. Perhaps saving face is more important to her than marriage.'

'Perhaps. I should also like to avoid a scandal, for everyone's sake, not least Sophie's, but I do not see how it can be done.'

'Give up this idea of marrying her and allow her to return to Leicestershire where she can revert to her true identity without anyone of consequence knowing she had ever repudiated it.'

'I will not give her up. Grandfather, apart from this bumblebath she seems to have fallen in, you have no objection to her as a granddaughter, have you?'

'None at all. In fact, it would delight me. She must have a great deal of spirit to have embarked on such a hoax and to have carried it off so successfully for so long.'

'But why do you think she did it? Was she coerced?'

'Do you think she is a young lady easily persuaded? After all, you failed to induce her to marry you and most young ladies would sacrifice almost anything for the prospect of one day becoming a duchess.'

'Not Sophie, it seems,' he said bitterly.

'No, but is that not one of the things you find so endearing about her, that she does not behave in a conventional way?'

Richard smiled wryly. 'Yes, of course, but what can she have been thinking about to have embarked on it in the first place?'

'What were you thinking about when you made that list of attributes a prospective wife must have?'

'Oh, I don't know. Not being duped by fortune hunters, I suppose.'

'Then you have your answer.'

A broad smile lit Richard's face as he realised what his grandfather meant. 'Do you really think so?'

'Only one way to find out, my boy. Ask her.'

As he rose to go, a footman came to the door to say that Mr Hundon wished to see His Grace and asked if he would receive him.

'Yes, yes, show him in.' To Richard, he said, 'You might as well stay, hear what he has to say.'

William betrayed nothing of his unease as he was shown into the room. He bowed slightly to both men and took the chair offered to him.

'Your Grace, I am indebted to you for taking the pains to alert me to what was going on in my own household. I need not say I am mortified by it all. How we shall come about without a major scandal, I do not know. I am doubly sorry that you and yours have been involved.'

'Oh, we shall contrive to endure it,' His Grace said, with a twinkle in his eye.

'That is what we must do too,' William said. 'We shall return to Upper Corbury almost immediately.'

'You surely do not mean to go before the young ladies' ball?' Richard queried. 'That would only fuel the flames.'

'You are not suggesting I should condone the deception? My lord, I cannot pretend to be my niece's father, I really cannot. I am a lawyer, a man of integrity. And Lady Fitzpatrick has been in such a quake ever since she discovered how she had been gulled, she is in no state to be hostess to a Society ball. She has been resorting to the laudunum and the brandy bottle and lies on her day-bed, hardly aware of what is going on around her.'

'It is not to be wondered at,' His Grace murmured. 'She would not have been my choice for a chaperon for two such lively chits.'

'But that is the answer,' Richard said suddenly. 'Lady Fitzpatrick has been taken ill, so you have reluctantly been obliged to cancel the ball.'

William turned towards the young man. 'I am sorry you were duped, my lord.'

'Oh, I was not. I knew some time ago. But Sophie does not realise I know. I have been trying to encourage her to confide in me, but she would not.'

'She is too ashamed, my lord.'

'Did she tell you I had proposed to her and asked permission to speak to you and that she refused?'

'No. She said nothing of that. I wonder what else she decided not to tell me? I expect she realised she had thrown away any respect you might have for her—'

'On the contrary, I can only admire her the more for sticking to her guns.' He stood up. 'Mr Hundon, if I go to Sophie now and can persuade her to consent, may we have your blessing?'

William looked startled and turned to the Duke. 'Your Grace…'

'Oh, do not mind me, my grandson knows his own mind and I shall not interfere.'

'But what about the scandal?'

'Oh, we shall contrive something. If not…' He shrugged. 'Give the boy your blessing, Mr Hundon, and let him be on his way. I fancy he is a touch impatient.'

William nodded and Richard left the room, calling for someone to saddle his horse. It was not far to Holles Street, but walking would take too long.

Even so, he was too late. Everyone, except Mr Hundon, had been late rising and it was not until Anne went to wake Sophie and found her bed empty that they realised she had left the house. Charlotte, worried by her cousin's state of mind, was at her wits' end and pacing the drawing-room floor until her father should return. When Richard was shown in, she almost flung herself on him.

'My lord, Sophie has disappeared and Pa—' She stopped and began again. 'She was upset last night and I am afraid…'

He smiled. 'I know. And I know why too.'

'You do?' She looked at him, wide-eyed in astonishment.

'Yes.'

'Oh. Do you think she had run away because she could not face you? Oh, dear, whatever shall we do?'

'Calm yourself, my dear Miss Hundon. If I know

Sophie, she has pulled herself together, made up her mind to make the best of it and gone off to Maiden Lane.'

'Oh, yes, I had forgot Maiden Lane. But she was not supposed to go unescorted, was she?'

'No, but she might have thought it did not matter, after all. Now, you wait here for Mr Hundon. I left him talking to my grandfather. I will go and bring her home and we will sit down quietly and work out a strategy for coming about.'

He sounded more composed than he felt about it. He had never liked the idea of Sophie going among the soldiers on her own and today, for some reason he could not explain, he felt a tremor of unease, of danger lurking.

He rode to Maiden Lane with all the haste he could muster, almost colliding with a carriage as he galloped out of the street. He hoped he was right and she really was at the refuge. Sophie. Sophie. Her name went round and round in his brain as he rode in and out of the traffic. Sophie. Sophie.

Chapter Eleven

'Major, how good of you to come.' Mrs Stebbings, clad as ever in a huge white apron over her black mourning dress, was her usual cheerful self. 'Your legal man came to see me yesterday. I want to thank you on behalf of the Association and of the men. It will make so much difference to know that this refuge will always be here for them and others like them…'

'Yes, yes,' he said, a little impatiently. He had arranged to buy the freehold of the property and set up a trust to administer it. He had also engaged a man to act as an employment agent, much in the manner Sophie had suggested. But just at the moment he was not in the mood to listen to effusive gratitude. 'Where is Mrs Carter?'

'Oh, Major, I am sorry, but you have missed her. She was here earlier, but she seemed somewhat distracted, a little out of sorts, and I suggested she ought to go home.'

'Was she alone?'

'She came alone, but I did not like to think of her

walking back unaccompanied, when she was obviously not feeling at all the thing and Sergeant Dawkins offered to escort her…'

'Dawkins!'

'Yes.' She stopped when she saw the startled look on his face. 'Why, is there anything wrong, Major?'

Richard gritted his teeth and told himself to remain calm. Dawkins was not an unusual name; there must be dozens of Sergeant Dawkinses and, even if it were the same one, he probably would not remember making that threat of revenge. And if he did, he had no reason to connect Sophie with the officer who had had him court-martialled.

'I certainly hope not,' he said. 'How long ago did she leave?'

'Oh, some time ago. Two or three hours, I should think.'

'Three hours! Good God! Are you sure she meant to go straight home?'

'That is what I understood. She said she was leaving town tomorrow and came to say goodbye. She said she would see that the rent was always paid, but I told her about the trust and how you had bought the house for us and she seemed very pleased and said it was just the sort of kind action you would take.' She paused. 'I do not know where she lives, but if you do, you could check if she arrived safely.'

'I have just come from there. She had not returned home when I left.'

'Oh, Major, you don't suppose anything has happened to her? I could have sworn Sergeant Dawkins was reliable.'

'I must go,' he said, suiting action to words.

'Please let us know she is safe,' she called after him.

He returned to his horse and sprang into the saddle. Sophie had told Mrs Stebbings she was leaving town; had she meant immediately and not tomorrow? Would she go on her own? Travelling alone would not frighten her, he realised that, but she would not be so inconsiderate of her uncle and cousin as to go without telling them or leaving a message.

On the other hand, she had been very distressed when he had last seen her and that was probably increased when Mr Hundon arrived and she knew her hoax had been uncovered. Was it worth checking the coaching inns which, considering how many there were, would take forever, or should he concentrate on Sergeant Dawkins? First things first—he must return to Holles Street; she might have returned in his absence and he was worrying over nothing.

But she had not. He decided to say nothing of his suspicions to her family, who were all distraught enough as it was, and offered to recruit all his friends to help search for her. He sent Luke to rouse Freddie and Martin and enlist their help in looking everywhere a properly brought-up young lady might be found: the shops, libraries and dressmakers, and the drawing rooms of acquaintances. He sent other men servants to check the coaching inns and set off himself to search the less salubrious areas of the city.

He went home, picked up a pistol and ammunition, told the butler where he could be contacted if anyone

should have news, then returned to the house in
Maiden Lane in a closed carriage where he told Mrs
Stebbings and those men who were in the house that
Mrs Carter had not returned home and he was afraid
for her safety.

'Did she say anything to any of you about where
she was going, or of any fears she had?' he asked.

'No, Major,' they murmured.

'We'll find her, never fear,' Andrew Bolt said. He
was a big, craggy-faced man with only one eye and
a hand missing, but neither disability seemed to trouble him much. 'If we have to search the whole of
London.'

'I think Sergeant Dawkins may have something to
do with it,' Richard added. 'He bears me a grudge.
Do any of you know where he might be found?'

None did, but the legless man, sitting by the door
on his trolley, pushed himself forward.

'I did see the sergeant talking quiet-like to a cove
yesterday, outside here,' he said. 'Didn't like the look
of him, thought they might be up to something smo-
key, like robbing the house, so I followed them.' He
grinned, tapping his wheels. 'I can move pretty fast
on these here round legs, when I choose to, and nobody notices me, bein' so near to the ground.'

'Where did they go?'

'Into an alley off Seven Dials.'

'That was yesterday?'

'Yes. I know it don't prove nothin', but if we could
find the other cove, he might lead us to the sergeant.'

'You can't go into Seven Dials in that flash rig,
Major, and that's a fact,' Tom Case said. 'You won't

take two steps before you're set upon and stripped bare. Besides, as soon as it's known you're looking for one of their number, the word will go round and every no-good footpad, pickpocket and cut-throat in the place will come to protect their own. It will take more than one man…'

'Are you volunteering, Trooper?' Richard asked with a smile. The man was skinny and stooped, but that did not mean he was weak, as Richard well knew. Like all of them, he was a good man to have with you in a tight corner.

'At your service, Major, and the service of the little lady.' It was a sentiment echoed by everyone present.

'I've got an old suit of clothes belonging to my husband, God rest his soul,' Mrs Stebbings said. 'I brought them here to give them to one of these men, but they might fit you. Very plain they are and a little shabby, but the better for that under present circumstances, wouldn't you think?'

'Thank you, Mrs Stebbings.'

She found them for him, and though the breeches were a little short so that his stockings barely reached them, and the cloth of the jacket was so tight across his shoulders that the seams began to spilt, that was all to the good, he decided. He rubbed dirt on his face, hands and boots, obliterating the shine which had taken his valet hours to produce.

After that, the search for Sophie took on the semblance of a military campaign, carefully planned. Men were dispatched to gather information. Others produced old muskets and rusty swords and expressed themselves willing to use them, but Richard, who did not think it was the right moment to ask how they had acquired them, forbade that. .

'This is England,' he said. 'Criminals must be punished according to the law. I shall use my pistol only as a last resort.' He smiled a little grimly. 'Though if you were to find anyone mistreating or showing any indelicacy towards Mrs Carter, I should not object to them being taught a lesson.'

'Then what are we waiting for, Major?' Andrew Bolt said.

Even more impatient than they were, he forced a smile. 'For our runners to return. Reliable intelligence is half the battle, you should know that. Going off at half-cock will lose us our prize.'

Sophie had no idea where she was. All she knew was that it was dark and it smelled horrible. Her previous worries faded into insignificance as she wondered if she was about to die. What she did not know was why. Who wished her harm?

How long had she been there? How long before she was missed? She had rejected Lady Fitzpatrick's admonitions and Richard's scolding about going out alone so often, it was possible those at home would think nothing of her absence until she did not return for nuncheon.

Richard would not miss her at all because she had sent him away, rejected his proposal of marriage and refused to give him a reason. This was her punishment, to be tied hand and foot, her mouth gagged with a disgusting piece of cloth, and left to die in an empty

room which stank of rotting garbage and excrement.
Where had Sergeant Dawkins gone?

Why was he conspiring with that dreadful, leering
giant of a man with a patch over one eye and huge
rough hands? What did they want from her? She had
offered them all the money in her reticule and promised more if they would only release her. When that
failed, she had asked them what it was they wanted,
had said she understood their problems and would try
to help them, that if they released her unharmed she
would not put the law on to them. Her only answer
had been guffaws of laughter.

She had accepted Sergeant Dawkins's offer to escort her home only when pressed to do so by Mrs
Stebbings, not because she was afraid of him—though
he did make her a little nervous—but because she did
not want him to know where she lived and who she
really was.

It was her silly pride again, she supposed, and the
fact that she had become so used to secrecy, to deceit,
that she kept on with it even when it no longer mattered. Her true identity would be the talk of the town
before the day was out. But would she live to hear
it?

Dawkins had walked beside her as they made their
way between the crowds in the market, pushing a way
through for her, yelling at the urchins who had recognised her as one of the two ladies who had thrown
coins for them. They wanted more. Dawkins clubbed
one about the face, kicked another and swore at them
all. Terrified, they fell back.

On the corner, Dawkins was joined by the second

man, who silently took up station on Sophie's other side; it was at this point that she knew something was wrong and became really frightened.

'Sergeant, I think I can manage to find my way home from here,' she said as calmly as she could. 'Thank you for your trouble.'

'Oh, it ain't no trouble,' he growled, pressing more closely to her, so that the smell of his unwashed body almost overpowered her. 'And we expect to be well rewarded.'

'Oh, yes, I am sorry.' She delved into her reticule for a coin.

'That!' He took it from her and threw it behind him, laughing as one of the waifs, bolder than the rest, dived on it. 'We'll have more than that before the day is out.'

They were opposite a narrow alley and the two men, each holding one of her arms, hustled her down it.

'Where are you taking me?'

'A short cut.' Dawkins grinned. 'A short cut to my just reward. I've got a score to settle.'

She had opened her mouth to scream, but that was a mistake. The second man clapped one enormous hand over her mouth, twisted her arm behind her back with the other and marched her forward. They left the busy market behind them and darted down one narrow alley after another. Tall tenements rose each side, blocking out the light and air. A few people stood about, but no one paid the least attention; they certainly showed no sign of wishing to intervene.

After a few minutes in which her futile struggles

weakened, they entered a doorway and she was carried, Dawkins at her shoulders and the other man at her feet, up several flights of stairs and into this room.

'Now, you'll stay 'ere until I come back,' Dawkins said when he had regained his breath. 'And if you're a good girl, Joe will bring you food and drink.'

She had made the mistake of struggling fiercely and yelling at the top of her voice, which resulted in her being tied and gagged and flung on to a filthy straw palliasse on the floor.

Now she was alone and her eyes were becoming accustomed to the gloom, she realised she was in an attic. There was a sloping roof above her, with some of the slates missing so that tiny beams of light played on the dust motes in the air. The room had no window and only one door and, apart from the mattress, the only furniture was a small table and a couple of rickety chairs with broken backs. In the corner lay a canvas bag and beside it a coil of knotted rope. It was unbearably hot and the gag had dried her mouth, so that she longed for a drink of water.

She heard footsteps on the stairs and Dawkins returned. He was carrying a small case from which he took pen, paper and a bottle of ink. 'Seemed to me that it would be better coming from you,' he said, in a chatty voice that took no account of her distress. 'I want you to write me a letter.'

She grunted and he sat down beside her on the mattress to look closely into her face while her eyes tried to convey that she wanted the gag removed.

'You want to speak, do you? Well, as to that, I

don't know. I'd need your promise not to yell out again.'

She nodded and he reached round her and untied the gag. She took several gulps of air but that hardly helped; the room was airless and she was parched. 'Water, please.'

He rose and went to the table where there was a jug and a tin cup. He poured water and came back to hold it against her face, but he made no attempt to tip it towards her lips. He grinned. 'You going to be good?'

She was so desperate for a drink, she would have agreed to anything. 'Yes, but untie me, please. I won't run.'

'Course you won't, there's nowhere to run to. There's the door and beyond it three flights of stairs and old Joe at the bottom of them and it's the only way out.'

He put the water down and untied her hands. She grabbed at the cup and poured the disgusting liquid down her throat, wiping her mouth with the back of her hand.

'I must say, for a genteel filly, you've got plenty of guts,' he said, watching her. 'A bit like my wife.'

'And what would you think of anyone who carried your wife off and held her prisoner?' she demanded.

'Couldn't do it. She died two years ago while I was stuck in Spain.'

'I am truly sorry.'

'Are you?' He looked closely at her. 'Maybe you are, so you won't mind writing a letter for me.'

'If it's only letter writing you want me for, you

could have asked me at the house in Maiden Lane. You didn't need to abduct me.'

'But this is a very special letter and the whole lay depends on you being hid.' He fetched a piece of broken floorboard and put the paper on it, took the lid off the ink bottle and offered her the pen. 'Write what I say.'

With a shaking hand, she took the pen and he began dictating. 'To Major Richard Braybrooke, Bedford Row.' He grinned at her gasp of astonishment. 'Go on, write it down.' He waited for her to do as she was told, then went on 'Dear Richard. Please do not try to find me or I shall be killed before you reach me.'

'Why do you think the Major would try and find me?' she queried, concluding he probably did not know Richard had come into a title since returning from Spain. 'He has no interest in me. We quarrelled.'

'Oh, you cannot gammon me, Mrs Carter. Or should I say Miss Hundon?'

'How did you find that out?'

'It weren't difficult. Followed you home, talked to the servants, watched the house, saw the Major visiting…'

'But he was visiting my cousin, not me,' she said, realising he did not know the whole truth, that she was not Miss Hundon, but Miss Roswell.

He laughed. 'One for the ladies, is he? It don't matter which one he was after, you were the easiest to pull in, bein' a mite more adventurous than the other. Aside for that, I've seen the way he looks at you. Now, go on writing.'

She dipped the pen in the ink again, just as heavy footsteps could be heard ascending the stairs. Dawkins scrambled to his feet and stood behind the door, drawing a knife from his boot. She held her breath, but it was only Joe who was tired of standing guard at the bottom of the stairs and wanted to know what was happening.

'You could 'ave got yerself killed,' Dawkins said, returning the knife to his boot. 'I told you to stay downstairs.'

'This is my room, I come to it when I want.' He looked down at Sophie. 'Ain't you got that letter writ yet?'

'Never will if you keep interruptin',' Dawkins said, returning to sit on the mattress again. 'Got that down, 'ave you?' he asked Sophie.

'Yes.'

'Then write this: "I shall be returned safely if you bring a thousand yellow boys to—"'

'Two thousand,' Joe muttered. 'Tell him two thousand.'

'He won't pay it,' Sophie said, guessing he meant guineas. 'Where would a major find that amount of money? And if he could, what makes you think he would pay it for my release? He would simply turn the letter over to the Bow Street Runners and forget about it.'

They looked at each other, wondering whether to believe her, then Dawkins laughed. 'Nice try, Miss Hundon. Now write: "Bring one thousand guineas to the steps of St Paul's tonight at seven—"'

'Two,' insisted Joe.

Dawkins turned on him angrily. 'I want him here, I want him to feel the lash as I felt it and if we're too greedy, he'll do as the chit says and hand the whole matter over to the law.'

'What do I care for your damned revenge?' Joe said. 'It ain't nothin' to me, what you did in the war, nor what he did neither. If you bring him here, to my lay, then my safe ken is blown and I need to find another a long way away and that takes blunt. He'll pay. Just look at her. She's a lady.'

'Yes, I am,' Sophie said, wondering what it was Sergeant Dawkins had against Richard. Whatever it was, it inspired powerful feelings of revenge stronger than mere greed. 'And a very wealthy one. I can give you more than Major Braybrooke who is nothing but a son of a second son, of no importance at all.'

She could see that Joe was interested. 'How much?' he demanded.

'You shut up and get out!' Dawkins shouted at him. 'Are you a cod's-head that you can't see she's trying to gull us to protect him? I want that man here. I want him to feel this.' He got up and went to the corner and picked up the rope by its handle. Sophie realised it was not an ordinary rope at all, but a cat o' nine tails. He swished it through the air a couple of times and then sat down again. 'I haven't finished the letter,' he said. 'Tell him to come alone and make sure he is not followed. If he brings anyone with him, I shall know of it and he may look for your body in the Thames. Tell him you know I mean it, beg him to come to your aid, say you are in mortal terror. Then sign it.'

She wrote slowly, trying to think of a way to warn Richard of what they planned for him. 'Come on,' he said. 'We ain't got all day.'

She wrote, her pen poised over the signature, but before she could write it, there was the sound of someone pounding up the uncarpeted stairs, making no attempt to be quiet. Joe hid behind the door, while Dawkins rose and faced it, standing poised with the lash in his hands, ready to use it. They could hear whoever it was banging on doors on his way up, shouting to the occupants.

'The Runners are coming down the street and they're searching all the houses.'

Joe flung open the door. A ragged man stood on the threshold, panting. 'If you've got anything to hide, you'd best make yerselves and yer booty scarce,' he said. 'The Runners are going from door to door looking for booty. I'm off meself.' He turned and clattered down the stairs again, but not before Sophie had recognised Tom Case. Was the refuge she had set so much store by, and worked so hard to create, nothing but a den of thieves? She cursed herself for her gullibility.

'I'm not waiting around for fool's gold,' Joe said, grabbing the canvas bag which clinked as he lifted it. 'But just you remember, you owe me, George Dawkins, and I shall find you, wherever you're laid up.' With that he disappeared down the stairs behind Case.

Dawkins was more cautious, but it was obvious he would be trapped if he stayed where he was. He stuffed the unsigned letter in his pocket, then bent to take Sophie's arm and hauled her to her feet, upset-

ting the ink bottle over her hand as he did so. 'Time
we was gone,' he said, pushing her in front of him
down the stairs, holding the cat o' nine tails at the
ready. 'We'll finish this somewhere else.'

When they reached the street door, he poked his
head out and looked this way and that, then up at the
windows of the tenements. There was not a soul in
sight. The cry that Bow Street Runners were in the
road had been enough to send everyone to ground.

'Right, you first.' He pushed Sophie ahead of him,
walking backwards himself. They had gone perhaps
twenty yards when an arm shot out of a doorway and
hauled her inside.

The next minute the street was full of men, some
of whom she recognised, and children, dozens of
them, converging on the cornered Dawkins, but Sophie was only half aware of them, as Richard, in an
ill-fitting wool coat and worn leather breeches, held
her tight against him. She felt breathless and weak
and almost ready to faint. 'Are you all right?'

'Yes.'

'Stay there.' He left her and ran out to join the men
who had Dawkins imprisoned by his arms. The cat o'
nine tails lay on the ground. Richard picked it up. His
expression was grim. 'So, this is what it was all
about?'

The man was struggling fiercely while the children
danced round, taunting him. Sophie, who had once
again disobeyed and ventured out to see what was
happening, was appalled to think Richard was going
to use the lash.

'Let me do it,' Andrew Bolt, said, holding out his

hand for the cat o' nine tails. 'It would give me the greatest pleasure.'

'No!' Sophie shouted, appalled. 'You must not do that.'

Richard turned and for a moment she saw the old humorous look in his eye, but it was gone in an instant when he saw her torn clothing, her lovely hair hanging down, the pallor of her complexion. 'I told you to stay out of sight.'

'But he didn't harm me, just frightened me a little. You must not take revenge on him in that way. Vengeance is not for mere mortals.'

'No, but punishment is.' He threw the rope down and took off his jacket. To the men who held Dawkins, he said, 'Let him go.'

They released him and formed a circle round the two men, while Tom Case took Sophie's arm to draw her away. 'Don't look, ma'am.'

But she could not help looking. Peering between the circle of men, she saw Dawkins put up his fists to defend himself, saw Richard deliver a blow past his defence which rocked him on his heels. Enraged, the man flung himself at Richard, who neatly side-stepped and landed another blow. Dawkins, reeling, came again and again but, though he did manage to land a punch or two, he was outclassed as a pugilist.

Even in the midst of her anxiety and anger, Sophie could admire Richard's muscular body, the quick reactions as he danced out of his opponent's reach. His grim expression had relaxed and she realised he was enjoying himself. Dawkins, in desperation, made a lunge for the discarded cat o' nine tails, but Richard, watching his face, saw his eyes turn to the rope seconds before he reached for it, and put his foot on it.

'Oh, no, you don't. Fight fair or not at all.' Dawkins lowered his head like a maddened bull and hurled himself at Richard to bring him down, but in the process he stumbled and fell forward, hitting his head on the cobbles. He lay still. Richard calmly put on his coat. 'Look after him,' he told the men. 'Take him to the infirmary.' Then he made his way over to Sophie.

'Do you never do as you are told?' He stood in front of her, looking down at her, blood on his face and hands, though she could not tell if it was his or Sergeant Dawkins's.

'Is that all you can say, my lord, after—'

'No, it is not, but what I have to say is best said in private. Come, my carriage is waiting at the end of the street.' He turned to the men, busy hauling Dawkins to his feet. 'Thank you, lads. You shall be rewarded.'

'We want no reward, Major, it was our pleasure to help the lady who has been so kind to us,' Case said, grinning. 'We wish you happy.'

'How did you know where to find me?' she asked, as Richard put his arm about her take her to the coach.

'You have the soldiers to thank for that. Davie saw Dawkins plotting with his accomplice yesterday and followed him to this alley. We did not know for certain if this was where you had been brought nor, if we were right, which house you were being kept in, and we dared not make a frontal attack because we were not sure how many men were holding you and if they would harm you if they were alarmed.

'But the waifs knew which house it was because one of them followed you. As soon as they saw me and recognised me as the man you were with a few days ago, they ran to tell me. After that, it was a matter of luring him out into the open.'

'He was using me as bait to have his revenge on you. He made me write a letter to you demanding a thousand guineas...'

'It is just as well he did not know your true worth to me or I'd have been left without a feather to fly with.'

'I told them I meant nothing to you,' she said, smiling at his declaration that he would give all he had to save her. 'I said you would not come yourself, which is what Sergeant Dawkins wanted. I said you would simply hand the letter over to the Runners and let them deal with it. But he would not believe me.'

'Then you are not as good a prevaricator as you thought you were,' he said, helping her into the coach. 'Holles Street,' he told the driver and climbed in beside her.

She lay back on the cushions and shut her eyes, every ounce of energy drained from her. She was safe, but now came the recriminations, the harsh words. And she deserved them. She had put herself and the soldiers at risk, had deceived Society, had involved her cousin in her duplicity, had shamed her uncle and put poor Lady Fitzpatrick in an impossible position.

'Before you say a word,' she said, 'I know I have been excessively foolish. I can only say I am sorry and very grateful for your timely rescue.'

'Save your apologies for your uncle and cousin, Miss Roswell, they have more need of them than I.'

Her eyes flew open. 'Did you say Miss Roswell?'

'Indeed, I did.'

'You know, then.'

'Yes, I know.'

'How did you find out? When?'

'The clues were there for anyone to see. Your spirit of independence, your lack of squeamishness, your fluency in the French language—all attributes lacking in your cousin, who was supposed to be the one who had come out of France in the middle of a war. And Freddie Harfield playing the gallant with you, while keeping his eyes firmly on your cousin. Need I go on?'

'No.'

'And then, of course, my grandfather twigged it right away. He tells me you are the image of your mother. She must have been a very beautiful woman.'

'I suppose the whole world knows now.' She was too weary to put up a spirited defence or recognise the implied compliment. 'I deserve to be vilified, but not Charlotte, not Lady Fitz. Not Uncle William.'

'No, they don't.' It was becoming increasingly difficult to be severe with her, when all he wanted to do was take her in his arms, to feel her soft lips yielding to his, to repeat his offer of marriage. 'As for the whole world knowing, His Grace will say nothing and certainly Lady Fitzpatrick will not, she is too mortified. She is returning to Ireland, I believe. And you must return to Upper Corbury.'

'Yes, I know.' She said it with a sigh.

'Tell me, how *did* you intend to bring this débâcle to an end?'

'I thought, once we were back in Leicestershire, we would simply resume our proper identities. The engagement of Mr Harfield and Miss Hundon would be announced and Miss Roswell would live in seclusion…'

'And what did you intend if you should receive an offer while you were in town?'

'I should refuse it, of course.'

'Why of course?'

'I could not accept it under false pretences, could I? I could not say yes and then tell the poor man I was not the Miss Hundon he thought I was.'

'Is that the reason you refused me?'

She did not answer and he took that as an affirmative.

'Was that the only reason?'

She managed a twisted smile. 'That and the list of requirements you put about. I did not, do not, conform.'

'And if I were to tell you that I was not deceived, that the name you adopted had no bearing on my proposal at all, and neither had that list? There is nothing I regret more than dreaming that up, unless it was telling Martin Gosport of it.'

She stared at him unbelievingly. 'But, my lord, you cannot possibly wish to marry me after what has happened. There will be the most dreadful scandal.'

'We have been looking for a way of cancelling the rest of your Season without causing scandal…'

'We?' she queried.

'Your Uncle William, my grandfather and I.'

'Oh.'

'You have been through a dreadful ordeal—that much we can make public—and it has left you unable to continue your Season. Miss Roswell—I mean Charlotte, of course—is too upset to continue without you and the whole family has gone back to Leicestershire.'

She smiled wanly. 'It is an ill wind that blows nobody any good.'

'In a few months' time—not many, because I am an impatient man—I shall present myself at Upper Corbury and the engagement will be gazetted between Miss Roswell and Richard, Viscount Braybrooke.'

'But, my lord...'

He lifted her grubby, ink-stained hand and put it to his lips. 'I do hope you are not going to reject me again. I do not think I could bring myself to ask a third time.'

Her lovely eyes had regained some of their sparkle. 'Oh, my lord...'

'Richard,' he corrected her.

'I am not sure if I understand. Are you proposing in spite of what I have done?'

'You want me on my knees? Then I go on my knees.' He slipped to the floor and took both her hands in his. 'You want me to say I love you. I say it. I love you, love you, love you, have done since the day I met you. And rather than being in spite of what you have done, it might be because of it, because of your compassion for others, your fearlessness, your independence which is far too pronounced for your own good, for...'

'Oh, Richard, please do not go on with that tarradiddle. And get up off the floor. It is dirty.' She laughed suddenly, realising that his breeches were already filthy, that his coat was torn and there was mud and blood caked on his face and hands.

He looked hurt for a moment, until he realised what she had said and joined in the laughter. 'Oh, Sophie, there will never be a dull moment married to you. You are going to say yes, aren't you?'

'Yes, Richard, yes, please.'

He resumed his seat beside her, putting his hands either side of her face and kissing her, tenderly, longingly, filling her with a surge of such happiness, she did not know how she could bear it. She was hardly aware that the carriage had stopped.

'Holles Street, my lord,' the driver said.

They were married at Madderlea six months later in a quiet ceremony attended by close family and friends, some of whom knew about the switch in identity and been sworn to secrecy. Mrs Stebbings and several of the soldiers who had known her only as Mrs Carter and were not in the least surprised that she turned out to be an heiress attended, along with the Madderlea villagers and the estate workers who had never known her as anything but Miss Roswell. Martin, amused by the way Richard had been hooked, had come, promising never to say a word to his mother, and also the new Mr and Mrs Frederick Harfield, who had married a month before. It was a happy day, the service solemn, the wedding feast gargantuan, a day full of laughter, as everyone toasted the new master and mistress of Madderlea.

Later, when the old Duke died, they would be expected to move to the Rathbone estate, but Madderlea would remain in the family, a home for their heir, the next viscount. But that prospect was years and years ahead, years they could look forward to with joy and more laughter, without secrets.

*   *   *   *   *

Perfect Summer

The perfect way to relax this summer!

Four stories from best selling
Mills & Boon® authors

JoAnn Ross

Vicki Lewis Thompson

Janice Kaiser

Stephanie Bond

*Enjoy the fun, the drama
and the excitement!*

Published 21 May 1999

*Available at most branches of WH Smith, Tesco, Asda,
Martins, Borders, Easons, Volume One / James Thin
and most good paperback bookshops*

FREE!

2 Books
and a surprise gift!

We would like to take this opportunity to thank you for reading this Mills & Boon® book by offering you the chance to take TWO more specially selected titles from the Historical Romance™ series absolutely FREE! We're also making this offer to introduce you to the benefits of the Reader Service™—

- ★ FREE home delivery
- ★ FREE gifts and competitions
- ★ FREE monthly Newsletter
- ★ Books available before they're in the shops
- ★ Exclusive Reader Service discounts

Accepting these FREE books and gift places you under no obligation to buy; you may cancel at any time, even after receiving your free shipment. Simply complete your details below and return the entire page to the address below. *You don't even need a stamp!*

YES! Please send me 2 free Historical Romance books and a surprise gift. I understand that unless you hear from me, I will receive 4 superb new titles every month for just £2.99 each, postage and packing free. I am under no obligation to purchase any books and may cancel my subscription at any time. The free books and gift will be mine to keep in any case.

H9EB

Ms/Mrs/Miss/Mr ....Initials.................................

BLOCK CAPITALS PLEASE

Surname...

Address...

....

....Postcode ....

Send this whole page to:
THE READER SERVICE, FREEPOST CN81, CROYDON, CR9 3WZ
(Eire readers please send coupon to: P.O. Box 4546, DUBLIN 24.)

Offer not valid to current Reader Service subscribers to this series. We reserve the right to refuse an application and applicants must be aged 18 years or over. Only one application per household. Terms and prices subject to change without notice. Offer expires 30th November 1999. As a result of this application, you may receive further offers from Harlequin Mills & Boon and other carefully selected companies. If you would prefer not to share in this opportunity please write to The Data Manager at the address above.

Mills & Boon is a registered trademark owned by Harlequin Mills & Boon Limited.
Historical Romance is being used as a trademark.

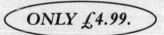